Chronicles *of an*
Occupational Prostitute

A Workplace Survival Story

Peechi Keane

GG Robins Books

Published by GG Robins Books

Printed in the United States of America

First Edition: May 2017

10 9 8 7 6 5 4 3 2 1

ISBN 978-0-9817555-0-2

Cover and book design by Andrew Benzie

Occupational prostitution remains a common phenomenon among employees and contractors. Fear of employer retribution or negative evaluation often keeps the truth from being told. Peechi Keane's novel, *Chronicles of an Occupational Prostitute,* artfully exposes the reality of occupational bullying and other forms of employee mistreatment and suggests practical guidelines for survival.

Franklin T. Burroughs, Ed.D.
Author and Professor

I have known this author for many years and was her confidant through many of the events that inspired this story. While told with some humor, the story describes an employment nightmare: an emotional and enlightening roller coaster with dramatic turns of events. Creating enjoyable reading from horrific circumstances takes real talent. Ms. Keane is to be commended.

Anonymous
Retired Office Manager

Abuse--a crime against the dignity of another person, whether female or male--should never be tolerated by a society that wants to live in peace. I congratulate Ms. Keane, for her courage, fighting spirit, and gutsy determination in telling this story, inspired by personal experiences. While *Chronicles of an Occupational Prostitute* reveals a prevalence of abuse and lack of respect for one's basic human rights, Ms. Keane's protagonist stands her ground and fights back, not only for herself, but for all employees who deserve to be treated with dignity in the workplace.

Cecilia Pugh
Author and Friend

Peechi Keane strikes home at the nightmares encountered routinely in dysfunctional workplaces. Her vivid descriptions mirror the injustices that occur and their ensuing frustrations. Well done, Ms. Keane.

Chloe Laube, Author
Dream On, Dancing Queen

Knowing Ms. Keane on a personal level has been an inspiration. Besides being a wonderful, loyal and cherished friend, she has been an enrichment and inspiration in my life. Learning from her that it is okay to say "no" to compromising, hurtful, or degrading treatment by a supervisor has been an eye-opener for me. Her book will cause a revolution! I am honored to have her book on my bookshelf.

A.S. who was "there" but lacked the courage

This story will stay with me for a long time.

Phyllis Houseman, Author
There is a Season
Romance Writers of America, National Award Winner
and Southern California Chapter Recognition

Dedicated to
Stephen and Christopher

Acknowledgments

Much love and gratitude to my immediate family, my spiritual and community families, my friends, teachers, editors, and those who have and continue to support me in the ways you do. To those who have read and debated segments as this book evolved, I thank you for your patience and inspiration. I will never be able to repay everyone's kindness and generosity.

Connie Cutrona, Barbara Durniak, Carolyn Gigoux, Sue Lewis, Charles Burke, Phyllis Fraser, Stacey Hinton, Jean McGraw, Diane Stangel, Mary Azevedo, Cindi Segale, Heather and Drew Bennett, Zeph Rose, Genia Pauplis, Mary Peare, Gale Haux, Marsha Beersdorf, Susan Mallah, Cherie Hallert, the late Marie White, Beth Guzman, Gwennie Preston, Chloe Laube, Cecilia Pugh, Amelia Schaller, Carol Calkins, Ann Marie Billotti, Christian Mammen, Sam Welch, Valerie Lau.

The creative members of my weekly writers group.
The gifted members of the California Writers Club.
My patient and capable designer, Andrew Benzie.

There are many more kind and wonderful people I have not mentioned by name. I am grateful to each and every one of you.

Prologue

A stained wooden spoon gripped in her pudgy little hand, a scowl permanently etched on her blotchy face, and an ear-splitting yell that could be heard behind the elementary school down the block, Celina Nowak, a petite Polish woman, was the perpetually miserable and angry matriarch of her Polish-American family.

Born to illiterate and unskilled parents who emigrated from Poland to the United States in the early 1900s, Celina expected her children to be quiet, do as they were told, or face harsh consequences. She threatened with that wooden spoon and struck for every infraction, and occasionally without provocation, trusting intimidation to produce compliant children. The children and their father lived in fear of her wild mood swings.

*   *   *

One night in her mid-seventies, while dining at the home of her first-born daughter, Celina poured a second glass of wine and began telling stories about her childhood. Her daughters knew their biological grandfather died when their mother was three and their grandmother remarried five months later. From comments made over the years, the girls suspected that Grandma and her new husband drank too much too often, ignoring or abusing their children.

Celina talked about the day when, as a small child, she spilled some juice. She dove under her bed to avoid a beating, but her mother grabbed her by the feet and pulled her out. In an alcoholic rage—as if that could be considered an excuse for this heinous act—her mother shook her hard by the arms and bit her on the shoulder. A week later, a visiting relative discovered the infected bite and took Celina to a doctor.

After another glass of wine, Celina talked about a stepbrother who beat her up and laughed about the bruises he left. Worse, with tears trickling down her cheeks, she talked about her stepfather who withdrew her from school at fifteen when her mother passed away. He told authorities he needed her at home to care for him, her brothers, and stepbrothers. Between occasional soft sobs, Celina whispered that he would come into her bedroom at night to "touch her and do things," telling her it was her fault "for being so pretty."

Celina went on to talk about her older biological brother who married, leaving her at sixteen and their younger brother at fourteen behind with their abusive stepfather and stepbrothers. Packing their belongings and making their escape, Celina lived with her older brother and his wife while her younger brother—too small and too young to work—remained homeless, living in a shanty village near some railroad tracks. Celina stole food and took it to him, always afraid someone in the encampment might steal it from her or hurt her. Her older brother eventually asked her to leave, after which various kind women took her in and supported her, one by one, until each also asked her to leave for stealing food.

*   *   *

Psychologically damaged, needy, and desperate for the love and affection she was denied as a child, Celina met and married an older man when she was eighteen. She anticipated that her husband would be so thrilled when she bore him a son that he would do the impossible and make her happy too.

But Celina's first child was a daughter.

Years later, she tried again to have a son but had a second daughter she named Irena, whom she resented because Irena was not the boy child she wanted so desperately. Bitter and hateful toward the child as Irena was growing up, Celina was unaware that she was replicating her mother's dysfunctional behavior. Irena's father often promised her he would "try something new" to get Celina to be less abusive, but nothing ever changed.

*   *   *

Celina eventually had her son. She doted on him and allowed him virtually unlimited freedoms, producing a self-centered and temper-driven child who adopted his mother's attitude and behavior toward Irena. When Irena reacted to his misbehavior—kicks to her shins his favorite pastime—Irena's mother punished her for "upsetting her brother."

Irena did her best to avoid her mother's rages and win her favor by becoming an overachiever. Granted a scholarship, Irena appealed for the additional financial support she needed to attend college and Celina refused. Unaware she didn't need parental support, Irena worked as a secretary until she and friends, inspired by the 1960s women's rights movement, left Massachusetts for Chicago.

Chapter One

Irena Nowak and her friends established themselves as successful executive secretaries working for presidents and other top executives along Michigan Avenue, known as the Magnificent Mile, close to Chicago's Loop. After sixteen years in Chicago, Irena was successfully and happily earning a living employed by a Fortune 500 mega-corporation. After six years with the organization, the holding company notified employees that they would be selling the unprofitable division and Irena and her co-workers would be "out-sourced," a benevolent way to say they were being fired.

She and co-workers had been hearing rumors about upcoming corporate changes. Some chose to find other employment sooner rather than later. But preoccupied and exhausted as she was by years of divorce proceedings ending her twelve-year marriage, and facing the bone chilling dread of financial devastation, Irena chose to stay until she no longer had a choice. Feeling like she already had cinder blocks on her shoulders, looking for a new job was more than Irena could manage at the time.

Debatably good news in this otherwise bleak situation was the week-long out-sourcing program for employees provided by Irena's employer that guided her away from business administration, where she spent most of her career, toward sales and marketing. Irena considered the unpredictability of sales commissions, cold calls, and rejection unacceptable and focused on the more stable yet still exciting field of marketing.

When the outsourcing program concluded, Irena asked human resources about an internal transfer to another division. Denied, she sadly accepted that it was her turn to start over elsewhere. Considering the number of years Irena spent recognized and rewarded in business administration, she hoped for the same kind of recognition and reward in marketing, wherever she might wind up.

*   *   *

With breakfast dishes pushed aside and children on the living room floor watching television, Irena sat at her kitchen table intensely combing through the *Tribune* want ads one sunny Sunday morning in her small but comfortable suburban home in Chenowith, where she and her husband had raised their children to date.

Discovering a want ad for a marketing coordinator for civil engineers, her stomach churned until Monday morning when she called to inquire. After a perfunctory conversation, the human resources representative invited Irena to interview later that week for a marketing position that had the potential to change the course of her professional life. She was giddy with anticipation.

Irena described herself as petite but curvy like her mother and grandmother before her. She had large blue eyes, wavy blond hair held back with a clip, and a smattering of fading freckles across a nose she thought was a little big for her face. She had a slight limp from a roller skating accident when she was nine years old, and considered herself blessed and cursed to be perceived as "cute."

Irena had been pursued by men in business over the years who pressured her for a relationship. Some seemed to view her as vulnerable or needy and wanted to be her knight in shining armor. Some seemed to view her as a sexual or financial target. When Irena resisted, some felt rejected and some retaliated. Irena dreaded a new workplace where she might encounter a new set of such suitors, but eagerly looked forward to the changes promised by a new career path. On equal footing with financial security, she looked forward to the transition from supporting others in administration to using her own creativity for the benefit of her employer.

*   *   *

On a cold and drizzly winter morning under a sky like the underbelly of a wet gray cat, Irena drove from suburban Chenowith to a part of south Chicago she never knew existed.

Irena's career in Chicago had been concentrated along Michigan Avenue, where many businesses occupied space in clean, well-furnished, high-rise buildings with secure parking; a relatively safe area with shops, restaurants, theaters and mass transportation nearby.

As she drove through the squalid neighborhood where she would interview, she noticed occasional street-level signs declaring that the Chicago Department of Planning and Development had identified the surrounding fifty-seven acres for mixed use redevelopment. She felt dwarfed as she approached a looming billboard illustrating the boundaries of the tentative five-year plan.

When Irena arrived at the neglected building that housed the engineering firm, she hesitated at the entry to the parking lot—a lot surrounded by a cinder-block wall punctuated by gouges, with spaces where mortar had fallen out between the blocks, presumably from the impact of careless driving. One length of the wall was listing and appeared ready to collapse.

The block wall had been sloppily painted with thick brown paint, gobs of which had dropped to the ground. The dried drops reminded Irena of dirty copper pennies. Weeds, dead for the winter and trampled flat, had grown between loose and irregular patches of distressed gray asphalt.

Like sentinels at the entry to the parking lot, two large, heavy-duty, orange dumpsters greeted Irena. Dented, chipped and filthy, both sported large, peeling green labels identifying the refuse collection company. Both were covered with sticky-looking stains and debris. One dumpster overflowed with cardboard and other recyclables. The other, filled with mostly organic debris, attracted a cloud of flying insects Irena could hear through her open car window. A horrific acrid odor assaulted her nose. And a mangy looking one-eyed cat of indistinguishable color crouched nearby tearing into what appeared to be a rat.

Dented and tarnished gray aluminum trash cans full of smaller rubbish were clustered near the dumpsters, and filthy green plastic waste baskets had been placed near access areas to the building. Irena prayed it was trash collection day.

*   *   *

Still in her car, with an unobstructed view, Irena took a long look at the three-story U-shaped clapboard office building that was painted brown with white trim around doors and windows, all seriously faded and flaking. The building curved around a courtyard of neglected flower beds with concrete pathways uplifted and broken by tree roots.

Visible along the open-air corridors of the building were doors emblazoned with unique signs identifying each tenant. Virtually every door showed the ravages of weather, the lower third swollen and delaminating from water infiltration. Worn door mats sat on coarse gray concrete with blemishes of aggregate exposed by years of weather and other abuse. That same deteriorating concrete formed stairways and landings adorned by wrought iron railings in need of sandblasting and fresh black paint.

An overflowing hardware store on an adjoining lot also needed a coat of paint, the white stucco dingy from neglect; its dead-weed-infested parking lot pocked by pools of gravel for make-do pothole repairs. Red, white, green and blue banners strung along the roofline flapped in the breeze, and an array of goods was piled up along an exterior wall, like an outdoor marketplace in a third-world country.

The images struck Irena as cruel metaphors for her life at the time, as she compared these surroundings to her employment out-placement, divorce, and family obligations.

Knowing the office building stood within the boundaries of future development, Irena anxiously wondered about the firm's future and her own if she were to be hired. Shivers of trepidation like ghost fingers crawled along her spine as she envisioned herself working in this seedy neighborhood, and she questioned whether she could face what may lie ahead.

*   *   *

Parking as far as she could get from the dumpsters and the listing wall, Irena checked her makeup before stepping out of the car, locking it, and approaching the building. Those outdoor corridors, illuminated by naked incandescent lightbulbs, may have provided overnight protection for the homeless, evidenced by the wafting odor of urine and scattered remnants of fast food packaging.

With sweaty palms and blood pounding in her ears, Irena needed to use a restroom, only to discover the building's outdoor-accessed restrooms locked. On the verge of giving up, she considered getting back in her car, hitting the gas, and returning to the comfort and familiarity of administrative support along Michigan Avenue.

Conflicted by repulsion and despair, excitement and apprehension, and overcoming the urge to flee to pee, Irena put one foot in front of the other and set out to find the door to the company where she would interview. Worried about a new career while going through divorce, and knowing she had three children to support, anxiety and desire collided, but faith calmed her down: faith that personal and professional achievements, relevant experience helping her dad market his retail business, and enthusiasm would win her this job as marketing coordinator. Regardless of the derelict environment she was facing, Irena trusted this interview to be her new beginning.

*   *   *

Standing in front of the ground-level door to Yutz & Dunne that cold, damp morning, the air seemed thick and Irena had difficulty breathing. Like a nightmare, the rundown door became the manifestation of some hideous beast about to consume her.

Irena did her best to dismiss the foreboding that threatened to paralyze her, and she reflected on the happy years she had spent in big business, despite the last six in an unstable and unprofitable industry where people came and went on a regular basis, voluntarily or involuntarily.

Staring at the tarnished brass name plate affixed to the door identifying Yutz & Dunne, Irena took a deep breath, let it out slowly, and attempted to enter. But overnight dampness had caused the wooden door and frame to swell and the door would not budge. Holding on to the doorknob, Irena shoved with her shoulder, first once and then again with more enthusiasm. The door gave way suddenly and Irena went flying into the reception area hanging on to the doorknob for dear life.

Regaining her composure and smoothing her disheveled hair, Irena noticed the large, frizzy-haired blonde receptionist sitting to her right. Wearing a faded blue pocket tee-shirt and no makeup, she thought the receptionist looked more like a gardener than an employee of a professional organization.

A partition of exterior grade wood sheeting, displaying several knots through glossy dark brown paint, separated Irena from the receptionist. An oddly oversized, shiny brass nameplate identifying the receptionist as Kitty Russell sat on a shelf atop the partition amid a clutter of sign-in/sign-out sheets, writing instruments, calendar, note paper, flowers, candy dish, etc. Had Kitty been a smaller woman, Irena might not have seen her.

A large, out-of-square print of a herd of sheep scattered across a green hillside, graced by a pale blue sky complete with innocuous white clouds, hung on a bright and glossy turquoise wall behind Kitty. Other walls in the reception area, devoid of décor, had been painted glossy forest green. Two lime-green-and-brown-plaid upholstered chairs sat across from Kitty, the arms gray and greasy. A small end table, colonial style like the chairs, separated them and supported a weathered brass imitation kerosene lamp with its lampshade askew. A rust-colored glass ashtray sat on the table for smokers, despite state-wide efforts to pass the Smoke-Free Illinois Act.

Short-napped and worn reddish-brown carpeting—spongy and gummy—covered the floor, sticking to Irena's shoes as she walked, and nearly causing her to stumble. A moldy odor wafted up from the carpet and lingered, insulting her sense of smell. Irena had a difficult time containing her revulsion as she compared this environment to previous work environments where she enjoyed clean, comfortable, and attractive surroundings. Disturbed by this organization's apparent disregard for sanitation and employee welfare, Irena, nevertheless, forced herself to get a grip.

When Irena flew in the door hanging on to the doorknob, the receptionist had been so startled she dropped the receiver of the old phone the company still used. Picking up the receiver and fighting back the giggles, she turned her back to Irena and continued with her conversation for too long before asking the caller to hold.

*   *   *

Irena explained why she was there and Kitty phoned Maxine Burns, executive secretary to Lupo Yutz, chief executive officer and company owner, to let her know Irena had arrived for her interview. Neither said a word about Irena's grand entrance.

Waiting for Maxine, Irena elected not to sit in either of those upholstered chairs afraid they had fleas or some other creatures lurking among the cushions. Maxine emerged a few minutes later to escort Irena to the conference room.

Entering through oversize double doors, Irena noticed that sunlight from two uncovered windows had faded the paint on the conference room wall to her right, a wall that supported an engineering design plan tacked directly to it. Numerous pinholes, dirty fingerprints, and hand smudges indicated that many other documents shared that wall over time.

Four dusty old fluorescent light fixtures hung from the ceiling, each containing three exposed fluorescent tubes that collectively sounded like a swarm of killer bees overhead. Industrial reddish brown carpeting, similar to the carpet in the reception area, covered the conference room floor. Worn and torn at the entry, the carpet presented a tripping hazard in defiance of Occupational Safety and Health Administration standards.

A mid-size rectangular conference table, with a chipped brown laminate surface and dull chrome legs, sat slightly off-center in the room, closer to the wall that supported the tacked-up engineering plan. Surrounding the table were five overstuffed swivel chairs, with stuffing like popcorn bursting from broken seams and cracks in the brittle brown vinyl. Distracting voices from adjoining offices penetrated the conference room walls from two sides.

Cal Chauvin, a licensed civil engineer in his early forties, awaited Maxine and Irena. Cal explained to Irena that he and Maxine would interview her, even though, if she were hired, she would report to the company owner, Lupo Yutz. Irena found it curious that Yutz was not going to participate.

Invited to sit, Irena pulled a chair up behind her and attempted to sit down. The swivel chair tipped over and slid out from under her.

The second test of her resilience in thirty minutes, Irena hung on for dear life, twisted her wrist, and landed on the floor squarely on her derriere. Red-faced, she picked herself up, pointed out the bent caster, and moved to another chair. Not seriously injured, Irena imagined some cosmic jokester having a great laugh at her expense.

A slender, attractive, middle-aged woman with deep blue eyes and short auburn hair, Maxine Burns was well-groomed and professionally attired in a tailored green dress adorned by a pearl necklace and matching earrings. Cal wore a short-sleeved cotton dress shirt hanging outside a pair of rumpled beige chino trousers. Worn and soiled running shoes adorned his feet. Irena wore a dark blue skirt and coordinating jacket with a pale pink blouse open at the neck. Small pearl earrings matched the buttons on her blouse. Mid-high navy pumps and a navy purse completed her outfit. She carried a brown envelope containing extra copies of her resume, just in case.

Smart, sassy, and ready to tackle the hard stuff, Irena never thought twice about reaching for a non-technical position that required a college degree. She qualified for an undergraduate degree but never applied because experience and enthusiasm had successfully carried her through her professional life so far.

Divorce and outplacement had undermined Irena's moxie, and she feared she might be perceived as a limp dishrag instead of the dynamic individual marketing demanded. Despite the doldrums, the sticky door, and the chair incidents, Irena did her best to appear the consummate professional, trusting experience and enthusiasm to serve her once again.

Cal, Maxine, and Irena spent about an hour discussing Irena's experience, work style, and preferences. Only in retrospect did Irena realize that Cal and Maxine barely touched on company needs and expectations. They learned about her while she remained vague about the company. The marketing position remained largely undefined, but Irena was confident she could meet expectations.

Cal told Irena that her background and personality "appeared to be a good fit for the company." When he and Maxine agreed that Irena should be hired, Irena maintained her professional demeanor while nearly bursting with joy. "But wait," Cal said in a curious tone of voice. "Lupo has to make the formal offer."

Leaving Irena and Maxine to make small talk, Cal went to fetch Lupo. His absence felt like an eternity. Rather than making small talk, Irena was hypnotized by the schoolroom-like battery-operated clock on the wall loudly ticking off the seconds. Cal arrived back in the conference room with Lupo sauntering in behind him, and Irena braced herself.

Short, pear-shaped, and middle-aged with thin gray hair, a thick neck, and gray-green snake-like eyes, Lupo oozed flash and dazzle. With manicured fingernails, a diamond pinky ring on his left hand, and reeking of cologne, he wore stylish round eyeglasses perched on his narrow nose, a designer suit, shirt, and tie, complemented by equally stylish black alligator shoes polished to a shine just shy of patent leather.

Lupo approached Irena with a grin and proceeded to look her over from head to toe and back up again. Irena responded viscerally, feeling like a call girl being evaluated for the night. She half expected him to ask her to turn around so he could see her from every angle; or perhaps open her mouth so he could check her teeth. Alternately, she felt like a canary within reach of a hungry cat, or prey for a cobra ready to lunge. She hoped her deodorant held up.

Based on her resume and whatever additional information Cal provided, Lupo offered Irena the position of marketing coordinator. Despite her response to Lupo, Irena felt like a kid who had just been handed a free all-expense paid trip to Disneyland. Struggling to keep her feet still, Irena accepted Lupo's offer and agreed to start work the following Monday.

The grin never leaving his face, Lupo enthusiastically welcomed Irena to the firm, shaking her hand and holding on with both of his soft warm hands a bit longer than she felt necessary. Feeling like a fish on a line, Irena was sure she saw a glint in his eye and imagined he was thinking, "Hot diggity! She has the qualifications and looks good, too. And she'll work for me. Yippee." As Irena choked on his cologne, the hairs on the back of her neck prickled, a wave of goose bumps came and went, and she felt a bit dirty.

The dissimilarity in the way Cal and Lupo presented themselves in dress, behavior, and body language, along with Lupo's creepy behavior, left Irena with feelings of foreboding she did her best to dismiss. She needed and wanted this marketing position for financial reasons and for the joy of new and exciting work. And so, Irena told herself to stop over-reacting—that Lupo was merely a man appreciating a woman—and she ignored the alarms going off in her head.

When the interview was over, Cal, Lupo, Maxine, and Irena went their separate ways exchanging smiles, waves, and see-you-soons. Irena left the building high on the adrenaline of anticipation; confident she had the skills, aptitude, and attitude for marketing; and certain she could meet the challenges of this new and exciting chapter in her life. Her spirit soared as she contemplated a new and exciting career while maintaining her home and raising her children as a single parent.

*   *   *

Irena learned that Yutz & Dunne had long suffered a south-of-mediocre image among competitors and clients in the engineering community. Lupo had been marketing the firm by entertaining clients at meals, golf, and the like, with lots of grandstanding and little substance. He believed the firm could maintain viability and be successful in an increasingly competitive market based on little more than spontaneous self-aggrandizement.

With limited success over a dozen years and motivated by declining revenue, Lupo and his partner George hoped to increase revenue by hiring Bernadette McCoy, a fifth-grade elementary school teacher, as the firm's first marketing coordinator. They apparently believed that a teacher—even a fifth-grade teacher with no prior office or marketing experience—could improve the firm's image and profitability by writing winning proposals with nothing more than verbal input from an engineer.

*   *   *

A competitive proposal is a written instrument employed to pursue revenue-generating contracts. Generally speaking, competitive proposals are formal responses to requests for proposals, commonly referred to as RFPs sent to select recipients. The more costly and complex the project, the more comprehensive the request for proposal, and the more complex the response.

In design engineering, at least, a proposal is usually coordinated by a proposal manager, who need not be an engineer. A proposal manager can be a marketing coordinator or marketing manager with writing skill, access to information, and a team of cooperative engineers and sub-consultants, all willing to do their part.

The proposal usually contains a persuasive summary prepared by the proposal writer and manager, followed by a detailed scope of work and cost estimate prepared by the proposed project manager (usually an engineer). Included in the proposal are supporting examples of the firm's most recent, relevant, and comparable experience and targeted resumes for suggested staff showing that each has relevant and ideally recent experience on similar projects, prepared by the marketing representative.

The project owner who issued the RFP reviews responding proposals, shortlists (selects) the apparently most qualified firms; then invites those firms and representatives from their team of sub-consultants to a competitive presentation. The proposal manager/writer/coordinator often develops visual aids for company representatives to use in the presentation and coaches the engineers regarding how to make the best impression. The firm emerging as the most qualified and desirable then usually enters into contract negotiations with the owner.

*   *   *

Bernadette did not use a computer on the job, compelling her to interact with Lunice, the word processor, or "typist" as Lupo referred to her. Lunice was the only employee with a computer, except for Lupo's secretary.

Engineers maintained autonomous records, as did the survey and accounting departments. And Lupo would rather be caught dead than share his files with prying eyes. When Bernadette needed substantiating data for a proposal or statement of qualifications, she had no choice but to interact with engineers and surveyors who were annoyed and frustrated when she repeatedly asked for information she previously sought but did not retain. Her proposals were much like Lupo's marketing efforts, with little substance, lots of grandstanding rhetoric, and lost opportunities.

Once Bernadette dispatched a proposal, the information she collected disappeared—lost in the infancy of Lunice's word processing cyberspace or disposed of—perhaps because a proposal that failed to result in a contract generated no revenue. A hard copy of a proposal that did result in a contract would usually wind up buried in a design engineer's project file located in his office.

Bernadette resigned after two years to go back to teaching elementary school, and Yutz & Dunne hired Irena to replace her.

*   *   *

Arriving for her first day of work shortly before eight on a cold and sunny morning, Irena wanted to believe the clear weather was a good omen. She parked her car in the unkempt lot and could not help but think about the parking garage at the Jansen Building on Michigan Avenue where she spent six years working on the nineteenth floor with its view of the Chicago skyline.

Irena approached the entry to her new workplace and, afraid she might have to do battle with a sticky door again, took a deep breath and cautiously turned the doorknob. The clear dry air allowed the door to open easily, and Irena took the first step on her marketing journey.

Kitty, the receptionist, again wearing a tee-shirt, greeted Irena and gestured the way to Lupo's office with her mug, splashing coffee on her desk. And Irena thought about the professional receptionist at the Jansen Building who always dressed impeccably with perfect hair and make-up.

Making her way to Lupo's office along corridors formed by cubicles constructed of grungy tweed partitions, Irena noted that nearly everything in sight was some shade of brown or gray. Old battered furniture and equipment appeared to fill every available space, like an over-stocked shop selling used office furniture and associated goods or a flea market forty years ago.

Cubicles contained dissimilar old wood or steel desks, credenzas, task chairs, and wooden side chairs, like those from some 1950s schoolroom or kitchen. Three- or four-shelf wooden or steel bookcases were piled high with reference books and papers, plus old blue-denim and black plastic three-ring binders with hand-lettered labels taped to the spine. Otherwise unoccupied cubicle corners held well-worn cardboard boxes containing rolls of engineering plans or blueprints standing on end, most with tattered edges having obviously been rolled and unrolled countless times.

An occasional shaft of sunlight from an uncovered window made its way into the seamy surroundings, in dramatic contrast to Irena's historical workplaces where architects and decorators designed well-lit office interiors that looked and functioned beautifully.

Cubicle occupants, men presumed to be engineers prepared to work in the field, wore blue jeans or khaki pants and casual shirts. Glimpses of shoes and clumps of dried mud on cubicle floors told Irena the field was often a muddy one. Irena considered herself, as marketing coordinator, a visual representation of the firm who needed to create a good impression on visiting clients. She would never adapt to the casual dress of these and other employees.

Irena arrived at Lupo's private office where the dramatic contrast between his work space and the rest stunned her. He occupied an immaculate, stylishly decorated, corner office nearly thirty feet square, like a royal crown room, where everything appeared new. Plush navy blue carpeting complemented buttery yellow walls. Coordinating draperies hung from bright brass rods and graced windows that formed a corner. Diagonally across the room, two tall and wide mahogany bookcases formed another corner providing space for a round conference table and four upholstered task chairs.

An over-sized carved mahogany desk, matching credenza, and black-leather-and-mahogany chair evoking a throne faced the door.

Two Queen Anne-style upholstered armchairs faced Lupo's desk. A dedicated stand held a fax machine. A matching stand, next to an ornate grandfather clock, held bronze sculptures. Fine art hung on one wall, portraits of family members on another. Irena hesitated in the doorway before stepping in, wondering if she should bow, genuflect, or otherwise offer homage.

When Lupo failed to acknowledge her arrival, Irena approached his throne-like desk and quietly said "good morning." Lupo responded with a brusque "good morning" but remained focused on his paperwork. Eventually looking up, he abruptly said, "You report to me, but you will work with Cal. Find him and have him show you around." He then dismissed her with a perfunctory wave of his manicured hand, his pinky ring glittering in the light of a desk lamp.

Irena stood there momentarily, trying to reconcile Lupo's behavior at the interview with this frosty welcome. His abrupt dismissal stung and her face burned as though she had been slapped. Her left eyelid twitched. For twenty years in business, supervisors and co-workers treated Irena as a professional in her own right. She wondered if courtesy was too much to expect at Yutz & Dunne. Determined to remain optimistic, Irena told herself not to worry, that everything would work out just fine. And off she went; glad at least he wasn't leering.

*   *   *

Irena found Cal in his informal and windowless office far from Lupo. While Cal served as engineering manager—the go-to contact for junior engineers with questions or in need of work—he also performed design as a senior engineer. Looking up from his desk strewn with plans, binders, and red pencils, Cal welcomed Irena amiably. His warmth disappeared and he became visibly agitated when she told him that Lupo expected him to show her around the office and introduce her to others. Cal's dismay, along with Lupo's hasty dismissal, left Irena feeling like an unwelcome intruder on this, the first day of what she hoped would be her new beginning.

Cal guided Irena around the ramshackle building pointing out that the firm occupied two-thirds of the first floor and a small amount of space on the third floor, some spaces connected and others not, forcing employees outside to move from space to space and floor to floor.

Dimly lit, decaying, and unsanitary-looking restrooms accessed by key from out-of-doors—unavailable on the day of Irena's interview—were provided on the ground floor for all building tenants. On hot and humid summer days or cold and stormy winter days, employees—especially those on the third floor—were challenged to decide how badly they needed to go.

Cal first introduced Irena to administrative support staff ("staff" the term used to differentiate rank and file employees from partners or principals). He then introduced Cassius Banker, chief financial officer, who maintained an office near Lupo.

Corralled immediately outside Lupo and Cassius's offices, were the accounting manager who maintained corporate personnel records, carried out payroll functions, and served as office supervisor; two accounting clerks who entered timesheet and other data; the receptionist who, in addition to answering phones, greeted visitors and connected them with appropriate staff or principals; and Lupo's executive secretary who catered solely to his clerical needs.

Cal then introduced other principals and key staff, including senior design engineers and the survey manager. Irena found it curious that no-one was introduced with human resources responsibilities.

Administrative staff, engineering, and the survey department were located on the first floor, with survey physically separated from the rest. Survey had their own entry to and from the outdoors because they needed space for equipment and because they tracked in the most dirt.

Lastly, Cal introduced Lunice Kali, the company's word processor. Lunice merely glared at Irena and said nothing. Having wanted to be promoted to marketing coordinator Lunice resented Irena immediately simply for being hired.

Lunice was assigned her own unique space apart from the rest of the administrative women. Theoretically, she provided the entire staff with clerical support, except for Lupo, who had his own private secretary. In her early thirties, tall and thin, Lunice had stick-straight light brown hair and bangs she constantly brushed from her eyes. She usually wore blue jeans, a sweater, and no makeup, and she rarely smiled.

Irena would soon learn that Lupo referred to Lunice as the company typist, perhaps because she used her computer like a typewriter. Unfamiliar with her computer's capabilities, Lunice produced text documents section by section, saving each section electronically simply by date and time created. She neither named documents nor created directories or subdirectories to organize her work. As a result, Lunice could locate electronic files for a week or so, but beyond that it was a crapshoot, presenting problems for everyone sooner or later. But as Lunice told tetchy staff, "I am the word processor, the producer of documents. Filing is not my job."

Unwilling or unable to organize and maintain work assignments on her computer, Lunice requested and was granted additional office space to spread out the paperwork associated with her assignments, ultimately graduating from a double-sized cubicle to a double-sized office the size of Lupo's.

Most staff, including design engineers, worked in small cubicles far from natural light. Lunice's office had four windows, two work stations, and two doors—doors she often kept closed "to keep out the noise," she said—on which she often posted do-not-disturb signs. With two of everything, including five-shelf bookcases, Lunice controlled what may have been three hundred square feet of horizontal surface area, always piled with papers. Visitors to Lunice's office faced visual chaos along with the smell of half-eaten sugar donuts and stale coffee on her desk.

*   *   *

After Cal introduced Irena to those in the office that day, he provided her with new-employee forms to fill out, advising her to deliver the completed forms to the accounting manager. Those forms contained purely factual questions for her and said nothing about corporate or personnel policies. Irena trusted she would learn about those policies later.

Cal then guided Irena outdoors, up an exterior concrete staircase, across a concrete landing, and back into the building on the second floor; then up a steep, narrow, interior wooden staircase to her work station on the third floor.

A crease between Irena's eyes etched its way into her forehead as she struggled not to over-react to her workspace—a cubicle at most six feet square squeezed between two similar cubicles, the three constructed along the short wall of a dimly lit modest room that looked like an attic. One small octagonal window well above Irena's desk provided a view of the sky and the only natural light. Sloped ceilings intruded into the workspace and that steep wooden stairwell punctuated the center of the room like a giant drain.

Rather than a desk, Irena was assigned an old wooden table with nicks and dents as though small children had banged on it for years. She sat on a similarly old hard wooden side chair with no cushioning for her back or bottom and no casters for mobility. Her only storage space was an empty, vintage, three-shelf wooden bookcase and a battered two-drawer metal filing cabinet. With no computer or even a typewriter in sight, the crease in Irena's forehead deepened.

Crammed along the wall across from the three cubicles and rounding the corners, infringing on any space not otherwise occupied, were apparently long-forgotten cubicle partitions, metal filing cabinets, and dated wooden side chairs, most in various stages of disrepair. There were stacks of flat tattered blueprints and boxes of rolled plans from long-completed projects, along with piles of old display boards and other used presentation materials. Considering the dim lighting and layer of dust covering most everything, little appeared to have been disturbed for years even by cleaning staff. Faded and dusty, it was impossible to tell the original wall color.

Revolted by the overall environment, Irena barely heard Cal tell her to get settled and he or Lupo would "get back to her." It took the better part of a week before either of them contacted her again and before she met her cubicle mates.

While waiting for Cal or Lupo to get back to her, and with her cubicle mates out of the office on assignment, boredom drove Irena downstairs looking for something to do or someone to talk to. Cal was too busy and she did not know anyone else well enough to approach, so Irena went back upstairs to glean what she could from what she had.

Her filing cabinet contained a dozen or so many-times-repurposed manila folders protecting tattered bits of formal correspondence and hand-written notes bearing dates at least five years old. The folders and documents sported smudged fingerprints, some were spattered, and many bore rings from coffee mugs. Cal explained that the filing cabinet had been assigned to engineers deemed marketers for more than a dozen years. Thumbing through this hodgepodge, Irena saw no potential benefit to keeping those bits of paper, as none appeared related to client maintenance or competitive proposals. But rather than dump what appeared to be trash, she retained them in the unlikely chance someone came looking for them.

Melinda and Pat were the young female engineers-in-training (recent college graduates with little on-the-job experience) with whom Irena would share this intimate space. The three women would work like hamsters among the debris, occupying a firetrap stoked with an over-abundance of fuel with no fire extinguisher in sight. These women would have been fried to a crisp in a fire or entombed under a pile of rubble in some other catastrophic event.

*   *   *

Working in such close proximity with her cubicle mates, Irena, Melinda and Pat bonded once they got to know each other. With little to do and no-one around to eavesdrop, the three women comfortably griped to each other. Irena complained about her furniture and about working in the figurative and literal dark. Melinda and Pat complained about disrespect, lack of work, and relegation to the attic, isolated from the men.

Irena knew she had been hired as marketing coordinator for civil engineers, but with no historical data to tell her what the firm specifically did or for whom, and with no job description for her position, Irena began her career in marketing frustrated. Cal eventually filled in some blanks and Irena took notes, giving birth to a fledgling resource of historical information.

Irena knew the moment she drove into the parking lot, long before she walked in the door, that working at this engineering company would be challenging. The attic made her skin crawl, but she knew she had to adapt to succeed. Even so, Irena longed for her previous ergonomically comfortable and well-designed work station that held everything she needed to accomplish her work: her comfortable desk and task chair, storage space, fresh circulating air, good natural and artificial light, and soft carpeting beneath her feet. Faith, hope, and the desire for a new career carried her forward as she gambled on an eventual win-win.

*　　　*　　　*

Attempting to settle in, Irena could locate no job description, tangible guidelines, evidence of previous proposals, or other useful or historical marketing information anywhere accessible to her. To learn what she could, she arranged to meet with her predecessor, Bernadette McCoy.

Meeting in the conference room, Irena and Bernadette exchanged pleasantries. A tall and friendly brunette in her forties with an endearing Irish brogue, Bernadette expressed her happiness to be back teaching because she had missed the kids. Irena expressed her happiness to be working in marketing. Both women seemed relaxed and comfortable despite their different life objectives.

Irena asked Bernadette about marketing records or reference materials left behind when she resigned, beyond the miscellaneous notes in the filing cabinet. "There *is* nothing else," Bernadette said, "because Lupo and George never asked me to save anything."

Irena nearly choked on her coffee.

While disposing of unsuccessful work efforts is a plausible concept, Irena was stunned to learn that Bernadette felt no compunction to retain any evidence of her work efforts, especially any record of winning proposals, or any notes that helped her compose those proposals. And she wondered who would condone such work habits. Bemoaning Bernadette's lack of initiative, Irena assigned the majority of blame to a poorly managed organization.

19

With nothing else to be said, Irena thanked Bernadette for coming in to see her, and the women bid each other a fond adieu.

Chapter Two

C al came to often invite Irena into his office for a friendly chat. But more than friendship, Irena needed guidance. One morning, nearly swallowed by his oversized upholstered side chair, Irena said, "I'm so frustrated by the lack of documented corporate information. I really need to know what I'm supposed to do, other than sit around and wait for something to happen or someone to approach me with a task. If I could just see any job description alluding to marketing, it might help me understand what I could or should be doing."

Cal explained to Irena that no job descriptions existed for anyone and, as though she had crossed some line, he added that "Lupo and George never expressed any expectations for Bernadette either," as if that logic made any sense. Accepting that there were no marketing guidelines, Irena focused on the positive—concluding that the absence of a job description, expectations, or guidelines left her free to do whatever she deemed best to prove her value to the company. Having entered Cal's office that day frustrated, she left excited by that perceived freedom.

Irena believed that her experience with image building, client contact, and complex filing systems—from her big business background and from helping her dad market his business—along with her ability to write, design, and produce persuasive proposals quickly—would help improve the firm's image, develop new business, and increase revenue.

To illustrate her plans and to cement her relationship with Lupo, Irena developed a formal proposal like one she might send to a client, and arranged to meet with him to discuss her ideas. Sitting across from Lupo in his sweet-cologne-infused office, Irena stated her belief that whether selling products or services, marketing is basically the ability to make friends who trust and respect you and are willing to spend money on what you have to offer. She then handed Lupo her proposal and briefly articulated her plan.

Lupo glanced at her presentation, thumbed through a few pages, then handed it back to her chuckling like she was a child showing him an art project. Changing his demeanor abruptly he said, "You work for me, and I'll tell you what you need to do." He handed back the proposal and pointed to the door.

Chapter Three

Mario Centoni was the first engineer Lupo and George hired when they established the firm. Now in his mid-fifties, of average height, with piercing black eyes surrounded by black eyebrows and long lashes, Mario wore silver earrings and looked spray-tanned. He once designed a lucrative waterside project along the central coast of Chile, and Lupo catered to him, hoping he might seek out, be awarded, and design another such profitable project.

Cal Chauvin, the engineering manager who interviewed Irena and became her supervisor, was the second engineer hired. Also in his mid-fifties, as were most managing engineers, Cal was tall and thin, with thick, wavy brown hair and a low forehead sprouting bushy eyebrows over dark brown eyes. Cal had aspirations of supremacy that put him on a collision course with Lupo. The two remained diametrically opposed on virtually everything, often going head-to-head in devious ways, as if to simply piss each other off.

Cal often complained to Irena about Lupo's controlling and deceptive ways. Even his body language demonstrated how much he disliked the man. And the feeling was mutual. Whenever the two men had reason to interact in Irena's presence, she could see Cal's jaw tighten and his temples pulse. And he spoke in staccato sentences as though he did not want to speak to Lupo at all. Every time these two men stomped away from each other in a meeting or in a corridor, Irena imagined steam shooting out their ears like dueling teakettles.

Cal expected Irena to report to Lupo like her predecessor, Bernadette, which she did for months. But when Lupo decided she required too much attention, he handed responsibility for her and marketing over to Cal while retaining overriding control and first dibs on her time for his special projects. Cal responded with a "fuck-you-Lupo," telling Irena to "make the position your own." He then avoided her for months just to screw with Lupo, probably hoping she would quit.

Trying to fulfill a marketing role in a firm with combative principals, no policies and procedures, and no reference materials, Irena felt like she had been placed in a dark room, blindfolded, and told to hit a target she could not see.

Effectively abandoned by Cal, Irena still had to deal with his resentment, Lupo's erratic behavior, and Lunice's growing resentment and hostility for not being promoted. Irena realized that employees at Yutz & Dunne were expected to sink or swim with no support. Fortunate for her, abandonment gave her the opportunity to consider the culture of the company at her own pace, to observe co-workers' often disturbing relationships, and to carve out a place for herself.

Cal eventually acquiesced to a future he could not avoid, one that included Irena, and found himself challenged to balance and satisfy the autonomous demands of engineering design with the interpersonal demands of marketing. Adaptation did not come easily and Cal held tight to his resentment. Frequently caught in the cross-fire between Cal and Lupo, Irena yearned to tell Cal he needed to get along with Lupo just as he had begun telling her she needed to get along with Lunice.

*　　　*　　　*

Lupo often tried to impress Irena with some tale of masculine bravado. Sometimes she failed to hear his approaching footsteps on the thin carpet outside her cubicle, but she always recognized the crown of his head bobbing along the top edge. Unable to escape, she would take a deep breath and settle back for the inevitable.

On one occasion, Lupo entered her cubicle with his usual panache, smiling broadly, and settled down in her faux leather side chair. He told her about an evening during the early days of his marriage when he took his wife Betty out for dinner at a popular steakhouse. While walking back to their car in the nearby parking lot, some young thugs, as he called them, made a comment about Betty that made him angry.

Lupo said he took Betty home, picked up his baseball bat, and went back looking for "those thugs." He ended his little story with a laugh, obviously proud of himself and his machismo. He never told Irena how the evening ended.

Lupo made other spontaneous visits to Irena's cubicle to manipulate her into performing assignments she considered repugnant. Whenever he started a conversation by telling her how much he respected and admired her, she knew he wanted something—usually for her to surreptitiously gather information from his partners.

Lupo would ask her to find out what his partners were thinking about or doing about blah, blah, and blah; or would ask her to find out if his partners would support him on blah, blah, or blah; adding the kicker, "Don't let them know I'm asking." When the task was complete, Lupo would reward Irena with more insincere flattery saying, among other things, that he knew he could count on her persistence and dependability. Irena wanted to retch, knowing she had little choice but to cooperate.

Irena knew that Lupo, as owner of the company, held her career in the palm of his hand, but it turned her stomach that he had so little regard for his partners that he would use her to spy on them, and so little regard for her, thinking she was unaware of his manipulations. Irena considered refusing to cooperate, but she did not dare risk Lupo's temper or possible termination, because fear of losing her ability to financially care for her children ruled her life.

Knowing it was impossible to change Lupo and how he interacted with his partners and staff, Irena would do what he asked, feeling like a hypocrite, often detesting him and herself in the process. She remained silent about her feelings and watched her integrity erode as she chose her survival over others'.

Compelled to contend with Lupo's manipulative and controlling ways and his flippant sexuality, she wanted to laugh out loud at his aging and feeble machismo as he followed her down empty corridors whispering sexual clichés from behind. "I don't want to get in trouble, but I'd like to have your swing on my front porch," or, "I'd like to have your slippers under my bed."

Irena coped and stuffed her thoughts and emotions into an ever-expanding metaphorical gunnysack, growing more and more disturbed—like a bird in a soundproof box, chirping and flapping like crazy, but nobody knew.

Chapter Four

A few weeks after being hired, Irena met Greedo Chienmale in the company kitchen—a kitchen that began life as a storage room, with abused steel cabinets and a deep industrial sink originally used to slop mops. Eating alone at the small table in this other-than-charming kitchen, wishing she could be anywhere outdoors, Irena noticed this blonde and muscular forty-something man checking her out. It did not take Greedo long to pull over a folding chair to make himself comfortable next to her.

Smiling broadly, he introduced himself as a field technician, "a surveyor or engineer without the professional title," he said. He explained that he assisted engineers and surveyors haul equipment to reconfirm property boundaries and plan digs for utilities after confirming no conflict with power companies. He also told Irena about his dedication to body building and floral design. Responding to his flirtatious manner, Irena heard, "I look great under these clothes," and, "I'm a sensitive guy who will bring you flowers." Shifting in his chair to make direct eye contact, Greedo asked Irena questions she wanted to believe were borne of simple curiosity.

Are you married? He asked.
I'm in the final stages of divorce, she replied.
 Where do you live?
I have a house in Chenowith.
What will happen to your house after your divorce?
I hope to keep it.
Do you have children?
Yes, three little ones at home.

Irena could almost hear the whirr of his brain and a red flag went up, but she told herself to stop being paranoid. They ended the conversation with smiles and encountered each other in the kitchen on occasion after that, casually chatting as they ate lunch.

*   *   *

The news of Irena's decree ending her marriage spread fast and Greedo invited her out to dinner to celebrate. Exhausted and depressed by job issues, divorce, and a sixteen-year-old dog dying of multiple myeloma, Irena's need for a friendly shoulder trumped her apprehension about dating this co-worker.

Greedo arranged a dinner date for the following Saturday night at an upscale French restaurant in downtown Chicago, where contemporary floral designs adorned glass-topped tables, delicious aromas filled the air, and classical music played softly. Greedo held Irena's chair for her to sit and took the liberty of ordering for both of them. Irena was impressed.

After that one-of-a-kind dinner date, Greedo began spending most evenings at Irena's home, casually dining with her and her children around Irena's oversized oak coffee table in front of her big-screen TV, a fire filling the living room with a warm glow and the smell of fruitwood.

In addition to theoretically wooing Irena, Greedo wooed her children. He played with them and surrounded them with stuffed animals after dinner, bundling them in blankets on the living room floor until they fell asleep and Irena put them to bed. Greedo became increasingly comfortable acting like a husband and father. His apparent tenderness warmed her heart.

Weekends without the children allowed time and opportunity for their relationship to grow. As she succumbed to his apparent tenderness, she also succumbed to his embrace. Years of divorce proceedings had frozen Irena's heart and body, but Greedo's tenderness and the warmth of his hands awakened a passion Irena had long suppressed.

*   *   *

On a warm summer weekend six weeks after their dinner date, Greedo and Irena went to Grant Park for a picnic. Sitting on a blanket near the fountain, they were occasionally chilled by a wind-blown spray of water. They drank wine from Styrofoam cups, listened to twittering birds, watched people at a nearby craft faire, and listened to strains of music drifting out of the faire grounds. Children walked by with their parents, leaving behind the lingering aroma of freshly spun cotton candy. Irena was more relaxed than she had been for a long time.

Taking advantage of a lull in conversation, Greedo leaned toward Irena and declared, in his soft-spoken, matter-of-fact manner, "I love you..." And without taking a breath or pausing for a reciprocal declaration, and with no reference to her children, Greedo went on to say, "...and I should move into your house as soon as possible. We should then get married. And when we get married, I expect you to put my name on the deed to your house, in exchange for sex and household chores."

Like a two-by-four to the side of her head, Irena thought:

Whoa, bucko! Why would I commit to a relationship with you or anyone else within weeks of the decree ending my marriage, especially after a contentious and expensive divorce? Do you think I can't survive without a man? Do you think I can't survive without sex? Or do you think I should trust you to help me pay off my legal fees?

With nothing further said, Irena allowed Greedo's proposition to hang in mid-air to die of neglect.

*   *   *

Greedo may have interpreted Irena's lack of response as acceptance of his proposition, because one evening shortly thereafter, after putting the children to bed, he and Irena sat on her living room sofa where, apparently feeling comfortable, he made certain revelations that freaked her out.

Greedo explained that the woman he married a few months ago, after a short courtship (whom Irena knew nothing about), had filed for divorce, but allowed him to stay in her home until he found another place to live. Greedo said he did not understand why she had a problem putting his name on the deed to her house. As the wife was pressuring Greedo to move out, he was pressuring Irena to let him move in.

Greedo went on to tell Irena about other wives, lovers, and children, revealing that he and his first wife had no children and divorced after five years: he and his second wife had four children when she kicked him out after an episode he refused to talk about. His third marriage produced two children and ended in divorce. Two more children were produced out of wedlock. Summed up, he admitted to four marriages, a fifth relationship, and eight children. Greedo told Irena she had nothing to worry about because, "I don't see them or have anything to do with them."

Irena had a difficult time keeping her lips together and her chin in place. Her aortic artery throbbed and her stomach thrashed like a washing machine full of rocks. Past behavior being a predictor of future behavior, the soles of Irena's feet began to itch.

*   *   *

When Irena failed to invite Greedo to move in, he rented a simple apartment—two-thirds of a detached and converted two-car garage—blocks from her home, apparently to wait her out. His dreary and windowless space displayed uneven walls painted a noxious shade of industrial green and a concrete floor painted steely gray. Greedo had the benefit of a small, well-used bathroom with a disagreeably moldy odor, and an efficiency refrigerator/sink/stove unit with only one working burner.

Greedo did not need much space because the sum of his material possessions consisted of two wooden side chairs, an old oak office desk, a drafting board, and a few flea-market finds—none bigger than a breadbox. He did not own a bed and reluctantly purchased an inexpensive plastic-webbed aluminum folding cot, counting on being in Irena's home and bed soon enough.

Following her divorce ordeal, Irena sought comfort in the company of this soft-spoken man she wanted to believe cared about her. But she soon saw Greedo in a different light when his proposition and subsequent behavior reminded her that life is full of risks and dishonorable people.

Three weeks after propositioning Irena and seven weeks into their ersatz relationship, Greedo began to apply pressure, asking her almost daily when he could move in. The more he pressed, the more she resisted. Realizing she was not the easy catch he anticipated, Greedo began seeking out other women even while continuing to pressure Irena.

*   *   *

While navigating her relationship with Greedo, Irena's sister Elaine came to visit from Massachusetts. After picking her up at O'Hare airport, the two women spent the day with Irena's children before dropping them off at their father house for their month-long summer vacation with him.

Irena and Elaine spent their first evening together getting Elaine settled in the guest room Irena recently redecorated in the shabby chic style they both liked. Morning sun would flood that east-facing room lighting up the fabric flora and fauna like an English garden.

Before retiring for the evening, Irena and Elaine relaxed with a cup of steamy, fragrant hot chocolate laced with peppermint schnapps. With each woman tucked into an overstuffed chair in Irena's living room, they debated Greedo and his pressure on Irena to marry him and put his name on the deed to her house.

Concerned for her sister's well-being and never one to mince words, Elaine pulled her feet out from under her and placed them squarely on the floor. Leaning in toward Irena, she said, "What is wrong with you? Are you crazy, dumb, or blind? Why haven't you dumped that gold digger?" Irena said, "I want you to meet him before I make a decision." And Elaine shook her head in disbelief. The women had a second cup of hot chocolate laced with schnapps and postponed further discussion. They watched a little television and went to bed early.

Irena and Elaine spent several days in Chicago checking out the local sights by foot, city bus, and local tours. They visited Buckingham Fountain, the Riverwalk, Navy Pier playground on Lake Michigan—and of course the Magnificent Mile where they took advantage of some quality shopping. Each day ended with a glass of wine over dinner, along with conversation about the sights that day and Greedo.

After mailing Elaine's large and heavy purchases back to Massachusetts, the women headed for Maui. The turbulent flight disrupted their thoughts of sunny beaches, palm trees, and ukulele music. An unanticipated drop in altitude caused their blue Hawaii and pink mai tai cocktails to rise up out of their plastic cups and come splashing down soaking and discoloring the fronts of their clothing. Sticky floors made for uncomfortable disembarking. Arriving in Hawaii smelling like fruity cocktails, they and the plane needed to be hosed down.

*   *   *

When Irena reserved their rental car, she asked for something "sporty." Waiting at the kiosk was a bright yellow Mustang convertible with a black top and double black racing stripes along the sides. They joked about feeling like a giant bumblebee and giggled like schoolgirls.

Irena and Elaine toured the island and spent hours sitting in the warm sun sampling tropical drinks on palm-fringed black sand beaches. After catching up about family back in Massachusetts, they debated Irena's relationship with Greedo.

"I don't need to know more about him or meet him," Elaine said. "He's a letch and a loser. You just need to dump him." "But...," Irena said, in a classic maybe-settling-is-not-so-bad attitude, "...I spent so many years on the defensive in my marriage trying to protect myself from events unfolding around me, events over which I had no control. I just want to relax and allow good things to flow into my life. Greedo seems like an easy man to live with, even if there is a lot that makes me want to run. Please...," Irena begged Elaine, "...just meet him first."

Greedo called Irena every night she was in Hawaii repeating his mantra. "I love you and want to move in and get married as soon as possible. When can I move in?" Irena would find some way to change the subject or tell him they would discuss it later.

Preoccupied with his own agenda, Greedo failed to realize that Irena never told him she loved him. But then, he probably did not care whether she loved him or not, so long as she married him and put his name on the deed to her house.

Having been in the throes of divorce for years, considering the hours she worked, and the little time she had to spend with her children, Irena was dog-tired, confused, and vulnerable. She flirted with the depression of a stereotypical divorcee with children, fearing that no man would ever want her with three children and a huge debt.

Irena continued to talk about Greedo on the flight back to Chicago, telling Elaine that she really needed someone like her, whose love she trusted, to give her a good shake to get her brain working again. "Let me know if you still feel the same way about Greedo after you meet him."

*   *   *

Back in Chenowith, the women decided to have dinner with Greedo and get right to the inevitable. Dropping off their luggage, they took showers, changed clothes, and showed up at Greedo's unannounced just after sunset. They parked across the street along the dirt embankment that served as a sidewalk, and Irena led Elaine around the beige garage to the patio between the garage and the house. When Irena told Elaine that Greedo lived in the garage, Elaine stopped short and looked at Irena with eyebrows arched high and her mouth half open.

Concealed by a six-foot-high chain-link fence woven with faded and flaking green plastic privacy strips, the two women, shorter than the fence by several inches, approached the patio unobserved, the smell of barbecue filling the air.

When they opened the creaky gate, they found Greedo and a woman sitting close together sharing wine at a table covered by a multi-colored striped tablecloth illuminated by several tea candles. Greedo's lady friend reacted with a startled yelp and reached for his arm. Both dropped their glasses, spilling wine and nearly dousing some of those candles.

Greedo looked at Irena, his face contorted, and uttered the uninspired, "What are you doing here?" Having pressured Irena just the previous evening to let him move in and marry him, Greedo had been fully aware of her arrival date and time. It had not occurred to Irena that Greedo would be anything but home alone waiting for her.

Her face hot with humiliation, Irena responded slowly, dripping with sarcasm, saying, "We just got back from Hawaii and I thought we might have dinner together. I wanted to introduce my sister Elaine and tell you about our trip. But I see you have a party going on here. We won't keep you from your plans." At that, Irena took Elaine's arm to leave and Greedo did nothing to stop them.

As Irena and Elaine approached the car, Elaine started to speak, but Irena cut her off saying, "Don't..." As sisters, Irena knew what Elaine had to say and Elaine knew that Irena understood.

*   *   *

Irena began to realize that her post-divorce stupor had made her easy prey for someone like Greedo who apparently believed in his formula for winning a woman's heart and home: tell her he loved her, demonstrate his love by having sex with her, demonstrate his generosity by spending lots of money on her even when it put him in debt, and show her what a great guy he is by helping out with chores around her home.

In return, Greedo expected that woman to demonstrate her love for him by taking him in, marrying him, and putting his name on the deed to her house. And, like any business arrangement, he saw no reason this could not happen in the span of a few weeks. Finding him with another woman convinced Irena that Greedo was prepared to bond with any woman willing to take him in and secure his future by putting his name on the deed to her home. Screw love.

"Greedo may have remained loyal like a dog," Elaine told Irena, "because loyalty may not have been too much to sacrifice for a lifetime of financial security. But while we may love our animals, wouldn't you rather have a man who loves you before a dog who licks your hand for a handout?"

That night, as Irena contemplated her children and her future, Greedo's recent revelations, and Elaine's observations, her image of good things flowing into her life became an image of raw sewage flowing into a cesspool.

But rejecting Greedo outright did not come easy for Irena.

*   *   *

Shortly after showing up at Greedo's apartment and interrupting his intimate little dinner on the patio, Irena asked him to have lunch with her. Under a bright and sunny sky, they sat on a concrete bench outside the office building. Birds flew overhead and clouds scudded across the sky. They dined on lukewarm hot dogs from a pushcart vendor.

Fighting off discomfort from the cold concrete bench, indigestion from the lukewarm hot dog, and wanting to exterminate Greedo like the vermin she now considered him to be, Irena told him as gently as she could, "I'm really not interested in getting married again. And since you seem so eager to remarry, we should stop seeing each other so you can find someone else." She resisted the overwhelming urge to tell him that hell would freeze over before she would ever consider marrying anyone even remotely like him.

Greedo stood up suddenly as if someone had goosed him. Likely upset because Irena wasted his time searching for a new woman to take him in, he accused her of being a "shameful kind of girl" who would have sex with a man she did not want to marry. *Shame on me,* Irena thought. *But Greedo obviously doesn't recognize himself as someone who would have sex with a woman so he can live off her money. Shame on him.*

*   *   *

After Irena broke it off with Greedo, he gave up on his neighbor—a renter no doubt—and redirected his attention to Gwen Fotch, another co-worker. Irena and Gwen ate lunch together on occasion and talked, as women often do, about themselves and men. Self-confident Gwen described herself as a greedy woman who "adored it" when men spent money on her.

Fifty-four years old, reasonably attractive, petite but oddly large-boned with thick ankles, Gwen had tightly curled light brown hair and pale brown eyes. Divorced at nineteen, having been married for a few months, she had no children, and of course owned her own home. Gwen responded enthusiastically to Greedo's attention.

Everyone in the office, including Gwen, knew that Greedo and Irena had been dating. On the way to their cubicles from the kitchen one day after lunch, Gwen took Irena into an empty cubicle. Glowing with pride and perhaps more, Gwen told Irena that Greedo professed his love for her. Boasting about his lavish spending habits, her tone of voice and body language clearly indicated that she saw Greedo as the trophy in some competition she was winning.

Irena wanted to laugh out loud.

She told Gwen about her relationship with Greedo, shared what she knew about him, and suggested she steer clear. Gwen rejected Irena's suggestion and refused to believe that Greedo ever told Irena he loved her, making Irena wonder what fantasy he concocted for her.

Greedo had pursued Irena for six weeks during May and June, and began to pursue Gwen in late June. He moved into her home in August and the two were married in September. Gwen, the heroine, saved Greedo from the streets of poverty and won herself a husband. He, more than likely, won a secure future by having Gwen put his name on the deed to her home. Five weeks after the wedding, Greedo resigned from Yutz & Dunne to work part-time at a local florist.

According to Mahatma Gandhi, "Earth provides enough to satisfy every man's need, but not every man's greed."

*   *   *

Irena faced the challenge of integrating the up of being in marketing, the down of her divorce, the up of her initial relationship with Greedo, the down of Lunice's resentment, the up of having time to get to know her new workplace, the down of discovering the hostility between Cal and Lupo, the up of recognizing a need she could fulfill, and so on—like riding a roller coaster.

Chapter Five

F
our of the six partners of this male-dominated engineering firm surprised the female employees with some "special entertainment" for National Administrative Assistants Day, spearheaded by the soft-spoken, close-to-retirement-age, detail-oriented Cassius Banker. Like Cal, Cassius fulfilled counterintuitive responsibilities as chief financial officer and human resources officer.

On the big day, portly Cassius, with his denim blue eyes, curly black hair, and mottled complexion, along with Cal, herded the women into an area of the office where several desks were arranged out in the open, where other partners and key staff, sans Lupo, had already gathered. One desk, covered with a festive tablecloth, held a full chocolate sheet cake, six bottles of champagne, and the necessary paraphernalia. Lupo's secretary Maxine served cake while Cal poured champagne.

Raising his glass in a toast, Cal said, "The partners want to take this opportunity to thank each of you *girls* for your hard work this year and show you how much you are valued." Cal grinned like a Cheshire cat and when Irena asked what was going on, he said, "Don't ask. Just wait."

When everyone had their fill of cake and champagne, Cassius asked the women to form a circle around some open floor space. He then stepped into the hallway returning with a young man in his early twenties about five foot six, slightly pudgy with dark shaggy locks, long sideburns, and a five o'clock shadow. He wore an old green pocket tee-shirt, ragged blue jeans, old tennis shoes, and carried a boom box on one shoulder. Irena thought of Chunky Monkey.

Cassius led the young man into the center of the women's circle and retreated to a doorway to join the men who were effectively blocking the exits should any woman try to escape the "fun." The women looked back and forth to each other like "What the hell?" while Cal and Cassius grinned broadly.

Putting his boom box on one of the gray steel desks, the young man turned it on to loud, pulsating music. Gyrating slowly at first, then more aggressively in time with the music, he began thrusting his pelvis and peeling off layers of clothing. First making eye contact, the stripper then looked each woman up and down pausing at strategic locations along their bodies, grinned and licked his lips lewdly. The women eyed each other like trapped animals.

Eventually stripped naked except for a green G-string that looked like it had seen better days, and dark chest hair that looked like a costume, he pumped his hips and otherwise drew attention to his presumed body parts. From the size of his package, Irena thought, *he must have a sock in that G-string.* Then he stripped off the green G-string revealing a red G-string. He stripped off the red G-string revealing a yellow one. Green, red, yellow: small, smaller, smallest. His package considerably reduced, there was no sock.

As part of his grand finale, the stripper cornered, rubbed, and bumped against some of the women trapped within the circle of desks. He thrust his hips in time to the music first face-to-face with his target, then bending away from her using his backside. The men roared with delight at the ladies' obvious discomfort. They even took pictures for the company photo files. Most women cringed, but remained where they were lest they be criticized later for being poor sports. *Thank God he couldn't reach me,* Irena thought later, *or I might have vomited.*

For the Christmas gift exchange later that year, Cal gave Irena a Chippendale's beefcake calendar and gave Cassius a pair of pantyhose for men, with an elephant's trunk for his appendage: the man's not the elephant's.

Chapter Six

O ther than hiring Bernadette to write proposals, historical marketing for Yutz & Dunne meant that Lupo would assign the title of marketer to an affable engineer with the gift of gab and dispatch him to entertain clients and potential clients. The affable engineer was expected to introduce himself, make friends, pick up the tab for lunch, dinner, or a round of golf, and see if he could generate work for the company. "He" because no woman ever held this position in this company.

That same engineer, cum marketer, would produce proposals incorporating braggadocio with little if any statistical substantiation, occasionally submitting an informal and unsolicited proposal in response to a rumor about an upcoming project. Like throwing leaves into a rushing river, no-one ever tracked these efforts.

With virtually no information readily available for new proposals or statements of qualifications, Irena was compelled to approach the engineers like Bernadette had. They seemed to believe that Irena's approach would mimic Bernadette's, because they reacted with resistance and even hostility.

Doing her best to be pleasant, Irena would sit in an engineer's guest chair or stand, depending on the degree of hostility she perceived. She would apologize for the interruption and explain that she had searched unsuccessfully for information she needed for a proposal, and ask if he had any project files containing a proposal or other documents with quantifying information. If not, she would ask if he could remember anything she could use.

She would also explain that she planned to minimize future interruptions by asking a question once, then retaining quantitative project information and other resources in a regularly maintained, user-friendly information management system readily available to employees.

She quickly discovered the depth of disregard staff had for Lupo, for Bernadette, and now for her. The engineer's body language and facial expressions prompted her to imagine his internal dialogue.

Oh no. Not you again.
(followed by a look of disgust and hostility);
Why do I have to go through this every time you have a proposal to write?
(followed by a slow sigh of exasperation);
I know I eventually have to do this, but I do not want to, and certainly not now.
(and a prolonged pause that felt threatening);
Let me calm down so I do not throw something at you.
(…or just plain uncooperative);
How can I get rid of you this time?

Engineers often brushed Irena off with an explanation as to why they could not take time to help "just then," and asked her to come back time and again. Irena failed to understand the on-going perversity, and the specter of chauvinism crept into her consciousness. To minimize further unpleasant confrontations, Irena tried requesting information in writing. Most engineers failed to respond. *Like trying to kill a swarm of killer bees with a slingshot*, Irena thought.

Few took Irena's efforts seriously because few took Lupo seriously, and Lupo had hired her. Lupo treated engineers with such disregard that they, like Cal, had a "screw-you-Lupo" mentality, doing no more than the minimum expected; and they considered providing Irena with information beyond their obligation.

Expecting Irena to help the firm be more successful without their participation, it seems none of them ever heard the expression, "If you always do what you always did, you'll always get what you always got." In the case of Yutz & Dunne, they got mediocrity. Frustration and despair gnawed at Irena and she in turn gnawed on her fingernails.

*   *   *

Even though Irena felt free to make a difference, she had little support from Lupo or cooperation from the engineers, and she had no tools. Despite fifteen years of computer experience before joining Yutz & Dunne, every time Irena requested a computer, technologically challenged Lupo would declare with increasing irritation that he would not spend money on a computer for her because computers used by "non-technical" women (i.e., those who were not engineers) were merely glorified typewriters. He insisted that Irena's "typing" be left to a "lesser employee;" i.e., Lunice. He refused to believe that Lunice's capabilities were inadequate to accommodate the scope of Irena's work products.

Three aging non-networked computers used by the engineers and surveyors, each on its own two-by-four-foot folding table, were located within a single cubicle near the high-traffic reproduction and word processing areas. With access to only one telephone, engineers and surveyors worked elbow to elbow amid the chatter and interruptions of passersby. Despite the pace of technology in other companies, Lupo clung to his pea-shooters long after competitors were blasting the marketplace with technological canons.

Pacing back and forth outside her cubicle in the attic one morning, after yet again being denied her own computer or use of the three computers downstairs, Irena complained to Melinda and Pat.

"I was under the impression I was hired for my abilities, including my computer skills. Lupo might as well cut off my fingers." Melinda pointed to a filthy old computer sitting on a small wooden table tucked in among the nearby detritus and said, "Lupo gave us that cantankerous old thing and you are welcome to use it."

The computer worked well enough and Irena was overjoyed, but soon dubbed the cantankerous old thing "the rogue" for its temperamental glitches, limitations, and isolation. However, the lack of networking left her free to develop a marketing database of relevant information with no-one able to view or access her files from another location.

This computer would become a focal point of contention, placing Irena in the cross-hairs of Lunice's insecurity and rage. Beyond the battle of the computer, Irena had to overcome the prevailing fear of change among Lupo, the engineers, and the surveyors.

*   *   *

Soon after Irena began using the rogue, Melinda and Pat resigned simultaneously. Disappointed that they had not told her in advance, Irena suspected that inadequate workload, inadequate tools, and the frustration of working in exile drove them out. Irena was despondent over being abandoned to work alone in that isolated and neglected third-floor space.

Melinda and Pat's departure seemed symptomatic of the gender bias at this firm where female engineers-in-training, field and office technicians usually resigned soon after being hired. Dissatisfaction ran rampant even among the few young female engineering school graduates seeking work experience, hired for a fraction of fair wages. Most left disheartened within a year after complaining to Irena and each other about condescension and mistreatment: except for Diane Lisbon, who lasted a while longer.

A capable and self-confident, high-energy, engineer-in-training in her thirties with a military background, Diane grumbled like the rest. Her complaints included a lack of respect and an inadequate workload she could complete in a few hours, leaving her with nothing to do. Diane told Irena that when she sought more work from her supervisor, he dismissed her, treating her like a pesky child.

Engineers-in-training traditionally go through years of progressive work experience under the supervision of a licensed engineer, only then qualifying to take the licensing test. Once licensed, they are typically recognized with a notable salary increase.

As an engineer-in-training at Yutz & Dunne, Diane earned less than her male counterparts. When she passed the exam establishing her as a professional civil engineer, the company denied her a salary increase comparable to that allocated to men who passed the exam—despite the Equal Pay Act of 1963, the yet-to-be-enacted-at-the-time Lilly Ledbetter Fair Pay Act of 2009, and the Paycheck Fairness Act still pending in 2016.

Diane met with Darrell Russell, her supervisor, to discuss the economic discrimination. He promptly had her salary converted to hourly wages and her workload reduced to a level that did not pay a living wage, forcing her to seek employment elsewhere.

Sue Montaigne, a youthful looking engineer-in-training, also complained to Irena that Darrell gave her little to do and disrespected her as though she did not have what it took to be an engineer. After mere months on the job, Sue resigned, "sick and tired of the comments about being a little girl in a grown-up world."

*   *   *

Condemned to the third-floor attic, Irena was frequently summoned to the first floor by Cal or Lupo. Neither man seemed able to communicate his needs over the phone or make his way upstairs.

Irena would descend that treacherous flight of wooden stairs from the attic, step outdoors to the concrete landing, then descend that equally dangerous flight of concrete steps to the first floor—on hot summer days, during spring rain, or clinging to the railing slipping and sliding on ice in winter—and do it again in reverse. Those calls from Lupo, Cal, and even Mother Nature began to feel like high-voltage electric cow prods.

The risk and discomfort of frequently descending and ascending those stairs, along with sitting on a solid wooden chair (despite providing her own cushions), lower back pain soon became Irena's constant companion. Pleading for a more comfortable chair, Cal would say, "We'll be moving to better quarters soon and things will improve." Waiting what felt like an eternity for that to happen, Irena's fingernails often left dents in the palms of her hands, and the crease between her eyes deepened.

*   *   *

Unlike other staff Irena interviewed, Cal cooperated and provided her with limited information about the firm's general history, projects, and staff. He explained that flamboyant and egotistical Lupo Yutz and his mild-mannered partner George Dunne, two aspiring young civil engineers with presumably equal financial and intellectual investments, founded the firm a dozen years before she joined the firm. George resigned the year before she was hired.

George and Lupo met periodically during Irena's first year to finalize George's transition out of the firm. Lupo negotiated to retain the company name and appointed himself chairman of the board.

Losing George as an invested partner, Lupo invited certain senior staff to become new partners, each to invest according to his financial ability above a certain minimum. Each was promised an equal and undivided vote on corporate matters, even as Lupo allocated ownership on a percentile basis relative to unequal financial investments.

Yutz & Dunne thus transitioned from a partnership of two to a partnership of six, with each new partner anticipating some degree of power and financial success. Lupo retained a fifty-one percent majority ownership and went on to emasculate his new partners by over-ruling many majority decisions, initiating an undercurrent of dissatisfaction, and igniting the long fuse of a firestorm.

*　　　*　　　*

Lupo's new partners had worked for years in relatively isolated servitude, subordinate only to Lupo and perhaps George. Still calling the shots, Lupo arbitrarily divvied up staff and assigned each new partner a group of subordinates including young engineers-in-training. He expected those partners, with no management training or guidelines, to become successful supervising managers overnight. And he expected their subordinates to thrive under the circumstances.

Aspiring young engineers were treated like nameless, faceless, interchangeable game pieces. They complained, even to Irena, about being arbitrarily hired, fired, and assigned and reassigned new tasks, even mid-task, with little discussion, guidance, or follow-up. Expected to succeed in a virtual vacuum, the engineering partners and their subordinates became the blind leading the blind, resulting in roiling dissatisfaction.

The narcissistic top-down belief that engineers are so intelligent and capable that supervisors do not need to provide guidance and subordinates do not need to receive any resulted in a culture of neglect that bled down through partners and staff like pus from an infected wound.

44

Psychologically healthy employees resigned in frustration and disgust for more valuable training and better working conditions elsewhere. Less healthy employees remained and grumbled amongst themselves, evolving like bumper cars at Coney Island, sooner or later adapting to an environment worthy of a psych ward.

*   *   *

Lupo bragged to Irena and others about being a reformed alcoholic and, like certain alcoholic personalities, he expected everyone to jump when he spoke. He dominated conversations, demonstrating little respect for others by dismissing and even mocking their opinions, often exploding at employees without warning, making cruel and hurtful comments.

Lupo was particularly abusive on Fridays when rumor was he drank his lunch. Conditioned by his unpredictable volatility, staff would avoid him after noon wondering if or when the hammer might fall.

Lupo often returned from his Friday mid-day meal and woe to anyone who crossed his path. He would find some reason to attack and then disappear, leaving the targeted individual dumbfounded for the rest of the weekend wondering what the hell just happened. Two out of three times, Lupo would apologize on Monday or keep the individual waiting until Tuesday, as though his apology absolved him.

Irena's first memorable exposure to Lupo's darker side occurred on a Friday afternoon after five o'clock, in concert with one of George's post-resignation visits.

Lupo had asked Irena to develop a statement of qualifications concentrating on roadway design projects including resumes of staff engineers with experience on such projects. No-one on staff could provide her with the necessary information, and Lupo told her that George, expected at five thirty, could do so.

Frequently required to work past dinnertime, Irena often left her children on their own to do homework and to eat pre-prepared meals plucked from the freezer for a quick thaw in the microwave, breaking her heart and steeping her in guilt. She promised her children this particular evening that she would be home to celebrate her daughter's birthday over dinner.

At five-forty-five, eager to leave, Irena wandered over to Lupo's office to see if George had arrived. Not seeing him, she said nothing, returned to her desk, and called her children to say she would be home soon.

At six-fifteen she again went to Lupo's office. Still not seeing him, Irena asked Lupo if George was still coming. Having seen Irena pass by the first time, he responded with a brusque affirmative that conveyed she was being a pest and she should just wait. Irena's cheeks burned and her fingers twitched, but she said nothing and returned to her desk.

At six thirty, having told her children yet again that she would be home soon, Irena returned to Lupo's office. Despite the pounding in her ears from her rising blood pressure, she calmly asked Lupo how much longer it might be before George arrived. Playing her sympathy card, she explained that her children were home alone waiting for a birthday dinner with her and she had already kept them waiting for more than an hour.

Responding with fire in his eyes, Lupo jumped to his feet, stormed around his desk and verbally attacked like a demonic pit bull. He jabbed a finger at her face and shouted that she had responsibilities to her job and she had better make a choice—his implied threat that she had better choose her job over her kids or she would regret it.

What the hell? One day this chameleon is laying on praise and the next day he's attacking.

Outraged by Lupo's behavior, yet wrought with fear and obligation to her job and her children, Irena overcame the inner demon that wanted to leap out of her chest, jump on Lupo's chest, and pound him into the ground after ripping his heart out. She knew the safest bet was to turn and walk away, but Lupo would not let her be.

Nipping at her heels and poking her every step of the twenty-five yards back to her desk, Lupo's final stab was an icy and sarcastic comment about being "free to go if she *wanted* to, to feed her *poor little babies*," his voice ending on the up in the unfinished sentence and implied threat that if she did, she was in deep shit.

George showed up within minutes of Lupo's tirade, provided Irena with the information she needed, and she left, dumbfounded.

Unaware of Lupo's tendency to behave like a raving lunatic, Irena feared she would be fired on Monday for even thinking of putting her children ahead of her job, even after the usual close of business. Grieving in anticipation of losing her newly won marketing position, Irena fretted over the weekend about how she would provide for her family. Come Monday, Lupo was pleasant and cheerful all day as Irena tiptoed around afraid to breathe. On Tuesday morning, he apologized, and Irena considered herself baptized.

*   *   *

Consistent with his crack-of-the-whip mentality, if Lupo imagined a grand or modest marketing product for some unique purpose, he expected Irena to drop everything, including her commitments to others. He expected her to produce the product virtually immediately with a bare minimum of discussion, demanding utmost secrecy even as he refused to divulge his intent.

Exiting the kitchen one afternoon, Lupo approached Irena and demanded that she produce what he called "a bible" of the firm's qualifications.

Standing within earshot of engineers, Lupo told her he wanted her to incorporate every service the firm did and could provide. He wanted her to confer with each engineer to pick apart his resume to explore his background and education. He wanted her to uncover previously unidentified experience, capabilities, and inclinations. And he wanted her to produce and include separate resumes targeting every capability identified for each of the thirty-plus engineers employed at the time.

Prior to this request, Lupo had made it pedantically clear that the firm provided one set of services to government agencies and another set to the private sector, lest Irena ever confuse the two. To avoid repercussions, she questioned him about the intended recipient, knowing that if she produced the "bible" for one sector including services meant for the other, he would want her drawn and quartered.

But Lupo detested questions because he considered himself always clear and direct and the questioner always a dolt, and he owed no-one an explanation for anything. So, when Irena questioned him, he cut her off twice and simply repeated his request in his do-not-ask-questions, just-do-as-you-are-told tone of voice. Irena wanted to smack him, but considering the potential repercussions, she merely gave him a malevolent glare and walked away, agreeing of course to do as he asked.

Having overheard Lupo's demands, virtually every engineer Irena approached made it clear they hated every minute of this investigation, just as they hated every minute of her research to acquire project information for the database.

Irena spent two months compiling the "bible" while under pressure by Lupo and others to fulfill her other obligations: most important, proposals under the demands of unyielding deadlines, which raised the temperature on her frustration simmering like soup on a stovetop.

Once completed and the monster document delivered to Lupo, Irena never saw or heard about it again. The "bible" was most likely a paper database for electronically illiterate Lupo's personal reference and rogue marketing efforts.

On a positive note, the exercise created a comprehensive source of information for Irena's emerging database. Nevertheless, the nagging fear remained that the document could come back to bite her.

*   *   *

Another curious aspect of Lupo's personality emerged when he hired a pretty young woman named Priscilla—with no marketing experience, no knowledge of the firm, engineering services, or staff—to assist in the development of resumes for a statement of qualifications focusing on subdivisions.

Shortly after hiring Priscilla, Lupo summoned Irena to his office to discuss the resumes she, Irena, had already drafted and delivered to him. Upon arriving, she found Lupo and Priscilla sitting at his conference table, resumes strewn about.

Before she could sit down, Lupo and Priscilla—animated by some conversation they were having before she arrived—began firing criticisms at her about format and content of the resumes, each jumping in when the other took a breath. Feeling like a duck under fire on one of Lupo's annual hunts, when the two of them took a simultaneous breath, Irena jumped in with her rationale. Lupo cut her off telling her not to be "so defensive."

Really? Defensive?

Three weeks later Priscilla disappeared and Lupo had Irena complete those resumes and produce the statement of qualifications. He had apparently been more interested in demonstrating his dominance before that pretty young woman than in the quality of the finished product.

*   *   *

Master of his realm, Lupo would tell anyone who challenged his style of management that Yutz & Dunne was his company to do with as he pleased; and employees including partners were likewise his people, like slaves, to do with as he pleased. Just ask him.

Whenever he sought an infusion of cash for some entrepreneurial pursuit, he attended a staff meeting and pressured engineers to increase revenue and profit, often pounding his fist on the conference room table for emphasis. Irena could see the engineers roll their eyes—out of Lupo's line of vision, of course.

Whenever he spouted his authority and superiority and demeaned others, Irena recoiled. He seemed to forget that staff put revenue and profit in the coffer to pay their salaries, business expenses, and provide him with profit he regularly spent on entrepreneurial side businesses, flagrantly taken up on company time and premises, conscripting company support staff.

*   *   *

Lupo resented paying salaries to Cassius Banker, chief finance officer, and Irena, marketing manager. He frequently pointed out that finance and marketing are overhead functions that fail to generate revenue to cover their salaries and make him some money—which was unacceptable.

In his impulsive entrepreneurial fashion, Lupo sought opportunities for Cassius and Irena to generate revenue. In addition to their regular duties, he twice committed them to start-up retail enterprises beyond the scope of engineering. Both enterprises failed because Lupo marketed the products, meeting with and alienating potential customers by pressuring them to purchase items he thought they should need and want. Both enterprises also failed because Cassius and Irena had little time or interest beyond their regular duties to be successful.

Chapter Seven

As one of many women who struggle to gain presence and respect in the workplace, petite Irena was periodically disregarded. She spent her student and adult life with goals and aspirations the same as most men: striving to be recognized as competent and even superior to others, to earn a market rate or better salary to support herself and her family, and to be respected.

Irena spent two years working at Yutz & Dunne's shabby structure in Chicago's redevelopment zone. She endured traffic disruptions caused by trucks entering and leaving project sites along her commute route, and tolerated a workplace made worse by the mud, dust, and debris blown in or tracked in from the nearby construction. Her work space was often covered with a fine layer of dust. Her eyes watered, she coughed a lot, and her clothing was filthy by the end of most days. She even had to keep her coffee covered or she would be drinking dirt.

While tolerating this environment and while trying to address the company's marketing needs, Irena had to adapt to personalities resistant to her help: people who treated her like so much window dressing. Those years might have been intolerable had Irena not reminded herself that she was performing new and exciting work to help her employer increase revenue and profit, while first and foremost providing for her family.

A top salary is usually an indication of recognition, reward, and respect for a job well done. For twenty years before Yutz & Dunne, Irena considered herself well regarded and well rewarded. She took a seventeen percent cut in salary for the privilege of working in marketing, anticipating that her meager starting salary would rise over time as she proved herself.

On her first anniversary, hearing nothing from Cal about an evaluation and possible increase, Irena approached him. He dismissed the fact that she had taken that salary reduction and said there would be no evaluation and no salary increase "for a while" because she was already earning twenty percent more than her predecessor. A few months later she was denied a three percent cost-of-living adjustment paid to all other employees.

*   *   *

Yutz & Dunne finally moved to bigger and better office space in a relatively new building closer to civilization and creature comforts. Excited, grateful, and relieved, Irena's lower back and derriere, in particular, looked forward to giving up her wooden chair for something more comfortable to sit on.

Irena packed up and transported her own limited resources and files. The movers accomplished the rest over a weekend. Irena arrived early Monday morning and walked around taking in the sights of the new space, all on one floor, that wrapped around a corner. She was elated that she no longer had to descend and/or climb two flights of stairs whenever Lupo or Cal summoned, and that clean and accessible restrooms were provided on every floor.

Lupo recreated his large and sunny throne room. The space outside his office also replicated the old: painted and carpeted in unimaginative shades of beige. Old furnishings, cubicle partitions, and other junk had been moved to serve employees at the new facility, the unusable moved to a storage room on-site.

Modest private offices about ten feet square formed the perimeter of the space and were assigned to Lupo's partners. Each office had tinted but otherwise uncovered windows, a door that closed, and was equipped like the old cubicles, with dreary furnishings and amenities.

Rank and file engineers, surveyors, and administrative support staff, including marketing, were assigned nine-foot-square or smaller cubicles constructed of grimy old five-foot-high tweedy partitions. Most were arranged back-to-back in double rows with a corridor between and around them.

Each staff cubicle was barely large enough to accommodate a desk, task chair, a two- or four-drawer filing cabinet, an open bookcase, perhaps a credenza, and a side chair, assembled tightly like a three-dimensional jigsaw puzzle. Anyone unfortunate enough to drop a document between a desk and credenza or other tightly wedged piece of furniture was challenged to retrieve it. The air often turned blue as individuals mumbled profanities in the process.

Once moved in and settled, Irena suggested an open house, and Lupo jumped at the chance to show off. Corporate friends, family, and especially clients were invited to tour the new facility. Posters with bulleted talking points and illustrations of completed projects were positioned around the office, as were refreshment stations where champagne and chocolate were plentiful.

Lupo boasted to anyone who would listen that the new facility reflected *his* firm's increasing success. Ever a whore in pursuit of prestige, Lupo regularly failed to acknowledge staff achievements, flaunting any earned prestige as though he alone was responsible.

Tugging on imaginary suspenders in puffed up self-importance, Lupo would assail listeners with the story about how he and George established the business in a dingy, cramped, two-office workspace above a commercial laundry in a questionable part of town. He would reminisce about office windows that were usually so steamy and dirty that he and George could barely see through them, and about the stucco exterior that fell off in chunks to be patched again and again. Then there was that moment when, real or imagined, one could hear Lupo say, "And look at me now."

Chapter Eight

Many if not most corporate employees in the United States had access to company-provided personal computers in the 1990s. Not so at Yutz & Dunne. Adapting to a workplace that had ten years to catch up to prevailing technology was frustrating for Irena, especially when her computer experience was rejected.

Lupo did not care how much quicker and more efficient it might be for Irena to produce her own work products if she had appropriate tools. He insisted that she hand-write proposals and statements of qualification on lined yellow pads, section by section, for Lunice, the typist, to produce a draft, which Irena then had to edit and send back for another go, often more than once.

Numerous sections of marketing documents, along with assignments from engineers, surveyors, and administration, remained in play, like ping pong balls in a lottery cage, rotating until a completed document dropped like a winning ball, theoretically ready for dispatch.

Before Irena was hired, Lunice had hoped to be promoted to marketing coordinator. No-one explained to her why she was not, and no-one informed Irena about Lunice's resentment. Irena's limited need for word processing support intensified Lunice's resentment, and Lunice engaged in her own little war to drive Irena out of the company, expecting to then be promoted.

Given Lupo's and her supervisor Mario's concessions to Lunice, Irena feared that Lunice could pull enough strings to get her fired. Lunice, too, seemed afraid Irena might cost her *her* job. Lupo and the partners cultivated this sick dynamic with their indifference.

Lunice's first line of attack against Irena was passive aggressive insubordination. Lupo ignored Irena's laments that Lunice, with various excuses, regularly failed to meet marketing deadlines and, despite her commitments during scheduling meetings, spontaneously re-prioritized assignments, sacrificing marketing.

Lunice pushed inflexible proposal deadlines leaving little if any time to proofread and cross-check content; forcing Gabby, the reprographics manager, to reproduce and bind proposals under crisis conditions. He then had to drive dangerously fast to deliver them on time. And Irena was held responsible if anything went awry. Irena pulled out her hair a few strands at a time over the years, often thinking about pulling out Lunice's hair, too.

Drip, drip, drip, drip, drip, drip, drip.

Lunice's lack of dependability felt like Chinese water torture.

When Lunice discovered that Irena was using the rogue computer, she complained to Lupo. And since keeping Lunice happy was high on his list of priorities, he insisted that Irena stop using that computer and take advantage of Lunice's services.

He mistakenly thought Lunice would be happy if Irena simply gave her more to do. But Lunice had plenty of work from engineers and surveyors and did not need more work from Irena.

Irena could not keep Lunice happy simply because Irena existed, and forcing her dependence on Lunice gave Lunice the perfect scenario to act out her resentment.

Trying to cooperate with Lupo, Irena would provide Lunice with hand-written draft documents on the ubiquitous lined yellow paper with directions for formatting. Along with limited hard clerical skills, Lunice would impose her own arbitrary formatting and Lunice's finished document would have little semblance to what Irena requested.

If Irena sent it back with corrections and/or reiterating the formatting she wanted, Lunice would complain to Cal, Lupo, and any other partner who would listen that Irena was "upsetting" her. Irena's education and experience trumped Lunice's background and she wanted what she wanted for good reason, but Lunice did not want reason; she wanted to be difficult.

Lunice had limited skills, but Lupo and the partners, in their clerical ignorance, accepted her as an expert, and no-one, certainly not Irena, was allowed to challenge that belief. Forced into subservience to Lunice with the directive to keep her happy, Irena was expected to lower her standards, compromise her capabilities, and endure Lunice's resistance to directives for typographical corrections, format, and production.

Like one more high-voltage cow prod to raw nerves, an associate principal pulled Irena into his office one afternoon to tell her that Lunice was "still complaining" about her and that she needed to "avoid the cat fights and resolve the problem."

Irena shot back, "What cat fights? What do you know about the truth of anything Lunice says? And who are you to counsel me?" Getting no response, she added, "How do you propose I stop that woman from lying about me?" After a stand-off with nothing further said, Irena left his office with another knot in her stomach.

Once more suffering the stink of the ever-present cup of stale coffee on Cal's desk during one of their friendly office chats, Cal reminded Irena that she needed to accept the fact that it was her responsibility to get along with Lunice and to find peaceful co-existence.

Outrage crept up the back of Irena's neck and she snapped, "E-freakin' GAD! Short of resigning, it is impossible to keep that madwoman happy when she is allowed to cross legal and illegal lines in her effort to drive me out of the company. And I am not going anywhere."

Even as she tried to keep Lunice happy, and even as the partners accused her of being an antagonist for wanting to work independently, if Irena wanted a marketing product completed on time, she often had to complete that work herself by taking advantage of the rogue computer.

Every time Lunice discovered Irena using that computer she would complain, and Lupo would underscore his demands telling Irena, with increasing irritation, that computers were "beneath" her and that there were "others to do that" for her.

Chapter Nine

I rena's stress and frustration began manifesting in muscle spasms and headaches that deepened the groove between her eyebrows. Despite the stress, she believed she could improve the marketing process and eventually the company's profit margin. But to do so Irena was sure she had to sever her association with Lunice. She could not do that without her own computer.

Refusing to cede her skills or be forced into mediocrity or failure by acquiescing to Lunice's manipulations, Irena bucked the system and continued to use the rogue whenever she could, because the frustration not to do so and the repercussions were more than she could bear. Her temples often throbbed as she clenched her teeth.

With twitching fingers, she imagined strangling Lunice every time Lunice caused her grief. She imagined strangling Lupo every time he chastised her for using the rogue computer. And she imagined strangling anyone who told her she had to keep Lunice happy.

By theoretically making Lunice available to do everyone's typing, and by insisting that everyone—not just Irena—keep her happy, Lupo bestowed power and control on the typist. Lunice was paradoxically elevated to queen of the realm, convinced that she alone as word processor should produce and be the final authority over all company documents, including Irena's proposals and other marketing documents.

And the tail wagged the dog.

*   *   *

One afternoon, after yet another confrontation with Lunice, breathing hard with anxiety and the desire to strike out, Irena steered Cal into the conference room where she felt they could speak freely, or where she could bash his brains in.

"What's up?" Cal asked, as Irena closed the door behind them and invited him to sit. "We need to have a chat," she said, doing her best to remain calm. "I am fed up with Lunice's hostility and her resistance to accommodating my grammatical and formatting requests. Were Lunice's skills tested before she was hired?"

Cal hesitated as though Irena had just asked him the most ridiculous question. A confused look crossed his face before he replied, "We're engineers. We don't do that."

Oh, my God! Oh, my God! Oh, my God! Irena began to comprehend that Lunice had been hired with only an assumption of skill—perhaps like everyone else in the company, including herself—and that the partners blindly supported Lunice as an authority.

After an ear-splitting silence during which neither Cal nor Irena volunteered another word, Irena rose and left him sitting in the conference room. She told herself she was working among idiots and it felt contagious.

Someone once said, "If you know ten percent more than the next guy, you're an expert." *Did no other employee question Lunice's capabilities? Did everyone accept whatever she produced in whatever manner and timeframe?*

Clearly, the partners and engineers knew less about what to expect from an employee with word processing responsibilities than Lunice did, which made her an "expert" until Irena came along and upset that cart.

Yutz & Dunne suffered a second-rate image in the engineering community due in part to what Irena considered Lunice's limited skills. Irena was convinced that the company would languish in mediocrity unless changes were made to improve the firm's image, and she considered it her duty to make those changes. Determined and confident she could succeed, she prepared for the challenges ahead, and rejected any niggling idea of resigning.

Chapter Ten

L unice's power resided in headaches that she brandished like weapons. Unhappy with anyone for any reason, she would develop a headache and clerical production would cease. She would leave the office to recuperate and stay away for a few hours, a day, two or three, often taking off a week or more each month. Lupo may have wanted everyone to keep her happy simply to keep her in the office.

Lunice had the privilege of hiring temporary staff to help her produce lengthy project specifications, or when she planned to be out of the office on vacation, etc. That privilege did not lend itself to hourly inconsistency like late arrivals, hours off mid-day, a day, two, or three off for a headache.

For years, Yutz & Dunne lacked any sick leave policy and workers were compensated for all sick time off, primarily benefitting Lunice. When a second worker began taking excessive sick time, compounding the impact on the engineers' and surveyors' ability to complete their assignments, staff grumbling became overt complaints, and the partners instituted sick-time limits, to Lunice's great dismay.

Irena was working with Lunice to produce a major proposal due at a client's office on a Wednesday afternoon at three o'clock. Lunice did not show up on time that morning or call in to alert Irena, the receptionist, or others waiting for their assignments, leaving everyone depending on her wondering whether she would show up, and if not how they would meet their deadlines.

By eleven o'clock, with sections of her proposal yet to be produced, Irena's anxiety was running high, and once again she felt the need to use the rogue computer to complete the proposal to be sure the client received it on time.

Lunice arrived at the office shortly before noon. When asked about being late, she responded as she did virtually without exception whenever she showed up late: that she "had a headache and couldn't get going early enough." Other times she might say she had a headache the previous night and couldn't get going early enough.

In addition to inconsistent arrival times, Lunice often left the office mid-morning or mid-afternoon for an unpredictable few hours. If discovered having been gone, she would simply respond that "she had a headache."

Irena had no doubt that Lunice's late arrival this particular day, with a major proposal due, was sabotage.

*   *   *

At nine o'clock every Thursday morning, the firm conducted the aforementioned "scheduling" meetings in the conference room, to plan and allocate computer use and word processing services for the upcoming week. Irena and Lunice would join the others, pulling in side chairs from nearby offices and cubicles to accommodate everyone.

Once gathered, impatient engineers and surveyors would begin mind-numbing negotiations, like a cattle auction, for hourly increments of Lunice's word processing time, and for hourly use of the three aging, stand-alone computers programmed and reserved strictly for use by engineers and surveyors. Once everyone agreed, including Lunice, she would produce and distribute copies of the schedule.

Keeping Lunice happy was in everyone's best interest to ensure assignments were completed on time. Too frequently, she failed to meet her commitments, bumping assignments to the following week. When anyone complained, Lunice would say, "It will get done next week. It's no big deal." Frustrated engineers and surveyors were forced to contact clients to renegotiate the timing for delivery of their design plans and accompanying documents.

But proposal deadlines could not be renegotiated, forcing Irena to meet those inflexible deadlines often working late into the night at the rogue. If the firm missed a proposal deadline, Irena knew she alone would be held responsible, which would generate Lupo's wrath tenfold that of using the rogue computer.

When faced with a deadline, along with an obstinate and unpredictable word processor, Irena would prepare for Lunice's snit when she learned Irena had not waited for her, and prepare for Lupo's wrath when Lunice tattled like a child.

Irena often felt like a hostage in a psychological horror movie, the magnitude of her frustration the perfect scenario for workplace violence. Why she never threw Lunice out a window remains a mystery.

*   *   *

Irena had been friendly and supportive toward Lunice in the early days as they commiserated over coffee or lunch. Lunice often complained about her difficult teenage children, her needy parents, her real estate problems, her unfaithful husband, and her migraine headaches.

Irena sympathized and offered Lunice the benefit of her experience as a former migraine sufferer. But Lunice rejected the idea that diet, stress or ergonomics might be responsible for her headaches. Instead, she sabotaged her wellbeing by regularly consuming donuts, candy bars, and coffee while she talked on the phone held to her ear with a shoulder as she "typed."

During those early days, co-workers often greeted each other with a courteous, "Hi. How are you?" Even clients who visited the office regularly engaged with staff, each no doubt anticipating the customary response, "I'm fine, thanks. How are you?" This greeting was a looking glass Lunice could not resist walking through.

Wherever and whenever greeted that way, by staff or client, Lunice would launch into what became known as the dreaded twenty-minute harangue. She peppered her response with hang-dog sighs and moans about her latest headache, her latest prescription that bothered her stomach, her plan to seek yet another doctor, and her rejection of any suggestion that diet, stress, or ergonomics might be involved. Perhaps Lunice believed she might lose control over the partners and staff if her headaches were cured.

Staff and clients began to avoid her.

During lunch at a local coffee shop, Lunice once confided to Irena that she was "addicted" to her husband, had to call him every couple of hours, and then had a hard time hanging up. Lunice said he was cheating on her but she could not confront him.

After paying the bill, leaving the coffee shop, and climbing into Irena's rattling old Corolla, Irena asked Lunice how she knew her husband was cheating. Lunice said she secretly taped a phone conversation between him and one of his girlfriends, and she was afraid of what he might do if he discovered she was spying on him.

Lunice then shoved a small white envelope toward Irena containing an answering machine tape, and asked her to keep it for her. Irena reluctantly agreed and Lunice watched Irena put the tape into her glove compartment under her owner's manual and other papers. Both forgot about it.

*   *   *

As Lunice's resentment at having been passed over for promotion escalated, she seemed to believe that Irena threatened her job security. When insubordination failed to drive Irena out of the company, and when Irena refused to conform to Lunice's manipulations, Lunice ramped up to poison Irena's interpersonal relationships.

She began spreading defamatory stories about Irena's sex life: exciting fodder for this otherwise staid engineering company. Lunice's defamation became a banquet of scandal feeding the lurid imaginations of co-workers, and Irena became the company slut because Lunice said so.

Irena's interactions with co-workers, male and female, became increasingly problematic, compounded by engineers influenced by the gossip, by Lupo, and by their experiences with Bernadette. More often than not, engineers subsequently failed to meet their commitments to provide Irena with technical work scopes and cost estimates for proposals.

As Lunice's defamation escalated, Irena pleaded with the partners to intervene. Not one man obliged to protect her from a hostile work environment—not Cal, her supervisor; not Cassius, the officer assigned human resources responsibility; not Griff Chimeric, the officer assigned responsibility for sexual harassment issues—did anything to counsel Lunice or stop her offensive behavior.

Griff and the other partners seemed to enjoy the titillating rumors, perhaps hot and bothered by what they chose to believe was truth. Instead of intervening, they laughed at Irena when she complained. They told her over time to "smile," "let these things roll off your back," "don't let it bother you," "stop the catfights," "stop whining," and "get a thicker skin."

Feeling increasingly helpless, months of distress and coping became years. Lunice was calling the shots and Irena had to accept the situation or leave. Refusing to leave, Irena did her best to rise above, say less, and cope more, but felt like she was being buried alive by a hostile mob.

According to French social psychologists Gabriel Tarde and Gustave Le Bon, mob mentality occurs when one or two people with hostile intent start an escalating movement against another, gradually incorporating others, that ultimately results in some form of catastrophe.

Lunice and Greedo's resentment manifested in hostile intent directed at Irena. Those in charge refused to intervene, leaving Lunice and Greedo free to say and do whatever they chose. Irena could only cope, resulting in chronic depression, an early symptom of a predictable catastrophe.

By failing their ethical, legal, and professional obligations to protect Irena from a hostile work environment, the partners fanned the flames of defamation. Where others would flee such an environment and never look back, Irena stuck it out, intent on proving her ability to succeed for the organization and for her family.

Chapter Eleven

Before the implementation of company e-mail, and because Lunice's phone was usually busy, and because she rarely delivered a completed assignment to anyone, staff had to travel to and from her work station to discuss their clerical needs, determine the status of or pick up their assignments. Each wasted trip Irena made drove her to distraction. By the third or fourth trip, she felt virtually homicidal.

In addition to socializing while trekking to and from Lunice, tall staff had a clear view over the tops of partitions and frequently interrupted those at work in their cubicles. Other trekkers stopped in the kitchen for coffee or a snack. Disrupted staff complained that they could not concentrate with the commotion, and others complained that the process wasted hours of everyone's time.

Arriving at the predictable traffic jam clogging Lunice's work area, some staff returned to their desks disappointed to try again later while others, more desperate, waited among the throng for Lunice's attention.

Irena imagined Lunice as a pompous, vacuous, female queen made of cotton candy, sitting high on a lofty throne well above the little people trying to climb the sticky slopes, clambering over each other trying to grab a piece of her, finding little in their hands if and when they got that far.

To mollify those who complained and to keep others at their work stations, Lupo responded in Gestapo fashion, imposing "quiet time" from nine to eleven o'clock every morning, when employees were prohibited from speaking or leaving their desks. Phone calls in and out were verboten, monitored by Kitty, the receptionist, commissioned as telephone gatekeeper. The standing joke among engineers and surveyors was that nine to eleven each morning was nap time.

Lupo, minus a whip, occasionally patrolled the office to enforce the rule. But the man had a short attention span and quiet time succumbed a few weeks later when foot traffic and chatter returned to pre-quiet-time levels. Certain employees demonstrated their distress by wearing highly visible, oversized neon purple or orange earplugs. The more generous staff maintained a fresh supply in saucers on their desks to share.

For years, like ostriches with their heads in the sand, Lupo and the partners neglected frustrated staff while supporting Lunice's pathos, ignoring the impact of her self-assumed supremacy and lack of dependability on company success.

*   *   *

Among the irritations chipping away at Irena's sanity was the on-going state of the company kitchen. Centrally located within the overall office space, like a box plopped within, the kitchen was the obvious go-to place for lunch or a momentary respite, especially on foul weather days.

Two kitchen walls formed a corner with diagonally opposing doors providing hasty travelers with a popular shortcut. Singly or in packs, travelers were like high-speed trains rushing through and disturbing anyone seeking solace.

Six side chairs with brown vinyl seats surrounded a narrow rectangular laminate table with indelibly spotted chrome legs. The table, situated close to the wall across from the cupboards, left standing room at the counter for access to two coffeemakers, regular and decaf of course, and the usual accoutrements.

The cupboards and walls were beige and the counter a shade of mustard that reminded Irena, the mother of three, of sick-baby poop. The countertop, like the vinyl floor, was often sticky by mid-afternoon.

With gray furry carcasses peeking out of plastic containers, the small white refrigerator regularly smelled like decaying animal corpses. Pink and white butcher-paper packages emitted unique odors and bled iridescent colors that would appeal to any fine artist. Nauseating smells often emanated through the open kitchen doors, most often the smell of burnt popcorn that lingered in one's nostrils and hair for hours.

The state of the refrigerator invariably led to a testy debate between administrative women and male staff about who would clean it out and decontaminate. Male staff inevitably won the stand-off as, sooner or later, a woman or two, fearing ptomaine poisoning, would do the deed. Plastic containers and paper packages would bite the dust, reeking in wastebaskets until removed by the overnight cleaning crew, perhaps wearing gas masks.

Chapter Twelve

L upo made it clear that he expected employees to be docile and compliant working for years with no job descriptions, no personnel evaluations, and no salary increases.

The absence of job descriptions allowed him and his partners freedom to make erratic and sometimes extraordinary changes to the scope of an employee's responsibilities with no prior discussion with the employee, whether the employee liked it or not.

The absence of personnel evaluations cost employees the benefit of recognition and reward for those who excelled, and gave Lupo and his favored partners freedom to ignore the need for counseling and/or consequences for those who failed to perform or worse, resulting in a workforce continually at odds with one another.

While employees at most firms are usually aware of their perceived value based on annual performance evaluations, in the absence of such evaluations at Yutz & Dunne, employees never knew where they stood. One might speculate Lupo feared confrontation with an employee who received a negative evaluation. Instead, he was afraid that an employee who received a positive evaluation might expect a salary increase.

Seeking a salary increase was like playing Russian roulette. An exceptional revenue-generating employee who threatened to resign might get a raise. But Lupo considered anyone else who expressed dissatisfaction with his salary, or anything else, to be a malcontent, and in his patent who-needs-you-anyway, like-it-or-leave attitude, he made it clear that malcontents should leave or be terminated.

*　　　*　　　*

Irena began deteriorating from the ravages of employment at Yutz & Dunne. She suffered from headaches—worse in the late afternoon when her emotional burden was heaviest—stomach pain after most meals—muscle spasms and chest pain whenever she had a less-than-amiable conversation or had to endure an un-resolvable conflict. And she lost sleep at night as daily events replayed in her mind on a loop over which she had no control. Her primary care physician, family, and friends regularly suggested she resign and seek other employment, but Irena refused.

Unsuccessful at alleviating her physical symptoms, medical care providers referred Irena to a psychotherapist. During therapy sessions, sitting in the same white wing chair week after week with tissues nearby for the tears that often spouted from her eyes, and facing the same lavender and gray contemporary watercolor painting, Irena shared her frustrations about work.

She described Lunice as a "hostile burden to endure each day."

She described Lupo as the primary reason the firm failed to thrive, and she doubted his qualifications to own and manage any business, much less a specialized one with strict industrial regulations and plenty of competition.

Irena also described Lupo as a man who resists recognizing, accepting, or effecting changes that might lead to success: a man who beats every bush with whatever stick is available demanding glory he believes is rightfully his, blaming everyone but himself for his lack of success. She called him a "vampire sucking the life out of her and other employees."

Irena described the partners as men who appeared to have no real interest in the day-to-day management of the firm. And she described her supervisor, Cal, as a man who wanted to be everybody's friend while remaining unresponsive to responsibility.

Irena especially wanted to explore why she tolerated such a dysfunctional workplace and to learn whether her assessment was reasonable, whether her employer and co-workers were as dysfunctional as she believed, or if she was the only "whack job."

The more Irena put the physical and emotional demands of her employment ahead of her family, her health, and her social life, the more frustrated and exhausted she became.

In addition to her passionate desire to provide for her children and the pleasure she obtained from the work she performed, Irena would learn there were other reasons why she tolerated such a workplace.

*   *   *

Irena learned that her dysfunctional birth family left her with lingering feelings of inadequacy and fear. As a child, she drove herself to meet or exceed real and perceived familial obligations, coping with mistreatment in exchange for love and acceptance.

As an adult, Irena reverted to coping with mistreatment. She failed to see this behavior as tolerating abuse. Instead, Irena prided herself on her ability to endure where others caved, and drove herself to overachieve in order to gain the recognition, reward, and success she craved. At Yutz & Dunne, she was on thorny but familiar ground.

In response to her desire to know more about why she remained committed to such an employer, Irena and her therapist explored American psychologist Martin Seligman's theory of learned helplessness.

Dr. Seligman hypothesizes that a subject, exposed to unpredictable rewards and punishment when pursuing a goal, will eventually stop trying, and will accept a lack of control over the unpredictable. The subject then copes or behaves stoically, refusing to expend any energy getting agitated over adverse conditions.

Dr. Seligman goes on to hypothesize that when opportunities arise to escape the adverse situation, learned helplessness prevents any action because the subject perceives no control. The subject subsequently exhibits symptoms similar to clinical depression.

Believing he or she is utterly helpless to change the situation, the subject ultimately chooses the worst-case scenario—up to and including death—rather than continue to endure or act upon the unpredictable.

Chapter Thirteen

Yutz & Dunne employed Griff Chimeric, a licensed land surveyor and partner, because quick access to and control over survey is integral to civil engineering design projects. Short, wiry, and bald with large ears, Griff sported whiskers that, at a glance, made his head look upside down. He usually wore rumpled clothing that he either slept in, left in a heap on a floor, or left in a dryer long after the dry cycle finished.

Griff pursued survey and safety issues with enthusiasm. But with no apparent expertise, training, or sensitivity to women's issues, he failed to live up to his responsibilities as sexual harassment officer with regard to Irena, Diane Lisbon, and other women on staff who complained about a certain male co-worker. Griff often made demeaning gender-based comments to and about women, and virtually every woman on staff considered him a joke.

For example: While Irena ate lunch in the company kitchen one day, sitting between Griff and Jim Sorento, a senior design engineer, Griff interrupted the meandering conversation and addressed Jim with his thumb extended toward Irena.

"Just look at the way she dresses around here," he said, referring to the fact that Irena wore skirts and dresses as opposed to blue jeans and old T-shirts like most staff. Jim's equally scornful response, "What's that supposed to mean?" And Griff blew off further conversation with a smirk and a harrumph.

Another time, Irena stopped by the reception desk to pick up a package as Kitty the receptionist was telling Griff and others that she was pregnant. Most knew Kitty had two children from her second marriage and the father of this new baby was her third husband. Griff walked away saying over his shoulder, "How many more husbands and kids are you gonna have anyway, Kitty?" She left the office in tears.

While writing a survey proposal after she was promoted from marketing coordinator to marketing manager, Irena prepared a utilization table—a form unique to the proposal process that demonstrates organizational and team diversity. The form identifies the number of managers, technical staff, clerical staff, and so forth, by gender and minority status. As female marketing manager, Irena included herself as—what else?—a female manager.

When Griff reviewed the table, he redlined her name saying, "You're "just a clerk and that's how you should be categorized." Griff was so focused on diminishing Irena, he failed to comprehend that identifying no female managers on the team (for there were no others) detracted from the team's image in an industry that values and rewards diversity.

And then there was the time when more than one co-worker told Irena that Griff announced to those assembled at a staff meeting during the weeks she dated Greedo, when both were absent, that she was "shacking up" with him. Those same co-workers told her that Rory Massai, a contract surveyor, leapt to her defense telling Griff to "Watch (your) mouth." The fact that Greedo was a gold-digging gigolo was apparently not mentioned.

By far the most egregious example of Griff's failure as sexual harassment officer was his long-standing refusal to investigate and/or intervene when women including Irena complained about a co-worker's deliberate, hands-on, sexual harassment.

*   *   *

Domenic Placido, laissez-faire partner, was a senior design engineer in his early fifties like most partners: mocked because of his reputed financial independence, and because he recorded what others considered excessive amounts of project detail. Domenic filled heaps of binders stored in and around his workspace.

Over six feet tall, blonde, tanned, and muscled, Domenic worked out every day at a gym near the office. Pontificating about the benefits of nuts and seeds, he usually had a half-eaten protein or nut bar on his desk or in his pocket. He periodically pulled out the one in his pocket and chomped on it—in a meeting, in a corridor, or whenever and wherever the mood struck.

More than anyone else, Domenic seemed to enjoy Lunice's stories about Irena, the two of them often observed in his cubicle sharing a laugh. Domenic baited Irena as she passed his cubicle, asking with a Cheshire cat grin if she heard what Lunice had to say about her that day, and then chuckle. Irena would return his smile and walk away, attempting to maintain a scrap of dignity.

At company events where food was served, Domenic would ask about ingredients in dishes he did not recognize, making it clear he did not eat garlic. Domenic believed that garlic was responsible for the Black Death Plague of the thirteenth century and some, if not all, of the outbreaks into the nineteenth century.

Domenic may have had his information backward, considering the story of four grave robbers who, in 1772, apparently immune to the disease, raided plague victims' corpses in Marseilles. The grave robbers had been eating garlic and infusing vinegar with garlic— later to be known as Vinegar of the Four Thieves—and used the infused vinegar for bathing, anointing their clothes, and breathing it through rags. Rather than cause plague, garlic appeared to protect them from the disease.

Domenic resigned from Yutz & Dunne to travel, returning eighteen months later as a rank and file engineer, occupying a cubicle perhaps twenty feet from Irena. Junior engineer Ricky Logan occupied a cubicle between Domenic and Irena, and could often be overheard chiding fifty-something Domenic about his age.

"What's it like being so old, Domenic?" "Good thing you work out. It's probably what keeps you alive." "Don't hurt yourself at the gym today." "Aren't you ready to retire?" Domenic did not complain, but because she was nearly the same age, Irena found Ricky's comments insulting and annoying. More salt to irritate her wounds.

*   *   *

Gabby Isakson served as reprographics manager, a title Irena had to work to wrap her tongue around. Gabby was responsible for general photocopying and for reproducing engineering drawings requiring more sophisticated techniques. Gabby also managed off-site storage of vital documents, ordered office supplies, and posted out-going mail. Most important to Irena, he reproduced, bound, and hand-delivered marketing proposals by car to clients and potential clients within a fifteen-mile radius.

The new office facility provided Gabby with a walled-in workspace about thirty-feet-square located at the physical center of the overall space next to the kitchen, with a doorway to the inner office and a doorway to the outer corridor. Within that beige space, counter-high cupboards, topped by a thirty-inch-wide laminate surface, surrounded and protected sensitive high-speed copying, binding, and postal equipment. The counter was often crowded with papers and miscellaneous office supplies.

Users of a less-sensitive, self-service copy machine, located outside the protected inner sanctum against a wall, were forced to navigate among file cabinets, stacked cartons of copy paper, shipping containers, a hand-truck, and an occasional bicycle.

Gabby liked to tell co-workers that he lost a lot of weight, but he continued to waddle when he walked as though his now-thin body still thought he was overweight. He retained a puffy little face crowned by thin black hair combed straight forward toward his high forehead, hooked nose, and bushy mustache.

In addition to his weight-loss story, Gabby also liked to tell co-workers that he once owned and operated a grocery store. When he could not make a go of the grocery store, he sold it and applied to Yutz & Dunne. One can only wonder what qualified him to work for an engineering firm.

Gabby boasted that, as part of his good business practices, he encouraged employees to talk about each other behind each others' backs. He argued that gossip is a healthy pastime that "gets things out in the open"—his right to freedom of speech.

Gabby obviously did not know that, while freedom of speech or expression may legally allow for gossip, exceptions include obscenity, breach of the peace, incitement to crime, "fighting words," sedition and defamation, including unverified and untrue negative gossip, or bearing false witness.

The line limiting freedom of speech or expression is drawn when gossip injures the reputations of individuals and/or organizations, when it is then defined as defamation, for which an injured individual or organization has the right to sue in Superior Court.

Most staff had frequent reason to find themselves in Gabby's area, to use the self-service copy machine, consult on a printing job, or request retrieval of files from off-premise locations.

As reigning king of gossip, Gabby took gleeful pleasure in holding court, cornering people to share what he thought he knew, or to encourage them to share what they thought they knew. Most employees were drawn in at one time or another as they passed through Gabby's area to or from reception or the restrooms. Master of his art, Gabby enjoyed agitating the cesspool, listening to and sharing hearsay, true or not, the juicier the better—so long as nobody was talking about him.

Second in line to the gossip throne was Kitty the receptionist who, like Gabby, was located in a high traffic area with frequent access to most staff. Gabby and Kitty were always ready to pounce on any tidbit of titillating tripe.

Given their affinity for the words, "Did you hear...?" Kitty and Gabby shared fact or fiction before their ears got cold. Neither, it appeared, ever stopped to consider that rumors tend to become exaggerated and distorted like the game of telephone, where one person whispers something to another at the start of the game and, when the game is over, that something has little if any semblance to what was originally said.

Fanned by Gabby and Kitty, Lunice's wild and salacious allegations spread rapidly. Both accepted Lunice's stories as true, or they simply enjoyed having something sensational to repeat, regardless of the source, intent, or consequences.

Every time Irena approached a group of two or more surrounding Gabby or Kitty and they stopped talking to stare, Irena took another blow from the hammer she felt driving her into the ground. According to American historian George Bancroft (d.1891), "Truth is not exciting enough to those who depend on the character and lives of their neighbors for all their amusement."

Chapter Fourteen

The early 1960s was a time when sexual harassment was widespread, a time when men fondled women in the office and otherwise objectified and demeaned them, and women were forced to tolerate such behavior to keep their jobs.

At first giggling at the attention, young women came to recognize certain behaviors as sexual harassment, and indignation gave birth to the 1960s women's rights movement. Young Irena watched in awe and admiration as Gloria Steinem, Betty Friedan, and others took on the mantle of contemporary warriors in support of women's rights.

Statistics for the 1960s illustrate the virtual exclusion of women from STEM career paths (science/technology/engineering/math). Statistics after 2000 show significant improvement in the numbers of women participating in STEM careers.

The Yutz & Dunne partners, themselves products of the 1960s, were like a bad dream for Irena in the 1990s. With gender bias rooted in bygone attitudes, the partners remained locked in attitudes like Madonna-whore complex, labeling women as either saintly Madonnas or debased prostitutes. Labeling Irena made her bad dream a nightmare.

*   *   *

Well after the formation of Lupo's new partnership of six, the partners held an election of officers. As untouchable majority owner, Lupo opted out of the process, content to remain as chairman of the board or reigning monarch. Resigned to a somewhat powerless relationship with Lupo, the partners nevertheless hoped to gain some control over the man who manipulated, controlled, and frustrated them with unannounced corporate changes peppered with temper tantrums.

According to Cal, as he shared with Irena after the election, no partner wanted what was expected to be the frustrating and thankless position of president. They were certain that Lupo, rather than exercise one vote, would continue to exercise his controlling interest to undermine officers and scuttle decisions he feared might undermine his authority.

Cal said that, after a long, drawn-out debate, he agreed to serve as president, as though he did the others a huge favor they should never forget. But Irena knew that Cal was thrilled. She also knew he triumphantly anticipated his impending supremacy. And she was painfully aware that his new position would put him on another and much more significant collision course with Lupo.

Irena remained obliged to both Cal and Lupo, each discounting the other's need for her time; each pulling her in a different direction with manipulating and self-serving half-truths, because neither could trust her relationship with the other. Struggling to keep them both satisfied, Irena adapted to their manipulations and often unrealistic expectations.

Someone once said, when you get to the end of your rope, tie a knot and hang on. Cal often proclaimed to be Irena's knot, but his declaration rang hollow time and again as he did nothing to improve his relationship with Lupo or protect her from Lunice.

*   *   *

Soon after assuming the presidency, Cal called Irena into his office to show off his impressive new carved oak desk, smaller than Lupo's massive desk but appropriate for Cal's smaller office.

After telling Irena about the deal he got, he reached across the top of the desk for some papers and held them out to her. Manipulative, unsympathetic, or simply naïve, Cal told Irena he wanted her to convince Lunice to participate in an executive assistant training program. *Right, and the sphinx will sprout feathers and fly, and the heavens will rain potato chips*, Irena thought. Losing her sanity began to feel like a foregone conclusion.

Considering on-going issues with Lunice, Irena wondered what Cal was thinking. Gallantly, perhaps he wanted to offer Lunice the opportunity to become more valuable to the changing organization to help her feel more secure. Foolishly, he may have believed she would be more receptive if this offer came from another woman, even a woman she hated. Optimistically, he may have thought that by having Irena present Lunice with this opportunity, Lunice might see Irena in a more authoritative light and be more cooperative.

Cal seemed to believe that if Irena offered Lunice this training, like some kind of peace offering, their problems would vanish, he could avoid getting involved, and he could come out looking like a successful peacemaker.

Cal seemed to believe, as much from delusion and cowardice as from his simplistic approach to management, that any issue between two women could be resolved if they just sat down and talked to each other.

Because Irena saw Cal as her only advocate, and because she unrealistically hoped that being cooperative, and perhaps even successful might trump the reputation Lunice was building for her, she agreed to do as Cal asked.

*   *   *

Lunice agreed to meet with Irena the following morning. Convinced she had little chance for success, Irena nevertheless picked up the paperwork from Cal's office, and hoped for a neutral encounter.

Finding Lunice sitting at her desk thumbing through some papers, Irena greeted her with the dread question, "Hi, Lunice. How are you?"

"Fine," Lunice responded in a cold, crisp monosyllable.

Thank heaven she no longer talks to me about her headaches, Irena thought.

Trying to engage Lunice in casual conversation before getting to the point, Irena asked, "So, what are you working on?"

"Nothing much," Lunice replied coldly.

This is not going to be easy, Irena moaned to herself.

Irena began by telling Lunice that Cal wanted to offer her the opportunity to participate in an executive assistant training program. "A great opportunity," Irena said, "because, if you complete the program, you'll not only become more valuable to yourself and to the company, but you might even get a raise." That last part was a stretch, but Irena wanted her attention.

Lunice slapped Irena down like a bug, telling her she was "not interested" in the paperwork and "not interested" in the program. "I was hired to be a word processor and that's all I want to do," Lunice said. And she turned her back to Irena in dismissal.

Perhaps Lunice realized her limitations and did not want to fail. Perhaps she was being difficult simply because she could. Either way, Irena wanted to fling something at the back of her head and then hurt Cal for putting her in this situation.

Chapter Fifteen

C al's craving for social dominance was as apparent to Irena as Lupo's craving for cash and control. Demonstrating a patronizing approach to management, Cal regularly offended Irena and other female co-workers by offering elementary information and assistance. He treated each woman like she was inferior, needed to be coddled, could only be delegated mundane work, and/or had limited ability to succeed in a challenging role left to her own devices.

Whenever she and Cal had a difference of opinion, a long, drawn-out debate would ensue. To end the debate, Irena would have to concede that Cal's opinion was more valid than hers, or that he was right and she was wrong. Her concessions would reinforce his feeling of superiority as her knight in shining armor—a man who could show her the way to success she could not achieve without him.

Irena struggled to control her fury in response to Cal's on-going inference to female inferiority, and his pursuit of gratitude for his condescending "kindness."

One model defines successful interpersonal communication as occurring only when both parties share information as adults. When either party assumes a parental/superior or child-like/inferior position, successful communication fails to take place. Cal had no idea how often the iron gates of non-communication came crashing down.

*　　　*　　　*

When Irena wanted to address issues concerning Lunice, Cal insisted on a conversation rather than a documented record of events. Irena was sure he wanted to avoid a paper trail that might demonstrate his unlawful failure to protect her from a hostile work environment. Irena preferred a documented record of events because she anticipated a need for that paper trail. They were deadlocked.

The more Lunice circulated stories about Irena, the more sleep Irena lost, the more enraged and depressed she became, and the more she pleaded with Cal to intervene. But Cal seemed unconcerned about her anguish, and she saw no evidence he took any action on her behalf. Irena believed that he and the other partners understood her distress, and chose not to get involved, viewing Irena as a troublemaker because she complained and sought help. They made it her responsibility to resolve interpersonal issues they considered unworthy of their time and attention—usually issues between or related to women—ignoring the fact that Irena could not resolve the issue without their intervention.

By entertaining Lunice's allegations, by failing to protect Irena from a hostile work environment, by failing to advise her of her rights under the circumstances, and by allowing hostility and defamation to run amok like a disease, infecting relationships and contributing to mob mentality, Cal and the other partners would likely have been considered complicit and liable in a court of law had Irena pursued such action within the appropriate statute of limitations.

Discussing Lunice's behavior with Cal resolved nothing. As he and the partners resisted her attempts to resolve legitimate interpersonal issues, her frustration intensified, along with her physical and emotional responses. Whether he liked it or not, Irena began documenting her distress and copying the partners. Cal berated her every time and gave her the silent treatment for a week or two.

Frustration, clinically speaking, is triggered by stress in the form of conflict or opposition. Frustration can result in passive-aggressive and possibly aggressive behavior. Lunice had no problem externalizing and directing her anger toward Irena as the perceived cause of her distress. But any attempt Irena made to externalize her frustration was counter-productive.

Unable to admit, even to herself, that she needed psychological help, Irena internalized much of her frustration, convincing herself that nothing was as bad as it seemed, and that she could overcome anything.

Psychological stress, physical stress, cumulative stress disorders, and stress management had all been on Irena's radar for years, but she considered those who sought psychological help for stress-related problems to be weak. Denying reality contributed to her deterioration as she remained trapped between professional heaven for loving the work she performed and interpersonal hell for despising the conditions of her employment.

In spite of repeated suggestions by those who cared for her to resign, Irena stubbornly chose to stay. And she suffered headaches. And she suffered stomachaches and ulcers caused by excess digestive acid. And she suffered stress-induced adrenaline spikes that made her more alert and able to respond to crises, real or perceived, but drained her physically. And she suffered involuntary muscle spasms weakening her ability to deal with stress. And she suffered sleep deprivation and its consequences.

Suffering this downward death-like spiral, Irena told herself that such was a small price to pay for the challenges of stimulating employment. It took years for her to realize that the psychological and physical pain she endured was her mind and body's response to the persistent frustration, fear, and anger she endured while coping with workplace bullying, abuse, and discrimination.

Chapter Sixteen

Yutz & Dunne's technological evolution began with the rogue, the first computer purchased by Lupo and George when the firm was established. As the firm grew, three non-networked computers were purchased, remaining the only computers available for use by twenty or so engineers and surveyors for more than fifteen years.

Lupo loathed the expenditure of money on what he considered unnecessary items for which he had no use, and probably resisted because he was and remained computer illiterate.

Eventually convinced the company could no longer compete in the marketplace without up-to-date appropriate and relevant technology, he reluctantly authorized the purchase of one or two new personal computers quarterly, whining about the expenditure at every executive committee and staff meeting. Griff Chimeric—in charge of survey, safety and sexual harassment issues—administered, installed, and maintained those computers.

Lupo believed that computers were only appropriate for technical applications. Consequently, engineers and surveyors received the first computers. He eventually authorized computers for the accounting department. And because the receptionist occasionally performed data entry for the accounting clerk, she received a computer. Gabby, the reprographics manager, received the last new computer to integrate with developing reproduction technology.

However, even after every other staff member received a personal computer, and even after Irena explained how much more efficient and productive she could be, Lupo refused to consider a computer for her, the marketing manager. He reiterated his assertion that, as a non-technical employee, she did not need a computer because he employed a word processor to do her "typing." Lupo refused to consider Irena's frustration at being forced to accept "typing" assistance she did not need.

Once engineers and surveyors were able to produce their own draft reports and everyday text documents, Lunice's workload naturally declined. Irrationally, she blamed Irena for her declining workload, adding this insult to her growing list of Irena's sins against her. Yet even as Lunice feared obsolescence, she refused to grow in other service to the firm, repeating her previous assertion that word processing was what she was hired to do and that was all she wanted to do.

*   *   *

As Irena's tolerance for issues concerning Lunice decreased, and without her own computer at work, she continued to bypass Lunice, taking advantage of the rogue as much as she could get away with. At the old facility, she had the isolation of working upstairs. At the new facility, she could slip into the unused cubicle that now housed the old computer. She even produced assignments on her home computer, consequences be damned. The products of Irena's efforts made Cal happy because her success reflected on him as her supervisor. Even so, he did little to support her during the computer war.

When Griff determined the first computer assigned to the first engineer was obsolete, he replaced it with a new one and offered the old one to Irena. The delightful surprise was almost terrifying as Irena wondered if Lupo knew about the offer.

Since tossing or recycling were the only other options being considered, perhaps Griff and even Lupo thought they were magnanimously giving her a piece of trash that might or might not work for her, with a care-less use-it-or-don't attitude. But Irena was thrilled. She knew that, if the computer actually worked and the programming was sound, she was on the brink of a breakthrough. She knew her ability to do her job would soar, followed she hoped by long-derailed respect and maybe even admiration.

Preparing the computer for Irena's use, Griff uninstalled engineering, survey, and other programs for which she had no use, and installed a suite of office programs giving Irena text, data, and graphics capabilities. He connected the computer at her desk and added Irena to the company network, and the computer performed without a problem.

Able to openly organize and produce her own work products, from her own computer, at her own work station, Irena looked forward to writing, designing, and producing her own proposals and marketing collateral without interference, and building a viable database of information. She no longer felt compelled to interact with Lunice.

No longer working surreptitiously, Irena re-committed to her goal of organization to reduce her frustration and that of those needing factual information. She worked toward completing her paper filing system and made her database available on the evolving company network. She eagerly looked forward to helping the firm increase its hit rate or quotient for success along with the associated increase in revenue and profit.

*   *   *

Once Irena finally possessed the fundamental tool she needed to accomplish what needed to be done, she was finally able to introduce the company to a systematic approach to inside marketing. She could easily compose, design, and produce more data rich and attractive proposals with a minimum of chaos, delivered with time to spare. And she could design and produce new and unique marketing collateral. Gratified, she looked forward to greater success for the firm and for herself, accepting the personal cost of employment at this company as the price she had to pay.

After long dealing with insubordination and sexually harassing defamation; after long being subject to snide comments and dirty looks; after long being counseled that it was her responsibility to get along—the tables began to turn for Irena.

Yutz & Dunne's image improved across the spectrum of clients, potential clients, and industry peers. The company began to win an increasing number of new contracts over respectable competitors referred to as "the big boys." Higher contract values produced increased revenue and associated profit. Backlog, or the accumulation of signed contracts awaiting execution, also increased.

Irena's user-friendly database provided her and staff with immediate access to information never before available and earned her the grudging praise of Cal, Lupo and others.

*   *   *

While enjoying the corporate and personal benefits of increased revenue and profit, Lupo showed up one afternoon at Irena's cubicle for one of his little chats. As he moved the binder on her side chair and settled in, Irena took a deep breath and waited for another long-winded, self-gratifying story.

But Lupo surprised Irena by telling her how much he admired her and what she had done for his company to increase revenue and profit. More so, he astonished her by inviting her to consider becoming one of his partners.

Holy crap! Irena thought.

The room spun, Irena's cheeks flushed, and she clenched her trembling hands in her lap so Lupo would not notice. She hardly heard the details, trying hard to ignore the music and jitterbugging elf in her head.

He told her to think about his proposition and they would talk more another time soon. Standing up and walking out of her cubicle, Lupo looked back and said, "You've earned it." Irena sat there stunned, thinking that all she had put up with had been worth it.

The allure of partnership felt like a huge compliment, but the elf stopped dancing in her head and her skin grew cold as she recalled Lupo's carrot-and-stick routine with others. She wondered if Lupo's offer was his way of encouraging her to do more of what she was already doing: working longer and more intense hours, producing more winning proposals, and driving up revenue and profit.

She wondered when he would try to convince her to invest in his company like the others, with thousands of dollars up front, or by taking a salary reduction for the dubious privilege of becoming one of his partners.

*   *   *

Meanwhile, Lunice continued to blame Irena for her diminishing workload. She intensified her attacks, determined to make Irena so unpopular and miserable she would finally quit. Irena's lamentations to Cal, Lupo, and Lunice's supervisor Mario meant nothing, because Mario supported Lunice unequivocally, defending her regardless of impact on the production of proposals and other time-sensitive marketing products. Lupo continued to demand that Irena "give Lunice more to do." And Cal stayed out of the melee.

Irena cooperated with Lupo to make work for Lunice, who superficially committed to Irena's assignments, then missed hard deadlines and ignored soft ones. She manipulated the truth to justify her actions, claiming she had too much work from engineers whose work had a "higher priority"—a policy that existed only in her mind. Whenever Irena followed up on a project or requested corrections or certain formatting, Lunice complained that Irena was demanding and uncooperative. And she continued to spread lies.

During a particular spike in Lunice's hostility, Irena was startled awake from a sound sleep in the middle of the night by the loud ringing of the telephone shattering the silence of her bedroom. Her heart racing, Irena listened as the male caller delivered a string of profanities and mocked a directive for an assignment she had given Lunice that day. When Irena reported the phone call to Cal and Cassius the next day, both men simply laughed.

Lunice went on to complain that Irena did not know how to delegate; that Irena discriminated against her by not giving her enough work to do; that work products Irena produced herself were assignments she was "taking away" from Lunice; and that Irena was "stealing her job."

Chapter Seventeen

L upo continued to measure corporate success—his success—not only by revenue and profit, but also by the number of people on staff. His simplistic logic told him that more staff brings in more revenue and therefore more profit—for him.

And so, a few weeks after his chat with Irena about partnership, with revenue and profit climbing, Lupo motivated his partners to hire sixteen new employees, increasing staff by nearly two-thirds. While still far from of his dream of three hundred employees, the number he equated to professional success, he believed hiring the sixteen would take him one step closer.

Among the sixteen were four talented engineers highly regarded in the marketplace hired as associate principals with the understanding that they would be groomed for ownership succession.

Mere weeks after expressing his pleasure with her accomplishments and inviting Irena to consider partnership, Lupo showed up at her desk for another chat. After buttering her up with his usual insincere flattery, Lupo told Irena he changed his mind and was hiring a "more seasoned, high-powered" marketing director as her supervisor.

Irena felt sucker punched. Watching him walk away, she noticed with some gratification that his glistening snakeskin loafers kept slipping off his heels revealing holes in his silky socks.

Hadn't Lupo just told her how happy he was with her performance? Hadn't revenue and profit been growing steadily? But Irena knew Lupo's hunger for revenue and profit was insatiable. No doubt, by his logic, if she could help generate regularly increasing revenue over time, then a "more seasoned, high-powered" marketing director, with Irena's support, should be able to generate even more revenue and thus more profit.

Even influenced by her professional organization, the Society for Marketing Professional Services, and supported by Cal, who often complimented her "good marketing instincts," Irena was aware that she hardly knew everything about marketing.

After agonizing rationalization, Irena decided to do her best to welcome the opportunity to learn directly from a "more experienced" professional. She looked forward to becoming a more valuable marketing professional herself, to being able to command a higher salary at this firm or elsewhere, and to being better able to provide for her family in the future.

Lupo's change of mind presented Irena with another crossroad where she might have been happier had she resigned. However disappointed and apprehensive, she sucked it up to face this next hurdle along her marketing journey.

Chapter Eighteen

Duetta Brummagem was the more seasoned, high-powered marketing professional Lupo and the partners hired. Duetta successfully negotiated a contract with Lupo giving her the title of vice president, an office next to his, and a salary more than double Irena's to perform work, the majority of which Irena was already performing. Duetta negotiated Irena's assistance in the bargain plus a clause guaranteeing her six months' salary if she were terminated for any reason within a year.

For all of her negotiating machismo, Duetta was a little over five feet tall, overweight with an oddly slender neck, thin arms and legs, and a scar along her fleshy left cheekbone. She wore only black and white, and with her alabaster skin and bright orange dyed hair, she resembled a carrot-topped penguin.

According to Lupo's secretary, the recruiter who identified Duetta provided Lupo with documentation about her history of interpersonal conflict. But with his eye on the dollar sign, Lupo ignored that history, hired Duetta anyway, and sicced her on Irena.

Irena had long been the object of a tug of war with Cal and Lupo pulling her in different directions. She now became the object of a more complex tug of war as Cal, Lupo, and Duetta claimed equal rights to her support.

Regardless of the challenges facing her, Irena loved marketing and knew the corporate culture. She predicted Duetta would not last two years, and further predicted that when Duetta left, she, Irena, would resume the marketing workload. She tolerated the situation, hoping for intermittent rewards, expecting the grand prize in the end, coming to feel like a B.F. Skinner pigeon pecking away in some operant conditioning behavior experiment.

*   *   *

Once Duetta settled in to her nicely appointed office next to Lupo's, it became vividly clear to Irena why the woman had a documented history of interpersonal conflict. Certain behaviors were merely irritating. Others made Irena want to run screaming out the door. Still others made her contemplate hara-kiri.

Duetta would shout at Irena to do something or not do something and then complain about what she had done or failed to do. Duetta often summoned Irena from her cubicle by phone simply saying "come here." Even if Irena was working on assignment for Lupo or Cal, Duetta expected her to drop everything, spring from her desk, and be at her side in an instant.

As soon as Irena would hang up, Duetta would call a second time. If Irena answered, Duetta would furiously demand to know why she was still there, why she was still answering her phone, what was taking her so long, and then tell her to hurry up, as though the world was on the brink of Armageddon.

When working with Duetta on proposals or other projects for clients with whom Irena had an established relationship, Irena would volunteer that the client anticipated and appreciated thus and so content. Duetta would cut Irena off, telling her she did not want her to think, she just wanted her to do what she was told.

Leaving the office for lunch or even the restroom, Irena was expected to call Duetta telling her where she was going and how long she would be away from her desk. Irena once went to lunch at noon without telling Duetta, and Duetta cornered her at the reception desk when she returned, like a disobedient child, snarling about leaving the office without telling her, because "I might have needed you for something." Likewise, Irena was not allowed to leave the office any evening without first obtaining Duetta's permission.

One week Irena booked two doctors' appointments: one prescheduled for herself weeks in advance and the other for a sick child. Irena notified Duetta well in advance of the day and time of the appointment for herself, and as much as she could for her sick child. With nothing critical on the agenda, Irena did not ask for Duetta's permission to leave for either appointment. She simply left when she said she would.

When Irena returned to the office after the second appointment, Duetta was livid on multiple fronts. She threatened Irena for not asking permission to leave. She told Irena that she was expected to be at her desk "all day every day." And that "two doctors' appointments in one week might just get you fired." Irena learned later that this last threat is considered workplace intimidation, possibly arguable under the federal Family and Medical Leave Act.

*   *   *

One day, Duetta called Irena to her office repeatedly to ask questions she could have asked on the phone. Each time, she complained that Irena did not get to her office fast enough. At home that evening while watching TV, well after dinner, with the kids asleep in their beds, Irena was startled by a knock on her front door. She opened the door to find Duetta standing there, reeking of alcohol, sobbing an apology for her behavior that day.

Duetta shoved a double-lined brown paper shopping bag full of beer and wine toward Irena, presumably as a gift to make up for her behavior, and then stood there mutely, apparently expecting Irena to invite her in. Irena accepted the bag, thanked Duetta kindly, but did not invite her in. *Bad enough she's in my professional life,* Irena thought. *I refuse to have her in my personal life.*

After an awkward moment or two, Duetta turned and left. The next day, perhaps because she embarrassed herself by showing up at Irena's home intoxicated and in tears, and perhaps because Irena did not invite her in to comfort her, Duetta intensified her demands and verbal abuse. Oh, that Irena could have smiled and let such things roll off her back.

*   *   *

As though Irena were her captive minion, Duetta periodically demanded that she go to lunch with her, insisting they go to a popular local bar and grill. The first time Duetta demanded Irena's company at lunch, Irena imagined an urgent project that needed their undivided attention.

Arriving at the restaurant, when the hostess led them to a booth, Duetta demanded a table, specifically requesting four chairs. Approaching the table, Duetta told Irena, a little louder than Irena thought necessary, that she would be teaching her "how to behave in front of men."

Several heads whipped around.

Really? Perhaps our dining neighbors think I'm a nun, Irena thought.

Duetta told Irena with a smug air of superiority that she would first teach her "where and how a woman should drape her coat." "Always on an adjacent chair. Never her own."

Demonstrating with exaggerated fanfare, Duetta folded her purple wool coat lengthwise and laid it vertically over the back and across the seat of the opposite ladder-back chair. The coat, worn at the elbows and frayed at the hem, belied her affected air of superiority.

As Irena began to sit, Duetta commanded that she wait again because she wanted to teach her "how a woman should sit down in a chair." Duetta appeared oblivious to the rapt attention of their dining neighbors, most chuckling into their napkins.

Did they think I just climbed out from under a moss-covered rock from the nearby creek or did they consider her a pompous ass? Irena wondered.

Her weight and stature puffed up to begin with, Duetta nevertheless fluffed herself up like a creature that does so to intimidate an enemy or seek a sexual partner. She pulled out her chair, smoothed her bottom, and sat down, deliberately dead square with the table, with her back as straight as the ramrod Irena suspected was... well, you know.

Continuing with her demonstration, Duetta explained how important it is for a woman to know "how to cross her legs in the company of men." She told Irena that, unless a woman is actually eating, she should be slightly away from the table with her legs crossed at the knee like a man, not at the ankle like a woman. Again she demonstrated.

Irena thought, *Duetta has those spindly legs, like her spindly neck, and can easily cross her legs at the knee. Not so easy for some of us. She reminds me of a penguin holiday ornament sitting on a shelf or mantle, with one spindly leg dangling over the edge and the other one crossed at the knee.*

Duetta climaxed by demonstrating, she said, "how a woman should drape one arm over the back of a chair like a man." She did not light a cigarette, but she did let out a deep breath and ordered a martini.

*   *   *

When Irena finally got to sit down and they ate, Duetta often shushed Irena, expecting her to remain silent while she, Duetta, discussed the benefits of being more like a man. Their audience, that Irena found impossible to ignore, continued to watch, listen, and giggle.

Back at the office, Duetta added a postscript to their lunch by insisting they rearrange the furniture in Irena's cubicle—important, she said, to "put a barrier between you and them." Irena wound up virtually trapped in a corner replicating the risk of her hamster's nest at the old office, where she would have been fried to a crisp in a fire or entombed under a pile of rubble in some other catastrophic event.

*   *   *

Commandeering Irena for other lunches at the same bar and grill, Duetta would insist on a booth effectively cut off from the rest of the restaurant—a booth with tall, red-leather-covered seats and a back topped with dark oak spindle trim—for privacy, she said. She would immediately order a martini, consuming two by the time their meal arrived.

Sitting directly across from her, Irena would watch as Duetta's nose, cheeks and the tips of her ears would flush, her eyes would glaze over, and her head would wobble. During these lunches, Duetta expected Irena to serve as psychotherapeutic doormat while she shared far more about her personal history than Irena wanted to hear.

As Duetta shared her woes, if Irena asked a question or made a comment, Duetta would mumble at her to "stop talking and just listen." Irena's alter ego wanted to snap Duetta's head off that spindly neck. Duetta often culminated her woes with her lament at having been unable to find employment in Atlanta where she had worked for nine years—*probably because her reputation preceded her*, Irena thought.

*   *   *

Irena worked long hours for Duetta—a total of a hundred and four over one seven-day period. With three children and virtually no time for a social life outside the office, Irena maintained a few friendships, despite the risks, within the confines of the organization.

Jed Molino, a personable single engineer, and Irena had an affable, bantering relationship and enjoyed each other's company. Trusting Jed's friendship only so far, Irena told him she did not trust anyone at work considering what others were doing to her reputation.

Irena and several co-workers including Duetta were gathered around the conference room table enjoying cake and champagne to celebrate someone's birthday. Having been inducted into the scandal-mongering mob, Duetta brought up the subject, in his absence, of sex with Jed.

Obviously led to believe that Irena was the company slut and therefore an acceptable target, she addressed the group saying, "Someone among us is sleeping with Jed." Without pausing to take a breath, she spun around theatrically to face Irena and said with syrupy derision, "Isn't that you?" And then, without pausing to take a breath, she told everyone present that she, in fact, had had sex with Jed.

Cackling as though she had just plunged a knife into Irena's heart, Duetta turned her back to Irena. Like mean girls everywhere, Duetta tried to convince those present that Jed and Irena were intimate and that she, Duetta, had successfully lured him away to have sex with her.

Unbeknownst to Duetta, Jed had already told Irena that he had had sex with Duetta, the poor guy not the first to be led astray by a conniving woman.

*   *   *

Before Duetta joined the firm, Irena represented the marketing department at monthly executive committee meetings. Once Duetta was hired, she barred Irena from those meetings. In fact, Duetta wanted Irena eliminated from the company.

Usually summoned to Duetta's office, Irena became suspicious when Duetta showed up at her cubicle minutes before an executive committee meeting. Duetta told Irena, "I have an idea for an invitation for the next client appreciation event. I want you to produce three different draft versions right now to take into the meeting for review." Presumably as an afterthought, Duetta added, "And don't worry about typographical errors." Up shot a red flag.

Duetta knew Irena would never knowingly allow a document she produced to leave her hands containing errors. So, standing over her in an anxiety-induced ambush, Duetta hurried Irena along, virtually prodding her elbow to be sure she made mistakes, refusing to allow her to make corrections.

When the meeting ended, Marc Fine, a sympathetic executive committee member, told Irena what happened at the meeting. He said, "Duetta complained to the committee about you, attempting to prove your incompetence with those invitation drafts. She offered to hire what she called a capable friend to replace you." Duetta failed to realize that the partners had worked with Irena for a long time and knew how competent she was or was not.

After Irena's talk with Marc, unable to control her outrage, she stormed into Cal's office sputtering, "I have endured that woman's volatility and abuse for six months and I refuse to take it any longer. Her charade to make me look incompetent at the executive committee meeting is the last straw. I love marketing and I do not want to leave, but if the partners prefer Duetta, I will resign if you grant me time to find another position."

Cal had been Irena's advocate for years and she needed him. But in many ways, Cal needed her too—enough for him to step out of his comfort zone to convince the other partners not to let her go. As a result, the partners created a new administrative position to retain Irena and keep her away from Duetta; and Duetta was advised that she could not hire her friend or anyone else.

Duetta was furious.

Irena was overjoyed.

*   *   *

Mae Mook, hired among the sixteen new staff members, was assigned the pretentious title of "records manager of paper documents for engineering," otherwise known as file clerk. Rather than pay fair wages, Lupo dispensed fancy titles, pleasing staff for a year or two until staff realized that a title was all they were likely to get beyond their hiring salary.

Just as co-dependents are said to gravitate toward one another, so perhaps do those who imbibe. Co-workers, tittering about Duetta and May slurring their speech and staggering at various company-sponsored events, dubbed them drinking buddies. Friends bonding, one might call it. But one could hardly call their evolving relationship a friendship because Duetta had ulterior motives.

Taking advantage of her position—a vice president after all—Duetta conscripted Mae—the file clerk—to watch Irena and find something to use against her.

Once the partners dissolved Irena and Duetta's working relationship, Irena relocated away from Duetta to a cubicle closer to Cal. In the process of cleaning out her desk and marketing files, Irena tossed useless old paperwork—most of which she had created—into a trash bin near her cubicle. Mae reported Irena's activities to Duetta who seized the opportunity to concoct a story for the partners.

While arranging incoming mail on Cal's desk the following week as part of her new administrative role, Irena discovered a memo from Duetta addressed to Cal and the other partners with her name—Irena's—on the subject line. The memo sat alone in the center of Cal's otherwise empty desktop in full view, no doubt where he had put it for her to see and read.

Given his distaste for such documentation, Cal might not have brought the memo to Irena's attention had she not seen it, read it, and reacted. And react she did.

Sitting in Cal's chair, she read Duetta's memo that began by accusing Irena of "sabotaging the marketing files" and stating that "she should be fired for such a crime."

Enraged, Irena stood up and started to pace. The more she read, the faster she paced. Heart racing and blood pressure rising, Irena could scarcely breathe. Her hands were shaking, her palms were sweaty, and an alter ego was prepared to strangle Duetta. Irena had to leave the office and walk around the building twice before she could calm down.

When Cal returned later that day, Irena found him sitting at his desk. Too angry to get too close, she confronted him from the doorway about the memo demanding a confrontation with Duetta. Not unexpectedly, Cal refused to participate. Instead, he advised Irena to "meet with Duetta and Mae to gather information."

Irena immediately arranged to meet with both women in Duetta's office at nine o'clock the following morning. Arriving at the appointed hour, Irena felt no fear or hesitation, her justifiable rage giving her every bit of the courage she needed for this confrontation.

Feeling like a warrior for the winning side, she entered Duetta's office and sat in an empty chair next to Mae. Both faced Duetta while Duetta sat facing the door from the protected space behind her desk. A window cast bright sunlight from behind, illuminating Duetta's orange hair like flames, making her look demonic in the shadows.

Duetta appeared stone cold with just a hint of a smirk on her pudgy little face. Mae's eyes were darting about nervously as she twirled a few strands of her hair with her left hand. Irena enjoyed seeing at least one of them squirm. Handing each a copy of Duetta's memo, Irena held hers aloft and got right to the point.

"What is this memo *really* about, ladies?" she said.

With feigned confusion and wide-eyed innocence, arms apart in staged comfort, Duetta said nothing but looked to Mae to respond. In that moment of weighted silence, an unspoken melodrama played out on Mae's face. Annoyance followed confusion before the light went on in her eyes as Mae realized Duetta had set her up and expected her to take the fall.

A look of betrayal and outrage spread across Mae's face as she grasped the far-reaching ramifications of the unfolding melodrama.

She then looked Duetta in the eye and said slowly and viciously, "That was the *last* time I will *ever* do *anything* for you." Leaping from her chair, Mae stormed out of the room as though by leaving she could escape the consequences.

After picking herself up off the floor, metaphorically speaking, Irena left right behind Mae, having heard all she needed to hear.

*   *   *

Reporting back to Cal, he then agreed to participate in a confrontation. In spite of his distaste for documentation, he advised Irena to write up the situation describing her on-going relationship with Duetta. With that memo in hand, Cal summoned Duetta to meet with him and Irena in his office.

Propelled by her ego, Duetta came ready for war, shouting her outrage all the way down the corridor to his office: that she, a vice president, should be summoned to his office, a mere engineering manager. Duetta was apparently unaware that Cal was assuming the presidency, and she had obviously forgotten that he was an invested partner, a company owner, and therefore her superior.

The meeting in Cal's office was nothing short of astonishing. He sat behind his desk while Duetta and Irena sat next to each other facing him, like Irena and Mae sat facing Duetta in her office. Duetta ignored Irena, ranting and raving non-stop, as though by simply never shutting up she would emerge the victor. Telling her to be quiet, Cal turned the meeting over to Irena.

Turning in her chair to face Duetta, Irena asked slowly and coldly, "Why did you write this memo and what did you hope to achieve?" Of course, Irena knew the answer, but she wanted to hear Duetta describe her motives: to say something in front of Cal: anything.

Instead, knowing Irena had Cal's support, Duetta responded to Irena with a silent glare that shouted, "I would sooner see you in hell." Behaving like the trapped rat she was, Duetta inched her chair backward until it hit the wall behind her with an audible thud.

Irena calmly told Duetta that she expected a written response for the partners describing how she planned to rectify the damage she had done to Irena's reputation. Duetta again responded with another silent glare that screamed, "When hell freezes over."

When the meeting was over, Duetta left Cal's office out of control. Her alabaster skin crimson with rage, she mumbled incoherently and flailed her arms all the way back to her office, like that carrot-topped penguin caught in a hurricane.

Several weeks after that extraordinary confrontation and eight months after Duetta and Mae were hired, the economy receded enough to provide the partners with plausible grounds to terminate both women. Despite the conspiracies, neither woman was fired. Instead, the partners announced that the receding economy made it necessary to lay them off.

During Duetta's time with the company, this "more-seasoned, high-powered" marketing vice president wasted huge amounts of money and alienated staff, consultants, and clients with her caustic behavior, in a futile attempt to increase revenue and profit. The firm honored her contract, and Duetta received six months' salary to leave. She raped the company and Lupo went down smiling.

*   *   *

After those eight months and not two years, Irena was "promoted" to marketing manager. She assumed ninety percent of Duetta's workload and resumed inside marketing responsibilities for then thirty-one engineers, when the ratio in the industry was one for ten.

Irena received no assistance or additional compensation, her salary remaining more than forty percent below her peers. She did not argue for more money because the company was supposedly in economic turmoil from a receding economy made worse by paying Duetta the equivalent of Irena's annual salary to leave. Convinced she could not win an argument for more money, Irena remained with the firm for love of the work and her belief that circumstances would eventually improve.

A year after Duetta's termination, Irena met with Lupo to discuss her ever-escalating workload, her unrelenting overtime under pressure to meet unyielding deadlines, her need for dedicated assistance, and her desire to foster continuity should anything happen to her.

Irena wanted Lupo to consider the risk of having only one staff member—her—knowledgeable about unique marketing systems and procedures: unique because Lupo chose not to invest in professional software and associated staff. After articulating her concerns, Lupo gave Irena a condescending smirk and said, "Don't worry about your job, Irena. There are plenty of hungry women out there."

Hungry women!

Irena wondered if anyone had ever hurt Lupo like she wanted to hurt him at that moment. In some alternate reality, Irena might have picked up one of his desk accessories to hurl at him or leapt across his desk to yank out the remaining tufts of hair on his balding head, and maybe even poked his eyes out. But all she could do when she regained control of her mind and body was stand up and leave the room in astonished disbelief.

*   *   *

It is said that co-dependents are attracted to one another by some undefined force, and that if you put two co-dependents in opposite corners of a room filled with people, the two will soon find each other. One might speculate that Irena gravitated to Yutz & Dunne by that same undefined force and that, in co-dependent fashion, she justified remaining on the job telling herself:

"I'm tough." "I can handle it." "I can cope." "I can improve the status quo." "They just don't understand." "I have always been able to endure and survive." "I can make this work for me." "I won't let them get to me, because I'm bigger than that." "This too shall pass." "What matters is how I do my job." "Things will get better if I just try harder, do more, do it faster, and do it better."

Co-dependency was critically the wrong paradigm for employment at Yutz & Dunne.

*   *   *

Irena was denied an increase on her first anniversary because she was making more than her predecessor. She was subsequently denied a cost-of-living increase.

On her second anniversary, the firm was doing well, in part the result of Irena's approach to marketing. Expecting an evaluation and an increase, her second anniversary came and went with no acknowledgement.

Taking a month or two to calm down and collect her thoughts, Irena approached Cal about the status of an increase. Cal told her she needed to justify in writing why she should receive a raise. The passage of time, of course, was an insufficient argument.

Researching the marketplace over several weeks, Irena presented Cal with a detailed written report comparing peer responsibilities and salaries. She articulated her achievements and included a formal request for a raise. The report sat on Cal's desk for months.

Too busy to make a fuss sooner, Irena eventually approached Cal about that report and a possible increase. Anticipating a long-winded debate, Cal instead said he would "see what he could do." More months passed, during which Duetta and Mae had been hired and fired and Irena was promoted.

The firm, having recovered from paying off Duetta and from her negative influence in the engineering community, was again winning more engineering contracts month over month, increasing revenue and profit. Clients praised Irena's work products directly to her and presumably to Cal and Lupo. She thought she was doing a good if not great job.

*   *   *

Three weeks beyond her third anniversary, Irena stormed into Cal's office. Throwing herself down in his guest chair, Irena addressed him sharply and said, "I have been with this company for three years doing everything expected of me and doing it well while dealing with substantial obstacles. Revenue and profit have been increasing steadily. I have had no evaluation and no salary increase for three years. What is going on and when can I expect a raise?"

Feigning magnanimity and probably realizing he could not stall Irena much longer, Cal told her he had already allocated an increase—of five percent—pausing perhaps for her reaction—then told her that five percent was "the best I can do."

Irena interpreted Cal's comment about doing the best he could as a deflection to Lupo as the cause of this economic insult, because Lupo held tight to the purse strings. Cal had to know that five percent after three years of increasing revenue and profit, much attributable to Irena's improvements to the quality of proposals and the process, was ludicrous and insulting. Five percent after three years even fell short of inflation.

Taking another tack, Irena asked Cal about promotion opportunities, which she presumed would be accompanied by more money. He shocked her by saying she would never be promoted again.

What?

When Irena asked why, he refused to elaborate, simply telling her that she "just might be happier" at some other company. Cal may have been thinking about Irena's relationship with Lunice. He may have been thinking about her relationship with Lupo and the engineers. But most likely Cal was thinking about the character assassination raging behind her back—character assassination he accepted as truth and did nothing to stop.

Irena refused to consider leaving. She refused to be driven out of a company by an insecure, jealous, and defamatory co-worker. She loved the work she performed. She knew that the partners knew that she was making valuable contributions to the success of the firm. And she was close to home for her children's sake.

And so, believing that right and justice would eventually prevail, Irena continued to tolerate a defamatory work environment where men were easily titillated by scandal; an organization that avoided personnel reviews and salary increases allowing them to engage in egregious discrimination.

Chapter Nineteen

While Irena was transitioning back to marketing and struggling to recover from Duetta's influence, a fifty-something married and unemployed engineering technician began hanging out in the office. Manny Handler's personal friend, Darrell Russell, a timid design engineer on staff, apparently told him that Yutz & Dunne had recently—over the last year anyway—hired several staff. Both apparently believed Manny could land a job simply by becoming a familiar face.

This pale, short, fire plug of a man was gifted by the cosmos with a pushed in nose and beady brown eyes. For several hours every workday for months, casually dressed in jeans and a collared tee-shirt, Manny would visit with Darrell, walk around interrupting and trying to befriend staff, or sit in the kitchen talking to anyone who stopped in for coffee or lunch. Irena saw no evidence the partners did anything to discourage him from being on company premises. They failed to consider that, by allowing him virtually unlimited access to the premises, they might be putting the company, male and female staff, at risk.

Every week or two, Manny would approach Cal, asking if there might be work for him. Each time, Cal would tell Manny no, and then almost, but not quite, complain to Irena with a silly grin on his face. Cal enjoyed being at the top of the pecking order where the buck stopped, in control of whether or not to hire Manny.

Manny's persistence eventually paid off. At first, Cal "threw Manny some work," as he put it, like the master of the house magnanimously throwing a bone to a starving dog. Then there were occasional projects that benefitted from a few hours of Manny's technical expertise in pedestrian street crossing design.

The firm had little need for his capabilities, but three months later Cal hired Manny full-time, succumbing to the thrill of his first hire. Like other engineers, Manny was responsible to marketing—to

Irena, a woman—to provide technical input for proposals involving his services.

Manny strutted around the office like an aging bantam rooster, boasting about his twenty-seven-year-old feather-weight boxing championship, as if this gave him credibility. Rumors surfaced that Manny had been unemployed for several years, having been terminated by a nearby city where, according to that city's staff years later, Manny had some kind of history there.

Rumor also had it that another public agency refused to hire him because of his reputation with women. Irena had no doubt that Manny's background and credentials were never investigated by anyone at Yutz & Dunne because, as Cal said, they're engineers and they don't do that.

The longer Manny remained with the company, the more offensive his behavior became toward Irena and other women on staff. After the women collectively complained about a girlie calendar Manny hung in the company kitchen, Manny argued his right to hang girlie calendars wherever he wanted.

Worse, Manny openly ogled women's breasts and bodies like a salivating animal. During any conversation, this man, with pores on his pushed-in nose big enough to hide beans, examined a woman down to her ankles and back up again, much like Lupo did with Irena during her interview. Manny also asserted his self-proclaimed right to send suggestive group e-mails. Complaining or asking Manny to stop these behaviors only seemed to encourage him.

While working on a proposal with Cal, Irena needed information only Manny could provide. Manny was out of the office and Cal asked Irena to search his network files for the information. As she did, she stumbled upon numerous strip poker games Manny had stored there, each with a different female name, and each with presumably different attributes. Irena did not check. When she mentioned her discovery to Cal, again he simply laughed.

*   *   *

When Manny was first hired, Cal assigned him a cubicle an arm's length from Irena's, so near she could hear him slurping his morning coffee and smell his after shave lotion. Pleasant enough at first, Manny struck up numerous conversations and occasionally invited Irena to lunch. She occasionally joined him.

After a few lunches together, Manny began waiting for Irena to leave work in the evening. He insisted on walking her to her car because, he said, it was dangerous for a woman to walk through a dark parking lot alone. Irena found Manny's concern quaint until she realized he considered a dark parking lot after work an ideal time and place to corner her in the shadows and pressure her for an intimate relationship. He said his wife was often out of town and "wouldn't mind" if they spent time together. He even suggested they go out on his family boat.

Concluding that Manny's pressure and persistence were likely the result of on-going speculation about her sexual behavior, Irena declined further lunch invitations. Her rejection made Manny mad and triggered a series of events that could, and perhaps should, have put Manny in jail.

Chapter Twenty

E mployment-at-will became an issue shortly after Manny was hired, perhaps motivated by Title VII of the Civil Rights Act of 1964 as amended by the Civil Rights Act of 1991. With no advance notice or discussion, every employee was asked to sign a simple, one-paragraph agreement and return it for their personnel file.

The agreement, produced in-house on company letterhead, stated that the employee accepted employment at will and gave the company freedom to terminate any employee at any time without reason, balancing the equation by stating that employees retained the right to quit at any time without reason—as if those were statements of true equality. The agreement conveniently omitted any mention of applicable litigious exceptions.

Virtually every state in the Union did and does maintain employment at-will, with litigious exceptions, so no legitimate need exists for such an agreement. The only purpose Lupo could have had for this self-serving and manipulative agreement was entrapment— to leave employees with no legal recourse if and when he chose to cross legal boundaries, act impulsively, and/or fire anyone, at any time, for any reason. Co-workers signed and returned their copies, but Irena considered the agreement contrary to her best interest and chose not to sign it, her decision not well received.

*　　　　*　　　　*

Lupo envied Carmichael Engineers, a local competitor founded the same year as Yutz & Dunne. Carmichael's success—with more than five-hundred owner-employees in twenty-seven offices—drove Lupo to distraction. He envisioned employing three hundred people in eight locations but, in business as long as Carmichael, Lupo employed thirty-something in one location.

Lupo refused to consider that Carmichael was successful, in large part, because they valued their employees and offered them a vested interest in the firm's success. He had difficulty comprehending that profit sharing and stock ownership can generate loyalty along with increased productivity and the ever-increasing profit he pursued.

But profit sharing, stock ownership, 401K matching contributions, and even bonuses were sacrifices Lupo refused to make. He expected those he hired to be bound in servitude by meager and unchanging salaries; and he used the crack of a verbal whip to drive staff to ever increase productivity, to earn him the profit to freely engage in entrepreneurial side businesses.

Lupo baited his invested partners with carrot-and-stick promises of ownership succession while maintaining tight financial control, allowing them limited influence over corporate decisions or budgets.

Those rare times when Lupo discussed corporate finances, under pressure to present an occasional state of the company address, he provided no factual data but badgered partners and staff to bring in more work for his ever economically failing company, whether that fact was true or not.

Lupo knew he needed staff to make him money, and he hated being dependent. Driven to punish those he depended on, he often mocked individual limitations and undermined morale in casual conversation and at executive committee and staff meetings.

When a partner, engineer or surveyor tried to engage Lupo in discussion, offer an alternative, or challenge one of his arbitrary decisions, Lupo said things like, "This is my company and you'll do it my way." "I don't need you or anybody else." "I'm doing you a favor providing you with work." "Be grateful you have a job." "There's always somebody else to take your place."

Whether or not Lupo could comprehend the impact of his words and actions, his attitude and behavior impeded loyalty and contributed to high turnover and variable profitability. Maslow's Hierarchy of Needs and theory of self-actualization were Greek to Lupo, who was unconcerned whether or not employees were satisfied with the work they did. Lupo was the antithesis of the man who said, "I am not the smartest, but I surround myself with competent people."

Lupo considered Yutz & Dunne to be his company exclusively; and regardless of partnership agreements, he allowed his partners a voice only so long as they agreed with him. Constrained as they were, the partners began to behave like rats in an overcrowded laboratory experiment, finding fault and attacking one another because they could not get to Lupo.

As the wildfire raged on, backbiting, badmouthing, and gossip typified corporate culture. Irena became convinced that principals and staff were destined to collide in some cosmic circus.

Over and over, Lupo demonstrated how little regard he had for his employees, male or female. He considered each individual easy to manipulate and/or expendable. He trusted unhappy employees to resign, move on, and never make a stink about anything. As a small company, less regulated by the Department of Labor than a larger company, that may have been the way it was.

But times were changing for Lupo and his company.

Chapter Twenty-One

L upo Yutz's quest for admiration and his imperative to drive up revenue and profit often motivated him to make autonomous forays into the marketplace to solicit new clients and new work. Comical when not irritating, most who knew Lupo agreed he could sell icebergs to polar bears, if only once.

Disregarding his marketing manager, the agreed-upon marketing plan, and his partners, and misrepresenting firm and staff capabilities, Lupo would create chaos back at the office by making commitments the firm was hard-pressed and often unable to fulfill.

When confronted about his random commitments, Lupo declared that he hired staff to do whatever he wanted them to do, and "they had damn well better" live up to his commitments.

Once those Lupo contacted discovered his misrepresentations, they viewed him with contempt. Upon any subsequent contact, if those he contacted were at all interested in his allegations, they would call Cal or Irena to confirm.

Cal and Irena began isolating Lupo from clients whenever possible to mitigate the damage he caused.

*   *   *

Business for Lupo was a contest requiring a distinct winner and a loser. He had to be bigger, he had to be better, and he had to win. Lupo seemed incapable of participating in a win-win situation. His win had to be someone else's loss, and someone else's win was an affront and he had to get even.

Yutz & Dunne once submitted a proposal for a roadway project for a local municipality. Losing a contract Lupo thought his firm should have won, he stormed the city's engineering department and browbeat the award panel. He seemed to believe on some primordial level that beating them up would change their minds. Good thing he left his baseball bat at home.

That city blacklisted the company and chose not to award a project to the firm for three years. Cal Chauvin was challenged to repair the firm's reputation, and a year or two later, the city resumed awarding work to the firm: that is, until Lupo called on the city engineer and reopened old wounds. That city never signed another contract with Yutz & Dunne while Irena was employed at the firm.

* * *

Lupo interpreted superficial admiration as respect. In addition to his upscale wardrobe, he cranked up the charm to woo anyone he considered potentially lucrative: a prospective client or a potential money-making engineer applying for a job.

If Lupo thought such an engineer was a catch—someone who might attract clients with deep pockets—he baited him (never a woman) with the perk of ambiguous but highly appealing marketing responsibilities. In Lupo's mind, those privileges included the freedom to wine and dine on the company's time and dime. He baited the bigger catches with the ego-gratifying title of vice president.

Lupo would capitalize on the new hire's name recognition and reputation while manipulating him with elusive promises of greater marketing responsibility and reward. He never warned Irena about his new hires or marketing promises, and he never considered the consequences. New engineers, hooked by Lupo's marketing lure, would show up periodically and cause Irena grief, believing she was a dedicated support employee for him until she made it clear otherwise.

One case in particular was Pedro Aqualina, a young, self-assured United States Naval Academy graduate engineer Lupo met at a County Engineers event. Eager to hire this Annapolis graduate who did battle with a five-o'clock shadow and hairy ears, Lupo lured him with those vague but appealing promises of marketing responsibilities.

Taking the bait, unaware of Irena's existing role and responsibilities, Pedro attempted to assume a definitive marketing role and a working relationship that was disruptive and insulting for Irena.

Calling a meeting of the partners to discuss his ideas, Pedro told Irena to bring refreshments. Increasingly sensitive to suffocating chauvinism, Irena commented about being *told* to bring refreshments versus a courteous request.

Pedro said, "Honey. It's either you or me, and since I've always been smarter than anyone I have ever worked with, I should make decisions for you."

Excuse me?

This was another man Irena wanted to smack. Fortunately for Pedro, he left the company a few months later.

Chapter Twenty-Two

When Lunice, the word processor, was out of the office, an anxious engineer or surveyor would occasionally ask Irena for a quick clerical favor. Provided she had no proposal deadline, that was okay with her.

Manny Handler, however, in a thinly disguised attempt to punish her for rejecting him, began an escalating deluge of trivial but time-consuming demands, as though Irena were obliged to support him in that fashion. The final straw was his command—not a request—to take his paycheck to the bank.

Irena refused, telling him that, as marketing manager, she did not have time to provide him or any engineer or surveyor with the kind of support he seemed to want. And she certainly did not have time to run anyone's errands. Not to be bested, Manny replied, "Oh, you think you're so big!" And like Duetta, he added, "You just need to do what you're told!"

And it was war.

*　　　　*　　　　*

Manny believed the gossip: that Irena was having random sex with random co-workers, and seemed to think he had a right to a piece of "the action," a right to control an intimate relationship with her, or at least the right to cop a feel. He was determined she would have sex with him, or he would continue to punish her for excluding him.

Passing each other in an unoccupied corridor or making his way to her cubicle where Irena might be working alone, with no witnesses of course, Manny would find some way to touch her—patting her shoulder, stroking her arm, rubbing her back, or putting his arm around her and giving her a little squeeze—depending on whether she was sitting at her desk, standing at a file cabinet, or walking around. Like a zap from a stun gun, Irena's brain cells would explode and she would pray to remember she was a lady. It was impossible to avoid Manny because his intent was to provoke her.

*   *   *

The partners had long been passively unresponsive or actively hostile to Irena's complaints about Lunice's defamation. She knew they would be equally unresponsive and hostile to her complaints about Manny's sexual harassment. Having never faced such offensive behavior, unaware of her rights, and with nobody in authority in whom to confide, Irena faced solving the problem with Manny on "her own.

She first tried to get Manny to leave her alone by writing him a note—*the least confrontational manner*, she thought. She composed a brief and informal handwritten message asking him to please stop touching her, and please stop suggesting they get together because their relationship was professional and not personal. She placed the note in an envelope and delivered it to his desk when he stepped away.

Once Manny read the note, he avoided Irena for a while, obviously annoyed. But within weeks, having gotten over his snit, he started taunting her again. One afternoon, Manny quietly entered Irena's cubicle, came up behind her, took her head in his hands, and kissed her hair. Startled, Irena whipped around in her chair, hitting him in the knees. Unfazed, he gave her a malevolent grin and strutted away.

With Cal and the partners' command that she "get along" making her fear for her security, Irena could not bring herself to slap him or, as she imagined, push him down a flight of stairs.

Days after the hair-kissing episode, Irena approached Manny asking, as coolly as she could and perhaps a bit sarcastically, "Do you have a minute to talk privately in the library?" Manny agreed without hesitation and Irena wondered what he thought might happen in that claustrophobic little room. Once inside, Irena closed the door and invited him to sit.

Taking a deep breath to keep her anger in check and her voice steady, Irena told Manny quietly and unequivocally that she wanted him to keep his hands off her because she was not his child, his wife, or his pet; and that continuing to touch her against her will constituted sexual harassment in the eyes of the law.

Very obviously not expecting Irena to say what she did, Manny's eyes narrowed and his brow furrowed. Dripping with sarcasm and challenge, Manny leaned back in his chair, puffed up his cocky little self, and said, "Too bad. I'm just a touchy feely kind of guy," implying that he would do whatever he wanted and she would have to put up with it.

Oh, the urge to strangle the bastard, she thought.

Responding in kind, Irena said, "My right not to be touched supersedes your touchy feely personality." At that, Manny rose abruptly, threw open the library door, and departed with a piggy snort. Later that day, the accounting manager told Irena that she overheard Manny tell another co-worker that "sexual harassment is a crock."

The day after their meeting in the library, Irena encountered Manny in an empty corridor. Keeping her distance, she hoped to pass with no interaction. Instead he accosted her. Shoving her against a wall, Manny trapped Irena by placing a hand behind each of her shoulders. Then, laying a bristly cheek against hers, breathing hard as if restraining himself, and smelling like garlic, he slowly and sarcastically—threateningly?—whispered in her ear saying, "If we lived together, I don't think we'd get along very well."

Irena heard that if they were a couple, he would beat the crap out of her.

Irena ducked out from under his arms and ran for the safety of the office and her desk, her heart nearly beating out of her chest. And with no-one in authority to support or protect her, she had to cope with and recover on her own.

Irena later wondered if his comment was supposed to be a come-on to some sadomasochistic relationship.

*   *   *

Losing her ability to cope, Irena absolutely had to let someone in authority know what was going on before she pulled out every last strand of her own hair, or Manny's, or pushed him down that flight of stairs. The logical individual to tell was Griff Chimeric, theoretically responsible for sexual harassment issues in addition to survey and safety.

In spite of her dread over involving a partner, and knowing Griff to be an insensitive clod, Irena approached him in an office full of muddy clothing, safety vests, an open toolbox, a tripod and various pieces of survey equipment. Clearing off the chair nearest the door, Irena sat on the edge and started talking.

Tentative at first, her story became a torrent spilling from her lips. Staring at her, perhaps in disbelief, Griff knew better than to interrupt. When Irena finished, she told him she was not asking him to do anything right then, but she wanted him to know what was going on. She added that if Manny ever touched her again she would seek corporate intervention. And then, in an anxiety-induced rush, Irena rose and left before Griff could say a word.

Griff did not follow up with Irena. However, he apparently told Manny she complained, but did not warn him to stop because, in or out of meetings, Manny took advantage of every opportunity to make snide and demeaning comments to and about Irena, witnessed by Griff and other partners who did nothing to stop him.

One staff meeting involved an assessment of needs for furniture, equipment, and space. Irena requested a four-drawer file cabinet, a lamp, and some office supplies. Manny said loudly, "Typical. All you ever think about is yourself."

What?

Never having learned how to successfully counter such barbs, much less in a room full of hostile co-workers, Irena once again overcame the urge to fling something at Manny. While struggling with his comment, Irena vacillated between imagining herself a warrior standing over his lifeless and decapitated body, one foot on his chest, offering a javelin to heaven in a victory salute with his head impaled upon it, and feeling like she was bleeding to death while everyone watched and did nothing. She decided to ignore his comment and get on with the agenda.

When the meeting ended and people were exiting the conference room mumbling amongst themselves, Irena stopped Cal near the doorway to point out what he had just witnessed. She pleaded with him again to do something about Manny's behavior.

Averse to what he considered distasteful women's issues that women should put up with or resolve on their own, Cal locked eyes with Irena, shook his head in obvious exasperation, and walked away, leaving Irena with the unspoken message that she was a pest, she should get over it, and she should stop bothering him. Cal seemed to think that neither the firm nor he would ever be held accountable for a hostile work environment.

Feeling like she had become the offender in some bizarre and painful twist of logic, Irena considered her options. Resignation would remove her from the offending situation, but considering her home, her family, and her hopes for the future, she told herself she had to endure. Accepting the situation as her cross to bear, Irena put up, shut up and, for the most part, left the partners alone, with intensifying psychological consequences.

*   *   *

It has been said that we as individuals have no power to change who other people are, that people will only change when they realize what they might lose if they don't, and that change may be less painful than loss. We cannot force other people to change: only how we respond. And we should refuse to feel guilty or defensive. If people choose not to change, we must stop forcing the issue causing ourselves stress. We must recognize that it is best to take things less personally. And we must try to accept that some relationships—like Lunice and Manny—are simply recipes for disaster.

Chapter Twenty-Three

C al wanted nothing to do with Irena's interpersonal issues, but he acknowledged her escalating workload, and supported her need for assistance. Or so it initially appeared.

Cal insisted Irena search for what he called "an un-carved block"—a woman with little or no skill, at entry level wage—a woman Irena could train with his input, as he emphasized. He refused to comprehend that Irena needed a competent, trained marketing coordinator to offload work, and not an entry-level, un-carved block, who would add to her already overwhelming burden.

Irena wondered whether Cal's request was because he felt superior around women he considered less capable, because he felt superior being generous to someone needy, or simply because he was cheap. Irena knew that if she agreed to Cal's proposition, he would be underfoot like a puppy, interfering and trying to impress this new hire with his manipulating amiability.

Irena also knew that the core of Cal's input would be teaching this un-carved block that getting along—or being subservient to his wishes—was more important than anything else. She also knew that Cal's proposition would compromise the little time she had to accomplish the work at hand. And she knew that she would be held responsible when proposal production dropped off and revenue and profitability diminished.

Unwilling to take the risk, Irena chose not to pursue this attempt to hire a marketing coordinator, knowing Cal would do nothing as well. And so, Irena continued without help rather than face the scenario Cal proposed.

*   *   *

Despite the impact of Irena's workload on her mind and body, she felt her share of pride when increasing revenue allowed Cal to engage the Chicago consulting firm of Nora Peet & Associates to assist with strategic and long-range planning. Nora and her associates, in consultation with the partners, organized and facilitated a day-long event at the upscale Natural World Lodge twenty-some-odd miles from Chicago. Lupo opted out. Irena was not invited.

According to Cal, the event began with each partner articulating his expectations of the meeting. Each then had the opportunity to offer suggestions as to how best to succeed in the year and years ahead.

Collectively, they identified strengths, opportunities, and risks; they acknowledged that the status quo was not a long-term option; and they agreed to move forward as a team. The process took the better part of a workday, and by four in the afternoon participants were headed home.

Two weeks later, Nora met with the partners to deliver binders to participants reviewing and summarizing topics addressed during their strategic planning session and presenting conclusions. The binders also contained guidelines for monthly workshops throughout the year to keep partners on track toward achieving their individual and collective goals in anticipation of the following year's session.

Nora pointed out to the partners that marketing is a vital component of the management process and therefore Irena should be included in the workshops and future planning sessions. Nora had no way to know that the partners were prejudiced toward Irena, having long been entertained and influenced by slander. She also had no way to know there was little chance the partners would engage Irena in any legitimate decision-making process.

Few, if any, workshops were held that year, despite Nora's suggestion. Irena was ignored. However, under the guise of inclusivity, Irena was invited to participate in the second year's off-premises strategic planning session.

Lupo again opted out. Nora remained in the dark.

*   *   *

On the first day of the two-day retreat the following year, again at Natural World Lodge, having enjoyed the solitude of her drive, a good night's sleep, and a power breakfast, Irena joined the group in the rough-hewn-oak paneled conference room in the main building. A large picture window overlooked a secluded wooded area where birds fluttered among tree branches in dappled sunlight.

The group convened around an over-sized oak conference table holding papers, water bottles, and vases filled with flowers. Nora welcomed the partners, acknowledged Irena's participation, and led a toast congratulating them for coming together for a second year.

After chinking water bottles, Nora walked around the table handing out agendas. Irena happily noted that Item 4(a) addressed word processing production and dependability, as she had suggested.

Nora guided the group to recognize accomplishments since the previous year's session including identification of corporate risks, opportunities and strengths; acknowledgment of options to move forward; and reiteration that maintaining the status quo or stagnating was not a long-term option.

And so, working in farcical cooperation at this off-site location, the group developed a statement redefining the firm's vision, mission, and core values, and progressed to developing objectives— the strategic plan—for the upcoming year.

*   *   *

The second day of the session, the group reconvened in the conference room. After a brief review of the previous day, Nora introduced Agenda Item 4(a), word processing production and dependability. With no-one else seeking the floor, Nora acknowledged Irena's upraised hand.

Trying to avoid a confrontation with Mario, Lunice's supervisor, Irena did not mention her by name and spoke from a seated position. She suggested that the firm might alleviate general staff distress over word processing production and dependability if a back-up plan were instituted to accommodate those days when word processing is unavailable.

Mario never let Irena say another word. He leaped out of his chair like his pants were on fire, placed both hands on the table in front of him, leaned toward Irena, cut her off, and spewed that she "did not have the right to talk about Lunice when Lunice was not there to defend herself."

Vesuvius erupted in Irena's head and she jumped to her own feet, ready to throw herself across the table to pound Mario's head into the table. Her vocal cords frozen, Irena screamed internally.

REEEAALLLY!!! If I, as marketing manager, do not have the right to discuss word processing as a function of marketing at a strategic planning session because the word processor is not here to "defend herself", what the hell am I doing here wasting my time? And why does she have the right to defame me when I am not there to defend myself? GRRRRR!

Cal, sitting to Irena's left, grabbed her by the arm and pulled her back into her seat as if to say, "Let it go." She did, fuming, sweating, and feeling like a prostitute for not speaking her mind. And the discussion of agenda Item 4(a), word processing production and dependability, ended as abruptly as it began.

Once again, Irena was rendered powerless, feeling as though any foundation she had built was in ruins. Nora, of course, had no idea what was going on. When she heard Irena's explanation in private later, she was speechless.

For the rest of the session, Irena mentally opted out.

Chapter Twenty-Four

I rena was working on three proposals the week before Labor Day. One of them, including street crossings to be designed by Manny Handler, was due Tuesday morning after Labor Day. Manny had agreed to provide his technical input by Thursday afternoon.

Irena realized at four-twenty on Thursday, after dispatching the second proposal, that she had not received his input, despite her reminders and Cal's repeated warnings to provide technical contributions at least two working days in advance of a proposal due date.

Tracking him down, Irena found Manny sitting alone on the conference room floor at the conclusion of an optional staff meeting, with partners and staff, including Cal, milling about. She knelt on one knee in front of him and asked about the status of his contribution for the proposal. Manny literally shouted that he had nothing for her, and if she had "a problem with that," she should go "talk to (my) boss."

Startled by his vehemence, Irena wobbled on her knee and asked why he was being so hostile. Again, he shouted saying that she was the one being hostile. He then stood up suddenly, knocking Irena over in the process, and stormed out of the conference room.

After picking herself up and returning to her desk to calm down, Irena tracked down Cal to discuss what he had just witnessed in the conference room. She found him standing outside his office where, before she could say a word, Cal chirped that Manny had already approached him saying he planned to apologize to her for his outburst.

Sure he will, Irena thought. *And those proverbial pigs will fly overhead in formation.*

Cal seemed to believe Manny's story and, with hydrochloric acid blazing through her digestive tract, Irena wondered if Cal also thought she was dim-witted enough to believe Manny would ever apologize to her for anything.

Irena knew that hell could freeze and thaw several times before Manny would ever apologize. What she did get from him were sarcastic smirks and body language that said, "Ha! Gotcha again!" ripping another layer of Irena's sanity to shreds.

Manny delivered his input to Irena twenty-four hours later, after five on Friday before Labor Day, for the proposal due at ten o'clock Tuesday morning. She therefore had to work the holiday weekend on a proposal to generate work for him.

Why did she not leave at five o'clock on Friday and simply refuse to produce the proposal? Why did she not let Manny assume responsibility? Because Irena knew as well as she knew her name that, no matter the reality, she would have been held responsible for the lost opportunity.

* * *

A month or two later, Manny again was obliged to provide Irena with technical input for a proposal including his services for a complex project that had the potential to generate significant revenue for the firm. Wanting nothing to interfere with getting the proposal delivered on time, Cal told Irena he would serve as go-between to keep the two of them apart. Manny and Irena therefore had no direct interaction.

As the proposal evolved, Manny delighted in yet another opportunity to cause Irena grief. Perhaps she should have seen this one coming.

Cal approached her saying that Manny was complaining that she was being rude and demanding. "And you believe him?" Irena said. "How can I be rude and demanding when all of our interaction is through you?" Saying nothing in response, Cal turned and walked away, apparently believing he had done his duty by warning her.

After Gabby left the office to deliver that proposal on Tuesday, Irena stood decompressing alone in the reproduction area. Manny entered, glanced around to be sure they were alone, then gripped Irena's arm forcefully and shoved her violently against the counter.

Pinning her arms against her body so she could not move, he brutally pressed his hot and sweaty body against hers in full frontal contact. His chest pressed hard against hers flattening her breasts. His legs forced hers against the counter. His hips and hardened penis ground down on her pubis. With his damp, hot cheek pressed against hers, his mouth close to her ear, he hissed sarcastic words carried on hot, moist breath. "You did such a great job on that proposal."

Struggling to free herself, Irena fled from the reproduction area out of her mind with fear and rage, feeling like she had just been raped. Manny's demonstration of power and control and his violent message were clear—like he said in the library—that he could and would do anything he wanted, including hug, touch and even assault her, whenever and wherever he wanted, and he would get away with it because there was nothing she could do about it.

No doubt Manny stopped in a bathroom to complete his man-business while Irena cried in the ladies' restroom. When she felt ready, she washed her face and headed to Cal's office, hiccupping along the way with a wad of toilet paper in her hand to sop up any errant tears.

Cornering Cal in his office, Irena demanded that he call Griff and Cassius to join them immediately. Seeing her face, Cal dared not refuse. Once the others arrived, as Irena sniffed and wiped her red and runny nose, she described what happened in specific detail and pleaded with them to make Manny leave her alone.

Having no idea how far beyond sexual harassment Manny's behavior had progressed, Irena did not think in terms of assault or police intervention. She trusted these men to do the right thing.

"I want you to witness me telling that son-of-a-bitch that if he ever touches me again it will be clear and deliberate sexual harassment and I will file a formal complaint with the appropriate authorities." The men remained mute as stumps.

Cal, Griff, and Cassius were obligated to take action, but rather than act immediately, Cal told Irena it was "neither the time nor the place" to deal with issues about Manny, and that the three of them would take care of the problem "in their own way."

What the hell is that supposed to mean? she thought.

Irena had been crushed by conditions of her employment for so long that even when she tried to take care of herself, she was convinced she had little chance to succeed. And so, Irena did not contact the police or any other authority outside the firm, perhaps in support of Seligman's theory of learned helplessness.

*   *   *

Days went by, then weeks. Whenever Irena approached these men, each had an excuse as to why he was unprepared to address the issue at the time. Each put Irena off and ignored the situation, no doubt hoping that sooner or later she or the problem would go away. After all, it had been that way for years, and they had little reason to expect it would be different now.

Imploring Cal and Griff one afternoon in Cassius' absence, Irena pleaded. "All I want is a minute for one of you to witness my third and final warning to Manny."

Magnanimously, Cal agreed to be a witness, but alas he claimed he had no time for the next two days and then he would be gone for a five-day weekend. Griff said, "I'm too busy, but perhaps next week."

Irena felt like they were playing hot potato with her brain. By avoiding their obligation to protect her, the partners gave Manny implied authorization to continue without consequence to touch her, snipe at her, undermine her relationships and work efforts, and perhaps even assault her again: just as entertaining Lunice's slander gave her implied authorization to continue.

*   *   *

While Irena was pressuring the partners to take action, Manny was making it his mission to bash her, intensifying the number and severity of his sarcastic remarks in and out of meetings. Most engineers found his antics amusing, unconcerned about how his behavior affected Irena. After one more malicious comment at one more staff meeting, Irena passed a point of no return.

When the meeting ended and co-workers were drifting away from a conference table littered with dirty coffee cups, Irena cornered Cal, Griff, and Cassius. With years of mistreatment driving her vehemence, Irena raised her voice and said, "You just witnessed

Manny's blatant hostility and hardly for the first time. I am done waiting and I demand that you do something to stop his harassment, hostility, and retaliation—and I expect you to do it *now*."

Looking like they had been struck by lightning, each, unbelievably, tried to pass the buck again. Inching their way toward the doorway to escape, Cal said, "I'm too busy. Griff will have to take care of it." Griff said, "I'm too busy. Cassius will have to take care of it." And Cassius said, "I'm too busy. Someone else will have to take care of it."

Irena blocked the escape route and refused to let them leave until Cassius agreed to do something. However, with unbelievable audacity, he said, "I'm leaving for a few days and I'll deal with this when I get back."

Fuck! Fuck! Fuck! Fuck! Fuck! Fuck! Fuck! Fuck! Fuck!

Colors burst behind Irena's eyelids like psychedelic splatter art. She refused to be put off again and demanded that something be done *immediately*. She followed Cassius from the conference room to his office where, red-faced with his own anxiety, he phoned an attorney for advice. Sitting on the opposite side of his desk, breathing hard, fists clenched, fingernails digging crescents into her palms, Irena glared at Cassius as she listened to every word he said.

He later told her that the attorney told him that employers are obligated by law to investigate swiftly (within days) when they first become aware of an incident of sexual harassment, whether or not the employee asks for help.

His comment triggered another explosion behind Irena's eyelids. She had made the partners aware for years that Manny was pressuring her to go out with him and retaliating when she refused. She had made them aware of his touchy-feely habits whenever he came near her, out of sight of others, of course. And she had recently made them aware of his assault in the reproduction room.

Had Irena been less exhausted, had she known sooner that she had legitimate recourse beyond the company with regard to sexual harassment and other hostility, and had she not been so afraid of losing her job and being unable to support her family, she might have taken legal action. But by the time Irena had a clearer sense of her rights and the company's obligations, she believed the statute of limitations had expired.

*   *   *

The attorney's comments precipitated a rush of phone calls and meetings resulting in a ludicrously brief internal sexual harassment investigation. As part of that investigation and despite his distaste for such documentation, Cal advised Irena to compile a written statement addressed to him, Griff, and Cassius about Manny's behavior and their history together.

Asked to identify the harm Manny caused her, Irena described a constant state of anxiety, loss of sleep, perpetual anger, and perhaps danger; a demeaning work relationship; and diminishment of her image in the eyes of co-workers; all of which resulted in physical manifestations.

Cal interviewed Irena and Manny separately in the casual comfort of his office. Cal told Irena afterward that Manny admitted to everything.

He then asked Irena what she expected from the investigation. She requested, in writing, that Manny be chastised, that he be made to apologize publicly, to discontinue his sarcasm and hostility, to stop demanding clerical favors, to attend sexual harassment sensitivity training, and advised that if he ever touched her again there would be serious consequences.

Good thing Irena didn't hold her breath.

Manny never apologized publicly or privately, and Irena never witnessed him being chastised, warned about his demands for clerical support, nor warned to discontinue his sarcasm and hostility. And she never saw any evidence that he was warned to stop touching her, because all these behaviors continued.

In Cal's parental approach to management, he simply told Irena and Manny, like children, to "stay away from each other." Yet they were expected to remain working in adjoining cubicles and theoretically cooperating on proposals.

A month after the investigation, in a feeble attempt to appear responsive to Irena's request that Manny attend sexual harassment sensitivity training, and to protect the partners from legal action, the company conducted a brief and optional cover-your-ass sexual harassment workshop, theoretically for all employees, in the conference room during the lunch hour. That workshop produced no noticeable change in Manny's behavior nor the partners' attitudes. Each disregarded sexual harassment, employment obligations, and human rights, perhaps thinking like Manny that sexual harassment is a crock.

Chapter Twenty-Five

Weeks after the sexual harassment workshop, without discussing it with her in advance, Cal enrolled Irena in a two-day American Management Association class entitled, "How to Manage People Who Don't Report to You, But Who Are Responsible for Doing Work for You." Seriously.

Once she completed the class and submitted a written summary to Cal, he directed her to meet with Lunice to "use what you learned to improve your relationship with her."

Did Cal forget how unsuccessful she had been at convincing Lunice to become an executive assistant? Did he really think Irena could reverse Lunice's resentment, hostility, vindictiveness, and paranoia? Did he have selective amnesia, forgetting the many efforts they had already made to keep Lunice happy?

Or did Cal think Irena was masochistic, seeking out Lunice's nastiness because she enjoyed being humiliated and mistreated?

Cooperating with Cal, like the obedient child her mother taught her to be, Irena called Lunice to set up a meeting and was pleasantly surprised when Lunice agreed to meet later that day: both apparently afraid of the repercussions of telling Cal that they did not want to play this game anymore.

Trying to be conciliatory, hoping for her cooperation, Irena agreed to meet in Lunice's office. Her desk covered with piles of paper, after a brief hi-how-are-you, they sat on rolling task chairs facing each other across a small metal work table that may once have supported a typewriter.

Reiterating Cal's desire that they improve their working relationship, Irena reviewed the American Management Association class curriculum with Lunice. She told Lunice she believed the partners had failed them by refusing to mediate their differences. Agreeing, Lunice relaxed until Irena added that, under the circumstances, they could either help each other or hurt each other.

Lunice took that comment as a threat, leading to an animated discussion about respective workloads, their work relationship, personal needs and wants.

Irena told Lunice that she and marketing needed to be able to depend on her and that she had no other concerns. Pulling herself up in her chair, Lunice whined that she did not like anyone complaining about her dependability. And she added that she resented corporate changes when she is not consulted first.

Really, Irena thought. *The word processor—Lupo's "typist"—wants to be consulted about pending corporate policy and other changes?*

Most astonishing, Lunice said she wanted freedom to miss deadlines, to work without supervision or oversight, absolute job security, and freedom to do, come, and go as she pleased.

Having never detected an iota of humor in Lunice, Irena accepted her demands literally and nearly fell off her chair. In a lightbulb moment, Irena concluded that either Mario had given her those freedoms or that Lunice was delusional.

During their meeting, each woman took notes and agreed to work together to submit a co-authored, co-signed agreement for the partners demonstrating their commitment to a better working relationship. Not yet sharing electronic files or using e-mail, Irena drafted a memo and gave Lunice a paper copy to contribute her input as they had agreed. Irena was surprised by Lunice's apparent willingness to do her part.

Two weeks later, when Irena followed up with Lunice, Lunice said she lost the first copy and needed another. Irena provided another copy and approached Lunice two weeks after that when Lunice said, "Don't rush me." *Hmmmm.*

Irena concluded that Cal had not spoken with Mario about any of this, nor had she, considering his hostility. And she knew in that instant that Mario was now in the mix, and that she had a better chance of success swimming across Lake Michigan in February.

Irena approached Lunice one last time when Lunice said, "Mario told me I don't have to do anything for you." And, as she enjoyed doing, Lunice turned her back to Irena in dismissal.

Strutting around the office later, Lunice gave Irena cocky grins and gloated, perhaps believing Irena would fail without her. But Irena did not need Lunice, and the less she needed her, the angrier Lunice became.

During one of their casual chats in his office, drinking bitter brew from the kitchen that passed for coffee, Cal told Irena that Mario, who considered himself next in line to Lupo's throne, had been deeply offended when he, Cal, was elected president and not him, Mario, in much the same way Lunice had been deeply offended when Irena was hired and she, Lunice, was not promoted.

Irena wondered if Cal and Mario were consciously or subconsciously using Irena and Lunice as pawns in their own interpersonal conflict.

*   *   *

As Irena continued to suffer physically and emotionally from the long and demanding work hours, Lunice's vilification, and Manny's harassment, she again threatened the partners with legal action. But her exhausting workload, family obligations, ever-present fear of poverty, and mounting depression impacted her ability to follow through, and nothing changed except that she felt more and more like she was disintegrating.

To survive psychologically and professionally, Irena did her best to distance herself from Lunice and Manny, using whatever means she could to accomplish the work at hand without some kind of reprimand from Cal or Lupo. As profitability continued to increase, Cal came to recognize and appreciate Irena's accomplishments, patting himself on the back by citing the great team they had become.

Irena's salary, which had risen a mere five percent in six years, continued to be an issue. But since she usually felt like a wet dishrag run over by a truck, she had little time or energy to argue with Cal.

Until year seven.

Two years has been defined as the industry burnout rate for marketing manager and/or marketing coordinator.

*   *   *

Highly motivated, Irena approached Cal in his office—calmly at first—reminding him of her compensation history and that she had been more than patient. He surprised her by immediately agreeing to an increase. The kicker though, as he said in the past, the best he could do was five percent. Irena wanted to send him straight to hell to be tortured and burned at the stake for eternity and then some.

Whether Cal was at fault for making such an offer, or Lupo was at fault for controlling the purse strings, given her contributions to profitability, Irena refused to accept that Cal could not authorize a more substantial increase. Having simmered over work conditions and salary for years, she boiled over.

"Five percent is not enough. I deserve more," Irena said.

"I can get you ten percent," Cal said.

"Ten percent is not enough either," Irena said.

When Cal failed to offer more than ten percent, Irena rose from her chair and headed straight to Lupo's office, consequences be damned. Storming in, she walked up to his desk where he was head down working on some papers. Without waiting to be acknowledged, she blurted:

"I am tired of arguing with Cal over money and I am fed up with being economically abused. A five percent salary increase every three years is insulting. I will not accept it. I deserve more. And I want more now."

Looking up and directly into her eyes, pausing perhaps to appreciate her courage, Lupo took Irena's breath away by asking her, "Does thirty percent sound fair?"

Holy crap, Irena thought.

The astonishment on her face and her stunned nod gave Lupo the answer he was looking for. While her salary would still be below market rate, Irena was not about to argue and give Lupo any reason to reconsider. He processed the increase while she stood there and Irena walked out of his office delirious.

Lupo may have believed she deserved a thirty percent increase. He may have been buying her loyalty. Or he may just have wanted another opportunity to make Cal look bad. Whatever the reason, Irena did not care.

Chapter Twenty-Six

S oon after Irena's thirty percent salary increase, the firm began to succumb to the cancer that had been festering among partners and staff since the partnership of six was established.

Contentious infighting approached crisis proportions among partners who had had their fill of Lupo's self-serving domination. Discontent produced snappy tempers when even the slightest disagreement could not be resolved peaceably.

Co-workers walked around with backs bent and heads bowed so as not to make eye contact with one another, lest that contact spark a conflagration. Revolution seemed imminent as the company teetered on the brink of collapse.

Lupo rarely attended meetings over the years to protect his autonomy by denying staff access to and interaction with him. Aware of escalating hostilities, he jumped the gun, so to speak, and called a meeting of his partners, the engineers, and the surveyors.

As the men gathered around the conference room table commiserating about what reason Lupo might have to call a meeting, he walked in. Standing at the head of the table, with his chin jutting out in a defiant stance, with no prelude, Lupo announced that he was dissolving the partnership effective immediately, despite contractual agreements.

After a moment of stunned silence, pandemonium erupted.

Irena learned from administrative staff located within view and earshot of the conference room that Lupo told those clambering to be heard that if they did not like the way he ran things, they should "vote with (your) feet."

Jeff Longacre, engineering manager at the time, expressed a few choice thoughts, resigned on the spot, and stormed out. His dramatic resignation signaled the beginning of the end.

Two more key staff resigned the following week, followed by the associate principals, one by one over three months. And in the final act of individuals long dissatisfied with and exhausted by Lupo's disposition, miscommunication, and misrepresentation, three partners resigned in quick succession: Cal Chauvin, president; Griff Chimeric, survey, safety, sexual harassment, and technology; and Cassius Banker, chief financial officer and human resources. In all, twelve partners and senior staff resigned from an organization of thirty-one. None were replaced.

Partners Mario Centoni and Domenic Placido chose to remain behind in rank and file positions.

Irena felt the earth tremble and the walls came tumbling down.

Chapter Twenty-Seven

T errified of unemployment, Irena applied for an advertised marketing position at Carmichael Engineers, the thriving competitor Lupo envied, dreading his reaction should he find out. In her stressed-out state of mind, Irena was doing the rational thing, but she was functioning in a haze, hardly in control of her thinking or her actions.

Riding the plush-carpeted and mirrored elevator to the fifth floor of the fashionably designed company-owned office building for an interview, Irena felt irretrievably removed from the esteem she previously enjoyed in such a workplace of style and grace, and tethered to the hades she considered Yutz & Dunne.

The impeccably groomed receptionist notified the human resources manager that she had arrived, and his secretary arrived to deliver her to his office. Sitting across a small conference table from him, Irena struggled to concentrate on what the man was saying. A conversation she had had with Cal kept interrupting her train of thought.

Cal once told Irena that when he was most disillusioned with Yutz & Dunne, he interviewed for a management position with Carmichael. Having crossed professional paths with their key staff over the years, he thought he was a good fit. Cal said his interviewer, perhaps this same person interviewing Irena, told him that owners and managers at Carmichael, along with other local competitors, reviled Lupo and his associates. And Cal was not hired.

As Irena tried to concentrate on her own interview, Cal's comments repeated in her head like a broken record: "Carmichael reviles Lupo and his associates."

Having lived in a state of despair for years, Irena was less than optimistic for herself. She knew she did not make the best impression with her interviewer; and when she was not hired, she told herself that, as Lupo's marketing manager for so many years, they reviled her as one of Lupo's associates.

Her confidence at an all-time low before she applied for the job, the interview sapped the last of Irena's strength. Consumed by lethargy, she chose to remain tethered to a sinking ship, and watched as the last fragments of her confidence floated away.

*   *   *

The great exodus of key staff at Yutz & Dunne and Irena's latest attempt to survive professionally were followed by Lupo's ineffectual control as sole proprietor. Savoring the relative tranquility, Irena continued to be responsible for inside marketing such as it was, including the weekly go-no-go report, monthly trend reporting, answering inquiries, and submitting proposals for small projects, the only opportunities presenting themselves.

Having little interaction with Lupo, Irena clung to hope for the future, and chose to believe he was quietly depending on her. In addition to Seligman's learned helplessness, Irena may have been suffering from Stockholm syndrome, where hostages irrationally express empathy and develop positive feelings for their captors, mistaking a lack of abuse as an act of kindness.

*   *   *

Cal and Irena had created a business development plan that paired engineers with clients, each engineer responsible for sustaining relationships by making a few phone calls each week. The plan included optional training to increase interpersonal comfort levels. When Cal resigned, Irena attempted to administer the plan alone.

Hostile and uncooperative engineers refused to make outgoing marketing calls and refused to take incoming calls from clients, many unhappy with the quality of design on their projects and/or unhappy about the lack of response to their concerns.

With no support for Irena from Lupo, no supervisor to motivate engineers to respond to clients, and no consequences for those engineers who failed to follow through, Irena did what she could to address client issues and watched her credibility erode.

She produced her reports to keep Lupo informed, but he too did nothing to follow through. Predictably, the firm received fewer requests for proposals with diminishing contract values. Backlog and profitability plummeted.

*   *   *

Eighteen months after the exodus—besieged by financial obligations to former partners; no management staff; young, indifferent, and mostly unlicensed engineers; and distressed because he could no longer pursue his entrepreneurial activities—Lupo began to emerge from his stupor.

Bypassing Irena, he began approaching engineers directly, demanding that they "make me some money." Those engineers had no idea how to do so and would not respond to Irena without support from him.

Believing Yutz & Dunne could no longer function under the circumstances, without so much as a conversation with Irena, Lupo embarked on a quest to hire new managers to restore the company and fund his entrepreneurial spending habits.

Naively optimistic, Irena believed a new management team would recognize and take advantage of her value, and together they would revive and restore the credibility and profitability of Yutz & Dunne.

Good thing she didn't hold her breath—again.

Chapter Twenty-Eight

At the same time Lupo embarked on his quest for new managers, Cal Chauvin, who resigned eighteen months earlier, contacted Jacques Strappe's architectural and engineering search firm seeking a new executive position in engineering. Cal told Jacques that Yutz & Dunne had been functioning without a president since he resigned.

Regardless of Jacques' search firm responsibilities and his engineering limitations, this personable, assertive, and self-serving man took advantage of the vacancy and promoted himself to fill the position.

Lupo had been impressed by Duetta Brummagem, his first "high-powered" vice president and marketing director. He became more impressed by Jacques' masculine charm, enthusiasm, and claims of marketing success. And so Lupo hired Jacques as his newest high-powered, high-priced, vice president and marketing director, Irena's latest supervisor, and the first principal of his new regime.

Lupo directed Irena to fully cooperate with Jacques, to continue responding to requests for proposals and statements of qualification, to continue producing her weekly and monthly analytical reports, and to continue regularly updating her database by interviewing engineers and culling payroll records.

*   *   *

A late-afternoon celebration was held in the conference room to formally introduce Jacques to staff. Champagne bottles, plastic champagne flutes, soft drinks, beer, cookies and pastries adorned a festive tablecloth hiding the ugly laminate-topped table.

Wearing neatly pressed gray chino pants, a plaid shirt and coordinating tie, his hair slicked back, his face a rosy pink with a broad smile, Jacques sat at the head of the table, clearly in his element. As Lupo introduced him as the new vice president and director of marketing "who will change the face of Yutz & Dunne," Jacques stood to tenuous applause.

An experienced presenter, Jacques told those assembled that he learned from his preacher father that business is most successful when it takes a divine approach. He claimed that his historic success had been, and theirs would be too, the result of charitable works, kindness, and generosity in the workplace. He promised good times and fun, including recognition and reward.

Slick, Irena thought.

Jacques went on to talk in non-specific terms about his successful "firm-building" experience, about his background in engineering with a focus on marketing, and about his hopes for the success of Yutz & Dunne—with his help, of course.

When he finished speaking, staff received him with open arms, some literally, like a ray of sunshine, and by many as though he were a conquering hero. Virtually everyone cheered and applauded as if the company team had just scored a winning touchdown.

Within weeks of convincing staff that he was such a good man who would do wonders for the firm, the veil of illusion began to fray as Jacques used shame to manipulate staff, much the way a preacher might do with his congregation or his children.

Irena felt a new and insidious wave of apprehension.

*   *   *

Granted carte blanche with the budget, Jacques spent money freely on marketing and quasi-marketing, widely disproportionate to his success rate. He encouraged Irena to follow his lead: to spend company money on fun in the alleged pursuit of business with little concern for limits.

Playing employers and spending significant amounts of their money in the pursuit of new relationships, hoping for new business, was Jacques' modus operandi. If and when challenged to justify expenses, Jacques absolved himself by claiming he was simply trying to achieve a goal, and that it was no sin to have fun while doing so.

Rumor had it that a previous employer went bankrupt less than a year after hiring Jacques for his "firm-building" expertise.

*   *   *

Adding predation to the picture of a preacher's son, Jacques cemented his image as one more smarmy addition to staff. During one of his face-to-face meetings with Irena in the intimate little library, he cozied up, looked her in the eye, and smiled that smile most women recognize in an instant.

Speaking in a velvety voice most women also recognize, he told her that he really admired her level of energy and commitment and knew she was a "passionate" woman, placing an oily emphasis on the word in an obvious double entendre. Irena believed that, with any encouragement, Jacques might have taken her hand and stroked it or touched her cheek.

Jacques was right, of course. Irena was passionate. Passionate about making a difference; passionate about her desire to succeed in the face of opposition; and passionate to be acknowledged, respected, and appropriately compensated.

*   *   *

During a marketing meeting in Lupo's office, Lupo requested Jacques' company on a series of marketing calls that would take five days and four nights. Turning to Irena, Jacques asked her to make local hotel arrangements so he would not have to make the long trip home each night, adding "...unless I can sleep at your house (chuckle, chuckle)." Irena ignored the comment. Lupo grinned.

Jacques did not yet have a company credit card and asked Irena to put the charges on hers, assuming she had one, which was not the case. Having long ago adopted an agreeable and cooperative persona, Irena's only goal was getting from day to day with the least amount of friction. And so, without giving his request much thought, she agreed and charged $632 on her personal credit card and told Jacques what she did.

Returning from that marketing foray, Jacques expensed the hotel charges among others and, according to the accounting manager, was promptly reimbursed. Irena expected to be promptly reimbursed as well, but Jacques kept her waiting for months. After several requests, and only after appealing to a higher authority, did Jacques reimburse Irena.

*   *   *

Once formally on the payroll, Jacques spent an occasional day at the main office and the rest of his time at various off-site locations, supposedly developing new business. He met with Irena for an hour or so every morning, most often by phone, to discuss ideas and assign tasks—so many that he forgot what they discussed one day and added more the next that often conflicted with the previous.

When Jacques realized that he could not keep his dos and don'ts straight, he had Irena spend another hour or so each day producing a spreadsheet documenting what he had asked her to do, not to do, and the progress of each assignment.

Jacques' tendency to hyperactivity and mood swings made the morning ritual a process that wasted precious time Irena might have otherwise used to accomplish something more worthwhile. As she continued the work Lupo expected, along with Jacques' frenzied assignments, the optimism she felt when Jacques was hired began to evaporate.

One overwhelming day, hurtling ever closer to the precipice of hysteria, Irena wrote in her journal:

> *The end of the day,*
> *nine hours at a computer,*
> *eye strain, eye aches, headache,*
> *profound weariness,*
> *anxious to put my head on a pillow and close my eyes,*
> *heavy limbs, stiff neck, shoulder cramps, backache,*
> *overwhelming desire to sleep,*
> *house guest, teenage children, dog, cats,*
> *demands from every direction,*
> *dirty dishes, no energy, must call it a day,*
> *but must still do some professional reading before it's over.*
> *Can I possibly stay awake?*

*   *   *

Exhausted by years tolerating Lunice's hostility and Manny's harassment, Irena approached Jacques during one of their face-to-face morning meetings, hoping for his help.

"I'm angry that the partners have consistently refused to intervene, expecting me to resolve problems with Manny and Lunice on my own. I can't change who they are and I'm exhausted. I have refused medical advice to take time off because I'm afraid I'll be fired. I'm a single parent with three children to support. I love my work, and I know I need to stay on the job to keep my job. I have toughed matters out long enough and deserve civility and protection.

"I have heard rumors that you and Lupo are considering reducing Lunice's hours. I'm sure she'll add that to her list of my alleged crimes against her. And I'm afraid she'll retaliate somehow. What can you do to protect me?"

Jacques looked at Irena, obviously contemplating how to respond. When he finally spoke, he said that Lupo had asked him to mediate the situation with Lunice, and he planned to give the situation some thought. He then moved on with his own agenda.

*   *   *

Meanwhile, the saga continued. In addition to Lunice's headaches that often kept her out of the office, she allegedly developed carpal tunnel syndrome, complaining on a regular basis to anyone who might offer her sympathy.

During a scheduling meeting, Lunice told staff that her doctor said she could only spend fifteen minutes of every hour working at a computer unless she had surgery, which she refused. With Mario and Lupo's apparent blessing, she remained on the payroll full-time, working for fifteen minutes then spending forty-five minutes hanging out, occasionally helping the receptionist open mail.

Frustrated engineers, with urgent assignments they could not produce on their own, had to factor in Lunice completing their assignments at the rate of fifteen minutes per hour, unless she hired temporary help, which she rarely did. When an engineer needed an occasional letter or memorandum produced quickly and Lunice was unavailable, he approached Lupo's secretary or Irena.

And Lunice complained that Irena was stealing her job.

*   *   *

Lupo, Jacques, Irena, and Darrell Russell (the young design engineer managing the paltry engineering department of the new regime) met in the conference room to discuss client maintenance.

Before Jacques joined the firm, Darrell and his subordinates had rejected Irena's encouragement to make weekly phone calls as part of the business development plan. When Jacques presented the concept of client maintenance in general and phone calls in particular as his own, Darrell and Lupo complimented his "forward thinking," like it was a new idea. To avoid confrontation and to protect herself from hostility, Irena did her best not to react to the sexism and chauvinistic dismissal of her and her ideas.

Once everyone had an opportunity to comment and plan for implementation, Jacques clasped his hands behind his head, tilted back in his chair, and said with enthusiasm, "OK, then. Let's get out there and sniff up some skirts."

As the words left his lips, he made eye contact with Irena, grinned and said, "Don't sue me for that."

*   *   *

Jacques worked hard to establish warm and fuzzy relationships. Once he had an ear, he dumped to elicit sympathy and compassion. Staff stopped asking Jacques "How are you?" the same way they stopped asking Lunice the same question.

With Irena often a captive audience, Jacques would talk about his then-current wife, his unhappy marriages, and his difficult teenage step-children from his first marriage. In an attempt to absolve himself of sexual misbehavior like he did fiscal misbehavior, Jacques justified lovers and female friends while married. He maintained that "different women serve different roles in men's lives," and he discounted the concept of emotional cheating, stating that only a physical relationship involving the heart is cheating.

Jacques seemed to believe that men should be free to entertain women, so long as they can argue to their partners that "it doesn't mean anything."

*　　　*　　　*

As part of Jacques' supervisory role, Lupo assigned him the task of evaluating competitive salaries for Irena, who received a five percent increase after three years and a thirty percent increase after seven. It had now been ten years.

Irena nearly wept with joy when Jacques told her that she would receive a fifty-percent increase, validating her previous exploitation and bringing her salary within spitting range of her peers. Given that Lupo agreed to the increase, Irena concluded that Cal had been the individual responsible for suppressing her salary, and she cursed him as she celebrated.

When Irena expressed her gratitude, Jacques responded with a smile and said, "If you're happy with this, just wait until I make you marketing director." She perceived a leer, heard a sexual intonation, and sensed an allusion to a liaison, hearing, "If you play my game (have sex with me?), I'll promote you and give you another fat raise." And, "You'll get more from me if you cooperate (wink, wink)," an implicit quid pro quo, or favor for a favor—a legally recognized type of sexual harassment.

Irena felt like she had just been bought.

*　　　*　　　*

When Jacques was in town, he often invited Irena and Fiona, Lupo's latest secretary, to attend "marketing meetings" after hours and over wine at the local bar and grill. Jacques told Irena that he invited Fiona because he wanted Fiona to help with marketing assignments. Irena began to think that she and Fiona were invited less to discuss marketing and more to entertain Jacques because he did not want to drive home during rush hour.

The three usually sat at a cozy table near the bar against a floor-to-ceiling stone wall surrounding a fireplace. After agreeing upon appetizers, Jacques would try to impress Irena and Fiona with his knowledge of wines, and then order something unique. They would talk about marketing for twenty minutes or so until each had consumed a glass of wine or two, at which time their marketing meetings degenerated into social chitchat.

Jacques, Irena, and Fiona consumed a lot of wine over time, not altogether unpleasant, with Jacques no doubt reimbursed by Yutz & Dunne.

It soon seemed to Irena that Jacques was using Fiona as a lure to make her feel comfortable in that after-hours environment. Likely intrigued and aroused by on-going speculation about Irena's sex life—*oh crap, not again*, she thought—Jacques seemed to think like Manny, that he might get lucky. Irena had hoped for a mutually beneficial professional relationship with Jacques: recognizing his inclination compounded her depression.

Irena believed that keeping Jacques happy was her last chance for professional survival at Yutz & Dunne, so she felt obliged to play his flirtatious game.

Calculating and managing her risk, Irena acted as though it was the three of them or none at those after-hours meetings, and she invited Fiona even when Jacques did not. The third time she did, Jacques pulled her aside, literally by the arm, out of Fiona's sight at the restaurant, to tell her that Fiona was only invited when *he* invited her.

And Irena continued to attend those "meetings" alone with Jacques knowing she was damned if she did and damned if she did not.

*   *   *

Jacques became increasingly assertive and sent Irena a greeting card about a man and a woman who were neighbors and their gardening efforts. The man's tomatoes ripened with embarrassment when he exposed himself. When the woman exposed herself, her tomatoes did not ripen, but the cucumbers grew huge. Jacques asked Irena if she would show him her garden.

Conditioned by Cal and perhaps society-at-large to believe that the only way she (a woman) could survive in business was to be nice and get along, Irena feigned amusement as she choked on the escalating sexuality of their ersatz relationship.

Afraid to lose her job, her income, and her ability to care for her family, Irena was convinced she had no choice but to tread lightly around the issue of a sexual relationship with Jacques. Seeing no satisfactory alternative, Irena delicately and noncommittally allowed him to believe they might eventually have sex. So long as he believed he had a chance, Jacques was Irena's champion. Otherwise, Irena knew she was toast.

*   *   *

When former partners Mario Centoni and Domenic Placido chose to stay behind after the exodus and fade into corporate obscurity, Lupo and Jacques promoted subjective and easily manipulated Darrell Russell—one of the sixteen hired during the earlier growth spurt—to vice president of engineering.

In his early thirties, with a few years of experience, Darrell remained the only other licensed engineer on staff besides Lupo, Mario and Domenic: and Darrell became the second principal of Lupo's new regime—despite poor interpersonal skills, limited leadership abilities, and an aversion to all things marketing.

While engineers obtain degrees and licenses based primarily on technical ability, many like Darrell are ill prepared for the real world of corporate engineering. According to the Carnegie Institute of Technology, even in engineering, only fifteen percent of financial success stems from technical skills. Eighty-five percent stems from what the Institute identifies as human engineering or people skills.

*   *   *

Darrell was a close personal friend of touchy feely Manny Handler, which did not bode well for Irena. With Manny egging him on, Darrell focused on Irena as the manifestation of his anxiety over the need to interact with clients. And he seemed to think if Irena were gone he might avoid any marketing responsibilities.

Having tolerated Manny's abuse for years, Irena now had both men snapping at her and making rude comments throughout the day, their combined hostility like an anvil around her neck. Irena appealed to Jacques for help, but Jacques used her misery as fodder for gossip in his bid for popularity, sharing her grief with others who then approached Irena for more of the juicy details.

*   *   *

Several months after promoting Darrell to vice president of engineering and second principal of his new regime, Lupo met Damien Hartless at a meeting of the American Society of Civil Engineers. Damien was a high-ranking military retiree who served as a senior officer at Carmichael, the engineering firm Lupo envied.

One day over lunch, Marc Fine, a long-time friend of Irena's who left Yutz & Dunne years earlier, told her that he, too, attended that meeting, and he shared his observations.

Marc said that when Lupo learned Damien was looking for a new job, he, Lupo, who virtually salivated over military types, followed Damien around the room during cocktail hour like a hound on a hunt. Marc said he was close by when Lupo cornered Damien and, in his typically impulsive manner, told him he was looking to hire a new president for his firm and offered him the opportunity, confident that Damien was the man to resurrect Yutz & Dunne.

And Damien became the third and final principal of Lupo's new regime.

*   *   *

Lupo relinquished his throne and crowned Damien the new king of Yutz & Dunne at a staff meeting, where he boasted about hiring this military bigwig and about the respect, admiration, and economic reward he was confident would follow.

Lupo told staff that whatever Damien wanted, Damien was to get.

Nobody knew how long Damien had been with Carmichael, or why he would leave such a prestigious organization to work for Yutz & Dunne. One might surmise that no-one investigated, because they're engineers and they don't do that.

Shorter than average and stereotypically military, thick and square with fifteen to twenty odd pounds in his barrel chest and belly and a compensating sway back, Damien looked neat and well-scrubbed, with crew cut slate gray hair. He walked with purpose wasting no time or words on anyone he deemed unworthy, which included most staff.

Lupo referred to Damien as "the Colonel" for weeks, bathing in the reflected glory of his military credentials, until Damien asked him to stop.

Lupo had remained on the fringe as marketing evolved over the previous decade and knew Irena's work products but had little idea what it took to produce them. He only knew that for years he had the freedom to drain profit to pursue his entrepreneurial pursuits, until his partners mutinied.

Charged with improving the firm's profit margin, Damien was ceded indisputable control over every aspect of the business including marketing, challenged by the impact of old partnership agreements and the drain of Lupo's entrepreneurial pursuits.

He had little idea how much money Lupo may have historically siphoned off for personal pursuits, or how much money former partners may have siphoned off in personal charges to corporate credit cards to even the score.

The joyful optimism promised by Jacques' hire evaporated in light of Damien's rigid military countenance. And by reinstating Lupo's web of secrecy, Damien obliterated the promise of good times to come, returning the firm to an atmosphere of doom and gloom.

Lupo had unbounded and somewhat schizophrenic faith in both Damien and Jacques as individuals, overtly supporting Damien's efforts to control the budget while covertly supporting Jacques' spending habits with their mutual pie-in-the-sky aspirations. Jacques and Damien therefore became financial adversaries, adding new tension to the atmosphere.

*   *   *

Damien first attempted to balance the budget and increase profitability by reducing payroll costs—slashing, burning, and clearing the field of those he considered non-essential staff—primarily women.

The accounting manager, her assistants, and the receptionist were safe. Lunice, the word processor, was on her way to the chopping block. Gone would be Lupo's executive secretary, Fiona. And Damien set his sights on Irena.

Before the key staff exodus, Yutz & Dunne enjoyed a slight competitive edge in the industry based on diversity and utilization of women in technical and management positions. Before Damien, a total employment count of thirty included eleven women, or thirty-seven percent. Irena was identified as management, but remained economically repressed.

After Damien cleaned house, the firm lost that competitive edge because no technical women remained on staff. An employment count of thirty-four included five administrative women, less than fifteen percent. Irena earned more money, but was excluded from intellectual participation.

Lupo had been urging Irena to call on certain clients to capitalize on relationships she had built over the years, hoping she might generate some revenue. When Irena sought Damien's authorization, he responded with a brief note telling her that "client contact is best left to an engineer."

Damien adhered to old school thinking that engineers were men, and an engineering firm's marketing manager or anyone who called on clients or potential clients had to be an engineer and thus a man to be successful. He even dismissed the benefit of peer-to-peer marketing, whereby Irena might call on other marketing representatives for team building awareness, just as they called on her.

Worse, Damien seemed to believe that engineering firms had no need for women outside administration, and that male engineers alone could accomplish any task necessary to manage and market a successful engineering company.

He was playing with fire.

*   *   *

Administrative, engineering and survey staff, for the most part, considered Damien a blustery, non-communicative, non-responsive military officer ill-equipped for corporate life, serving out time at Yutz & Dunne until he could retire and collect social security benefits in addition to his military pension.

Engineers and surveyors labeled him a reluctant communicator who failed to manage by holding himself above day-to-day concerns. Damien wanted to run a tight military operation in a hands-on/total-control, but hands-off/don't-get-them-dirty approach. After all, military subordinates are theoretically programmed not to question authority and that was the way he wanted it.

Damien had little tolerance for subordinates and no tolerance for women. He was an icy non-communicator with Irena, not only because she was a woman, but also because she was a non-billable employee and the common denominator of controversy.

Biased like the former partners, he discounted and ignored Irena's appeals for help with Lunice and Manny's hostility, defamation, and sexual harassment, perpetuating a hostile work environment.

*　　　*　　　*

The new principals dismissed Irena from intellectual participation and basically ignored her. Damien and Darrell scorned the need to pursue new and repeat business. They scorned the need to maintain relationships with existing clients. They tolerated subordinate engineers who refused to make courtesy calls. And they rejected the concept that more contracts come from satisfied clients than from new clients: satisfied clients being those who not only get value for their money but also believe they are appreciated and cared for. Darrell accused Irena of being "sappy."

Meanwhile, Damien expected Irena to satisfy Jacques' exorbitant task-based expectations and, at least for the time being, and despite his disdain for the process, he expected her to continue with information acquisition and management, updating marketing materials, and compiling her regular statistical and analytical reports.

He also expected Irena to respond to requests for proposals and statements of qualifications as they arose, assigning engineers she thought best qualified, copying but not otherwise involving him, Jacques, or Darrell, while avoiding personal contact with clients.

In addition to denying Irena participation in marketing discussions and banning her from meetings, the new principals were unresponsive to her written requests for information. Making matters worse, not one would commit as principal in charge or project manager for those projects she was expected to pursue

On occasion, when Damien decided Irena should pursue a more significant project, he rarely informed her more than two days in advance, allowing her no time to develop a worthy proposal. Those slapdash efforts resulted in lost opportunities, and Irena became the scapegoat for diminishing backlog.

* * *

As that first year of the new regime slogged on, Irena's interaction with and respect from Damien, Darrell, and even Jacques—who had begun to seriously pursue Irena sexually—slipped further away as they discounted, ignored or disparaged her contributions to marketing and contract success.

For ten years, Irena successfully served as marketing manager and marketing coordinator for twenty-four to thirty-six design engineers when industry standard was one for ten. Jacques added hyperactivity to Irena's excessive workload, but at least he agreed she needed help.

The marketing budget they co-developed before Damien was hired allocated funds for a marketing coordinator. When Irena identified a candidate, Damien disallowed the hire—Irena's second denial of assistance.

Determined to persevere and survive as a woman among men who did not want her there, Irena succumbed to escalating dissociation—a coping or defense mechanism to help tolerate, minimize, or master psychological conflict and stress.

* * *

On his quest to eliminate women, perhaps Damien's most ruinous decision for Irena and for the firm, was formally severing her ten-year relationship with Lupo. Rather than discuss this decision, Damien wrote Irena a memo advising her that she was no longer to participate in any discussions with Lupo about marketing, business development, or any other topic.

For years, Lupo had at least a passing interest in Irena's monthly business analyses and trend reports. He was most interested in the weekly go-no-go report that analyzed and evaluated requests for proposals and other immediate opportunities for which the firm had credible staff and experience, his interest of course piqued by the potential revenue.

Before Damien was hired, Irena and the partners met weekly to discuss opportunities in the go-no-go report and decide which to pursue, evaluating factors that would contribute to winning a contract or not. After Damien was hired, he wanted Irena to continue with her reports but to discontinue sending them to Lupo. He wanted her to send them only to him, Jacques, and Darrell.

Doing as instructed, Irena received no acknowledgement or feedback and was eliminated from relevant discussions. She never knew whether Lupo was made aware of winnable opportunities, or if Damien kept him in the dark to protect himself when he did nothing to pursue those opportunities.

Although Irena often attempted to engage Damien, Jacques, or Darrell in conversation about worthwhile opportunities, after three unsuccessful attempts, in order to protect herself from repercussion, she relegated associated paperwork to a large black box under her desk she labeled "The Black Hole," a mounting reservoir of missed opportunities.

*   *   *

One week, Damien convinced Lupo to address a staff meeting to badger engineers to work harder to bring in more money. That same week, two noteworthy and lucrative projects presented themselves. Irena highlighted those projects in her weekly go-no-go report, but heard nothing about pursuing them.

Knowing the firm had the experience and staff to win the work, knowing she needed time to write and produce winning proposals, and knowing time was short, Irena approached Damien.

Standing at his desk waiting for him to look up and acknowledge her presence, when he finally did, Irena brought up pursuing the projects. She expressed confidence that the firm could win both based on qualifications and experience, and she urged him to allow her to pursue them.

One might have thought the man was mute. Drilling Irena with hate-filled eyes, he sat there stone-faced and silent. Irena broke the silence, perhaps failing to avoid the sarcasm surging through her brain.

"I really think we need to talk to each other to be successful," she said.

Damien's face and neck turned crimson and he responded with another long silent glare that shouted, "I do not have to talk to you." He then turned his back in dismissal, like Lunice, or more like a four-year-old stomping his foot and running to his room.

Yutz & Dunne did not pursue those projects and Irena came to understand that she should keep her opinions to herself, because Damien enjoyed shooting himself in the foot.

*   *   *

Lupo told staff that whatever Damien wanted, Damien was to get. Likewise, whatever Damien said not to do was not to be done. And he had forbidden Irena from interacting with Lupo, which appeared to be a case of Damien telling Lupo to "just trust me." Irena contemplated who might have been the puppet and who the puppeteer.

Before he hired Damien, Lupo never seemed to trust any business associate, and he maintained a web of secrecy until his partners mutinied. Irena questioned why he would turn over his business, wholly or in part, to anyone.

Lupo may have had high hopes for help from this retired military bigwig, but he may just as easily have been the puppeteer in this drama to reinvent his company—pulling Damien's strings, compelling him to maintain a web of secrecy so he, Lupo, could remain out of the limelight, keep his hands clean, and dictate events, which may have accounted for Damien's nasty disposition. Whatever the reality, Damien consistently rejected Irena's marketing contributions and denied her intellectual participation.

And so, performing like one more puppet in the show, Irena operated by rote and continued to do in isolation much of what she had done for years, to the extent she was allowed or able in her state of mind. Still on the job and receiving a paycheck, Irena told herself in wavering delusion that she must be doing something right.

*   *   *

Damien hired Arden Champion, an accountant, as the company's chief finance officer to replace Cassius Banker, who resigned with the others. Corporate policy at Yutz & Dunne continued to assign human resources to a finance officer in the absence of anyone with appropriate qualifications.

Tall, thin, in his mid-forties, with gelled and spiked blond hair, Arden wore lipstick-red plastic-rimmed eyeglasses and, except for Damien and Debbie Lewis, an accounting clerk and agreeable young mother of four, Arden was disliked by most employees because of his abrupt and combative demeanor.

Rumored to have been Damien's long-time friend, co-worker, and devotee at Carmichael and elsewhere, Arden was conservative and uncommonly loyal, following Damien's orders like the good little soldier Damien expected.

Fiscal conservatism and a goal toward profitability are admirable qualities for any corporate officer. However, while Damien and Arden were counting pennies, Jacques continued to spend lavishly on client contact, marketing, and pseudo-marketing meetings.

*   *   *

Drama continued to swirl around Lunice. Adding to her hostile insecurity, headaches, and unaddressed carpel tunnel syndrome, she allegedly fell off a chair while sitting at the reception desk during one of her forty-five-minute breaks.

She went out on state disability and filed for workers compensation. Deposed in the process, Lunice alleged that Irena, who never served as her supervisor, discriminated against her by not giving her enough work to do.

A copy of Lunice's deposition showed up in Irena's in-box one morning with a note from Damien telling her that she was required to submit to a responding deposition to be taken in the Yutz & Dunne conference room two days later. Minutes before the deposition, Lupo's attorney coached her to give only yes or no responses to questions asked.

Damien, Arden, Lunice's attorney, and Lupo's attorney were present to witness Irena's deposition that proceeded smoothly until the deposing attorney asked Irena, "Is it true you were having a sexual relationship with Cal Chauvin, president at the time?"

Literally on the edges of their seats, Damien and Arden were waiting for the "ah-ha" moment, eager to hear Irena confess under oath to having sex with Cal.

"What?" Irena sputtered. "Where did that come from? I read Lunice's deposition word for word and saw no such reference."

The attorney replied brusquely, "It was in there. Just answer the question."

When Irena denied the allegation, the scornful looks on Damien and Arden's faces told her they thought she was lying.

Given the long-standing speculation about Irena's sexual behavior, she concluded that Lunice, to fortify her claim of victimization, had asserted to someone along the way that she, Irena, was allowed to discriminate against her because she was having sex with Cal.

When Irena re-read Lunice's deposition very, very carefully that evening, there was no such reference. The question about her sexual behavior was obviously asked—legally or illegally—simply to satisfy Damien and Arden's prurient interest.

Before disbanding, hoping to illustrate that she was not the enemy Lunice portrayed her to be, Irena offered Lunice's answering machine tape, long buried and forgotten in her car's glove compartment.

Irena explained that, years ago, Lunice confided in her that she secretly recorded a conversation between her husband and an alleged girlfriend and entrusted the tape to her as her friend, both forgetting about it until now.

One of the attorneys accepted the tape, asked a few innocuous questions, the gathering disbanded, and everyone left the conference room.

Three weeks after Irena's deposition, Yutz & Dunne terminated Lunice, and contact between the two women ceased. But Irena has no doubt Lunice will forever hold her responsible for her termination.

Someone once said, "The greatest pariah a gossip, the deadliest weapon the tongue, the most worthless emotion self-pity."

*   *   *

Floating about in the miasma of Irena's tenth year with Yutz & Dunne were Damien, a militant who wanted to control the war but stay out of the trenches; Jacques, a self-serving financial and sexual wastrel; Darrell, a marketing-phobe; and Arden, Damien's loyal subject. Lupo had become virtually invisible.

Damien and Arden continued to count pennies. Darrell did little engineering or marketing. And Jacques charged exorbitant expenses while Lupo held open the money bags anticipating an abundant return on his investment, from which to extract profit for his entrepreneurial pursuits.

These men refused to interact with Irena and made untimely, unsuccessful, and virtually self-destructive marketing decisions.

Had Damien terminated her after her deposition, Irena would not have been surprised. But, with her marketing self in a virtual coma, she knew that, as the last individual of either gender in the firm with clerical capabilities, these men needed her as their automaton to attend to incoming marketing inquiries, alerts to upcoming projects, requests for statements of qualification, and requests for proposals: and as their scapegoat.

*   *   *

By disregarding years of increasing revenue and profit year over year before the mutiny, by disregarding marketing policies and procedures developed along industry guidelines, by disregarding the need to nurture client relationships, and by encouraging design engineers to reject her marketing contributions, Irena imagined Damien and Darrell saying, "We don't need no stinkin' marketing support. We're engineers. We can do anything."

Damien did not realize he was positioning the company to be left in the dust, stuck as he was in the good ole' boys' marketing ideology of the 1970s and 1980s, when virtually all that was necessary to win a contract was perhaps taking a fellow engineer in a position of power to play golf or to lunch. Sadly, no-one but Lupo cared enough any longer to make even that much of an effort.

*   *   *

Lupo looked to Damien as his economic savior, and Damien aimed to live up to that expectation. Unwilling or unable to reconcile Lupo's melodramatic behavior with the exodus and financial state of the company, Damien instead focused on marketing as the primary drain on revenue.

He discounted Irena's contributions to eight years of success prior to the exodus. He ignored her present-day monthly analyses, refusing to consider that downward trends mirrored the attitudes and behaviors of engineers.

Rather than accept Irena and marketing as a small price to pay for the greater financial gain to be achieved, he gagged her, tied her hands, and set in motion a thinly disguised plan to eliminate her. Sentenced to professional death, Irena had become little more than a mute shadow in the dark.

Years of success at Yutz & Dunne had been achieved by overcoming marketing chaos with organization and pre-planning. Damien reverted to chaos with no apparent appreciation for what was being sacrificed, and he set the scene for corporate failure, apparently unaware of the adage that those who cannot (or choose not to?) remember the past are condemned to repeat it.

*   *   *

Like Lupo, Damien pressured engineers to "market" and "make money." And like Lupo, Damien thought inexperienced young male engineers could intuitively divine what to do, how, and when, and do it successfully without guidance, supervision, or evaluation, while managed by a leader like Darrell with interpersonal phobias.

Damien tolerated or perhaps encouraged Darrell and those engineers to disregard Irena's content and design for proposals and statements of qualification. He scorned the concept of business development and tolerated engineers who not only recoiled from maintaining professional relationships but also failed to follow up on commitments made to clients during negotiation and execution of projects.

Those clients, feeling neglected at least and offended at worst, began dropping Yutz & Dunne like a hot rock.

Even with his "marketing" demands, Damien required no quantification of engineers' marketing efforts. Instead, perhaps to increase revenue, he pressured them to charge one hundred percent of their time to active projects, thus providing them with the perfect opportunity to avoid marketing and to misrepresent the truth.

*   *   *

Darrell Russell chose the companionship of two unlicensed subordinates for social support: Irena's touchy-feely nemesis Manny Handler and young Ricky Logan. The three, dubbed musketeers by staff, spent lots of time together during the workday drinking coffee in Darrell's office or visiting in the kitchen, their voices easily overheard demeaning co-workers then laughing out loud like children. Darrell, Manny and Ricky often targeted Irena, but few were safe from their barbs.

When Irena exited Darrell's office after a brief meeting with him and Manny, she turned back to ask a final question, to find the two pointing at her, sneering, and giggling like third grade boys.

Making do without the answer, Irena went back to her desk where, twitching with rage, she phoned Jacques and told him what happened. She told him she planned to talk to Damien, even knowing how futile that would be. Jacques advised her not to do that, and not to feel bad because "nobody likes Manny."

Irena eventually came to the painful realization that she had devoted ten years to a company that had come full circle, reverting back to the insignificant organization that hired her so long ago: a firm with aging principals who disrespected women; a firm with a shoddy reputation in the industry struggling to win the smallest of contracts; a firm with a small and mediocre cadre of engineers who refused to call on clients or potential clients because they had no idea and were unwilling to learn what it takes to win new contracts.

As the year drew to a close, Irena acknowledged with a broken heart her powerlessness to change Damien or Darrell's thinking and her inability to ever again influence the company's future.

Chapter Twenty-Nine

A fter eleven years, watching years of organization, success, and nurtured relationships falter and die, Irena began a ghostly death spiral, sinking further and further into depression.

Barely able to get out of bed each morning, the more Irena contemplated the outcome for the firm and for herself, the more she inched toward professional and psychological death, never quite sure if she was losing her grip on reality or finally seeing reality for what it was.

Irena's greatest problem was refusing to believe what her senses were telling her. Isolated and maligned, she felt broken and terrified that she was about to lose everything, including her professional identity.

Often encouraged by her care providers to take time off to heal, Irena refused, paralyzed by the fear of losing the work she loved, the income it paid, and her ability to provide for her family.

Damien precluded Irena from contacting clients, even as those clients were calling her to express their dissatisfaction with the engineers and their service. He ignored those clients; he continued to ignore her reports; and he blamed her for dwindling backlog. Jacques continued to pressure Irena for sex.

Irena became convinced that Damien, Darrell, Jacques, Lupo, and Manny were dangerous to her career and perhaps even her person. Afraid they had the authority and/or power to do what they wanted with her, Irena lived in daily fear of displeasing them, incurring their wrath, and losing her livelihood.

Of course, she had already displeased them and incurred their wrath, but she was still getting a paycheck. Therefore, she told herself she was still making a contribution, and she clung to her unrealistic fairytale belief that if she held on long enough, everything would turn out fine.

Irena hung on because she loved her work—work that took advantage of and benefitted from the organizational best she had to offer, her ability to write persuasive copy, and she was earning a living as a writer, truly her dream job. Having her professional life and accomplishments rejected after ten years of a successful fusion of need and solution was excruciating for her.

American psychologist Abraham Maslow believed human motivations generally move in ascending order through a pattern involving the satisfaction of physiological needs, safety needs, feelings of love and belonging, esteem, and ultimately the achievement of one's full potential, otherwise known as self actualization. Irena felt like the poster child for a distortion of Maslow's philosophy.

In response to the intense drama playing out around her, dissociation left Irena with little memory of her eleventh year with Yutz & Dunne other than her desire to survive. Like a prostitute who sells her body for money, Irena had sold her soul for her place in this unworthy organization, and the devil made her do the things she did next.

Chapter Thirty

I rena began her twelfth year with Yutz & Dunne feeling like a lab rat in an experiment to see how much frustration it would take to kill her. She had become a shell of a person: unwell, taxed to her diminishing limits, and barely able to keep her eyes open.

The principals considered her a woman who simply couldn't take it. And they were right. Irena *couldn't* take it. "It" being an organization of men who flagrantly disrespected employees, most especially but hardly limited to women, approved of mistreating them and isolating them from support, and eliminating them if and when they complained.

Irena believed that her survival depended on keeping Jacques happy. As he pressured her for a sexual commitment, she had disturbing dreams and knew she would not be keeping him that happy.

During one of his office visits, Irena suggested a glass of wine after work. After a few of his flirty and suggestive compliments, having danced around his verbal foreplay for months, Irena told Jacques they would never have a sexual relationship.

Once rejected, as Irena anticipated, he ignored her phone calls and ceased interacting with her, even though he remained her supervisor of record.

*   *   *

While Irena was dealing with Jacques' sexual pressure, he and Lupo were leaning heavily on Damien to authorize a relatively huge sum of money for what they referred to as a "glitzy marketing campaign," proposing to serve as the on-site engineering department for an emerging Illinois city.

The contract was worth seven million dollars, huge for Yutz & Dunne. After weeks of negotiation, the firm won the contract and installed Jacques as on-site engineering manager.

The firm celebrated amid questions about Jacques' background and license. Once again, it seems the principals failed to check Jacques' credentials because they're engineers and they don't do that. When research indicated Jacques never possessed the professional engineering license he claimed, Irena and others speculated about his ignorance or misrepresentation, even as he continued to misrepresent himself.

Within weeks of settling in at the city, Jacques hired his then-current wife and a step-daughter to work for him. Shortly thereafter, rumors began filtering back to Yutz & Dunne about Jacques' offensive misbehavior on the job.

His city secretary, Trish, a Yutz & Dunne employee on paper, complained to the city manager about Jacques' harassment and hostility. And Jacques reputedly commenced an illicit relationship with Trish's assistant, Lola, exposing his wife and daughter to the consequences.

The city manager faxed Damien a castigating letter, not marked confidential, which—in keeping with the company culture of no-holds-barred gossip—made a rapid-fire excursion around the office.

The city manager said that if Damien did not respond appropriately to Trish's complaints, the city would consider the company non-responsive to contractual obligations. He said that Trish was not the only person to complain about Jacques' misbehavior, and that Yutz & Dunne had already been warned three times.

The city manager pointed out that the company was obliged to take remedial action and that, if they did not, the city would view inaction as negligence. Further, should Trish file a claim against the city, the city would assert its indemnification rights.

Not long after the letter reached Yutz & Dunne, the city manager kicked Jacques to the curb, stating that he should have nothing further to do with serving the city, had no reason to be on city premises, and had no business contacting other city contractors or city employees.

Yutz & Dunne promptly terminated Jacques' secretary, Trish, in apparent retaliation; and Jacques enticed Lola, his alleged paramour, to leave with him to work at his newest Yutz & Dunne-subsidized field office.

Field technician Jenny Rodriguez, the last technical woman remaining on the payroll, returned from assignment at Jacques' field office commenting to the wrong people about inappropriate behavior she witnessed between Jacques and Lola. Shortly thereafter, Jenny's hourly workload was reduced and she began to struggle financially.

Even after losing this lucrative contract, Lupo continued to have faith in Jacques' opportunistic approach to life and business, so like his own, and continued to support his spending habits, Damien be damned. Lupo trusted Jacques with pie-in-the-sky naiveté to bring in another municipal contract like the one he lost, similar to the way he trusted Mario Centoni to bring in another waterside project like the one in Chile.

*　　　*　　　*

March found Irena near collapse, feeling like the glue holding her together was dissolving and she was falling to pieces. Responding to the continued urging of her care providers, Irena took a much-needed, never-before, two-week vacation. When she returned to the office, an eerie calm prevailed as if people were afraid to speak in her presence. Manny and Darrell's nastiness yanked her back to reality.

Meanwhile, Damien was advancing his plan to creatively eliminate Irena to avoid paying her the company's standard severance. After all, Irena had been with the company nearly twelve years and severance would cost Yutz & Dunne three months of her salary.

By virtue of his position as president, and having isolated Irena from Lupo, Damien believed he had garnered the freedom to eliminate her with little if any interference. But he had no legitimate reason to do so. And Damien's goal was further complicated by the

179

fact that Irena had not signed Lupo's employment-at-will agreement allowing them to fire her "at any time for any reason."

Virtually every state in the Union, including Illinois, is and was an at-will employment state, and Damien could have terminated Irena with or without that agreement, after dealing with sticky little litigious exceptions like gender discrimination and retaliatory discharge.

Chapter Thirty-One

During her twelfth year, Irena found herself at a fork in the road leading to the peace of resignation or a war of confrontation. She chose war.

Abandoning fear and driven by psychological forces beyond her control, Irena took up the arms of documentation and threat, overcoming the certainty that her confrontational behavior would be professional suicide and would cost her all opportunity for future employment.

Preparing for impending death on the battlefield, Irena refused to die quietly and charged ahead screaming in her head like a banshee.

Her first volley consisted of persistent appeals for help in real time. She documented each and every act of hostility perpetrated by Darrell and Manny and copied every principal and key staff member with a need to know and the power to intervene. She refused to allow their behavior to continue in isolation, and she refused to allow any principal the opportunity to ever say, "I didn't know."

Irena's documented complaints about Darrell and Manny made Damien mad, in much the same way her documented complaints about Lunice made Cal mad.

The principals by now should have been worried that Irena was creating a paper trail to illustrate their failure to protect her from a hostile work environment. Why they did nothing to protect themselves by rectifying the situation remains a mystery. They probably assumed that eliminating Irena was their solution.

Well past her second, third, or even fourth point of no return, and giddy with the release of frustration pent up for years, Irena perversely enjoyed provoking Damien and the others with her barrage of documentation. Of course, they ignored her.

If not insane, Irena's behavior could have been considered imprudent, but she delighted in irritating them. No doubt, the more she documented Darrell and Manny's behavior, the more acutely non grata she became. But she no longer cared. All things considered, attack was what Irena had to do.

*   *   *

In response to the screeching silence from the recipients of her individual communiqués, Irena sought a coup and constructed a ballistic missile of sorts. She composed an all-inclusive, one-time dump of grief and pleading for help, confident the document would later serve as evidence in some legal confrontation.

She summarized pertinent issues and described individual events as she perceived them. She included a description of the frustration she experienced as a result of harassment, gender bias, and discrimination. She reiterated Lunice's defamation, Manny's sexual harassment, and Darrell's on-going verbal abuse. And she lamented the lack of acknowledgement and support by management staff.

She summed up her accomplishments, stated that she did not deserve to be treated so poorly, begged for help, and offered reasonable suggestions for resolution.

Irena directed her missile at Damien as president, Jacques as her immediate supervisor, and Arden as human resources officer. No-one had been designated sexual harassment officer after Griff Chimeric resigned or Irena would have included him.

She could not include Lupo because that would give Damien reason to immediately terminate her for disobeying his direct order to stay away.

Damien, Jacques, and Arden behaved like those three little monkeys with their hands over their eyes, ears, and mouth. No-one heard, no-one responded, and no-one lived up to obligations. Instead of "see no evil, hear no evil, speak no evil," their passive aggressive mantra was: "I do not see it, I do not hear it, and I will not talk about it." They seemed to believe that, so long as they played dumb, they could avoid responsibility.

Although allowed to continue her work, such as it was, Irena expected her catalytic ballistic missile to trigger a hard-core bitter battle to her professional death. Her brain felt like a ping pong ball during a game—smack, smack, smack, smack—back and forth, rational and irrational. As she donned her mental chain mail, Irena imagined herself rolling on the floor laughing hysterically at the concept of defeat. Madness was setting in.

Meanwhile, Damien continued to build his case to eliminate Irena by hiring a consultant to evaluate her work efforts beyond the production of proposals and statements of qualifications.

Denigrating the go-no-go process—scorning information acquisition and management—mocking regular reporting and trend analysis and regular updating of marketing collateral—and cancelling client appreciation events—Damien wanted the consultant to substantiate his belief that Irena was wasting time on useless and expensive undertakings.

He wanted confirmation that Yutz & Dunne could survive and thrive without dedicated marketing staff.

And he wanted confirmation that Darrell and subordinate engineers could write and produce winning proposals from static resources while avoiding interpersonal contact with clients and potential clients.

*   *   *

Toward the end of April, Irena had become so dissociated, dehumanized, and easily manipulated from fatigue, frustration and depression that Lupo's secretary Fiona—still on the job—managed to persuade her to foster a unique celebration for National Administrative Assistants Day. Fiona told Irena that nothing had been done the previous year to celebrate. Irena accepted Fiona's comment to mean that the entire administrative support staff had been ignored.

Fiona convinced Irena to approach the principals about a luncheon, and then prodded her to expand the proposed outing to include a shopping trip allocating each participant twenty-five dollars for a self-selected gift.

Like the virtually mindless puppet Irena had become, she did Fiona's bidding, overlooking the possibility that Fiona alone had been ignored by Lupo.

When Irena e-mailed Jacques, Damien, and Arden asking for consideration of Fiona's plan, not mentioning Fiona's name, she did not consider the potential consequences. The men ignored her e-mail, as she should have expected, and passively denied the event with no plans made, no details worked out, and no invitations issued.

Arden, Damien's favored finance officer with human resources responsibilities, accused Irena (by way of gossip behind her back that made its way back to her, of course) of fostering a gender issue because she never mentioned Gabby Isakson, the male reprographics manager, when she mentioned the administrative support staff.

No longer passive when goaded, Irena responded to Arden's comment with an e-mail to him and the other principals providing details of her proposal along with an invitation list that included Gabby.

Arden returned Irena's e-mail with contemptuous and provocative comments inserted and highlighted for emphasis. That e-mail, abstracted below, was later used as legal evidence of corporate hostility.

Arden: Thought you had a proposal to get out today?

Irena: ...your comment about my fostering a gender issue has been stuck in my craw...

Arden: Seems like a lot of things stick in your craw!

Irena: ...firm culture has been... to use Administrative Assistants Day...to acknowledge the admin staff including the reprographics manager. Lupo would refer to taking care of his girls, and the reprographics manager was always included...

Arden: Aren't you offended by this statement? I understand the reprographics manager was included one time. (The reprographics manager was always invited and participated once. Irena was always invited and participated once.)

Irena: ...My approach... was to rekindle the acknowledgement of these individuals because a year went by with no acknowledgement...

Arden: How do you know?? And is it any of your business??

Irena: ...I don't expect, need or want to be included... because I am not an admin staff member... as defined by this company.

Arden: I consider myself to be one so what are you?

Irena: ...I feel the need to write because I perceived Arden's distaste for what it seemed he considered my begging for acknowledgement for myself...

Arden: You are correct.

Irena: ...I think it is important for... employees... to be recognized...It makes for improved morale. Whether all staff gets acknowledged or not is not the issue here.

Arden: OK, so what is the issue???

Irena: ...I think it is in the firm's best interest to acknowledge these individuals... lack of acknowledgement can be actively negative...

Arden: So can e-mails like these!!

Irena: ...Thanks for taking time to read this in the positive and helpful spirit in which it is written...

Arden: ...destructive, time wasting. I consider this to be the last word on this subject and any subsequent e-mails or other correspondence will be disregarded and unread.

*   *   *

Later that month, Damien assigned Darrell as principal-in-charge for three proposals, for projects Damien eagerly wanted to secure. He apparently tolerated, authorized, and perhaps even encouraged Darrell and his subordinates to disregard Irena's content and design in an attempt to determine if Darrell and his subordinates could succeed without Irena's marketing support.

Darrell wrote, designed, and produced those three proposals, perhaps with help from subordinate engineers, because no-one but Irena remained on staff with appropriate clerical skills. Fiona, Lupo's secretary, had fallen, broken her arm, and was out on state disability.

Apparently seeking no-one to review or critique those proposals before dispatch, all three were rejected, and Yutz & Dunne lost any opportunity to participate in competitive interviews—the next step in the contract award process.

Livid to learn the proposals were rejected, Damien held Irena responsible.

Rarely speaking to her, he nevertheless called her into his office to chew her out. Like a snake, Damien hissed, "Don't tell me. I know you wrote and produced those proposals. You and your poor workmanship are accountable and responsible for the loss of those contracts. You alone are responsible for the associated drop in marketing success. End of discussion."

What? she thought.

Trying to explain that Darrell refused her help and rejected her contributions, Irena offered to show Damien what Darrell rejected, but he refused to look or listen to anything she had to say. And, as he seemed to enjoy doing, he turned his back to Irena in dismissal.

Irena lost a few more brain cells.

Damien hired a second consultant to evaluate Darrell's proposals, but Irena would not be made aware, nor included in any discussion, until September, five months later.

*   *   *

The absolutely marvelous news of that atrocious April, and the thrilling highlight of the decade for Irena, was touchy-feely Manny Handler's resignation.

Manny could not leave the building his last day of work without taking a final poke at Irena, leaving a heckling poster at her desk showing a picture of a coyote strangling a prairie dog. The poster said, "Never miss an opportunity to shut up."

Regardless, Irena was ecstatic to conclude eight miserable years of exposure to this abusive and controlling, sexually predacious, annoying bastard.

Within weeks, little Ricky Logan resigned to follow Manny, just as he had followed Darrell to Yutz & Dunne. And gone were two of the three musketeers. In Irena's dysfunctional and naively optimistic delusion, she had hoped that with Manny and Ricky gone, she and Darrell might put the past behind them and work together to win new contracts.

It is said that mental illness is when one does the same thing over and over, each time expecting a different outcome.

Isolation only served to heighten Darrell's insecurity, and when Damien again encouraged him to "market," Darrell became even more anxious, agitated, and spiteful.

Continuing to target Irena as the manifestation of his angst, Darrell aimed a stream of demeaning public attacks at her in unadulterated Manny fashion. Irena continued to document every incident, making Damien, Arden, and Jacques aware: of course, to no other avail than assuaging her anger and building her paper trail.

*   *   *

Unsuccessful at getting Darrell and his engineers to submit winning proposals, Damien did an about-face and began exerting extraordinary pressure on Irena as marketing manager and Gabby as reprographics manager to create, produce, and deliver an unrealistic number of proposals. He seemed to think the only thing necessary to become more profitable was submitting as many proposals as humanly possible, apparently thinking of them like pasta: if you throw enough at a wall, some will stick.

Damien was unaware that the pasta-approach sacrifices quality and content, which undermines a firm's image, resulting in fewer requests for proposals, and thus fewer contracts—in a classic case of diminishing returns.

By issuing his dictum and cranking up the pressure to "just send out those proposals and bring in those contracts," Damien was echoing Lupo's simplistic demand to "just make me some money."

*   *   *

Under Damien's pressure to produce more and more proposals, Gabby and Irena began showing signs of human limitation. Even at their breaking points, Damien threatened them with "perfection or else." Under these conditions, still in April, Damien experienced what he considered a major crisis.

Gabby reproduced, collated, and delivered a proposal to a local client, minus the all-important cost estimate. The client, who could have rejected the proposal for the omission, called Damien, who went berserk.

Stomping to Irena's desk, he glared at her in unbridled rage and threw a note at her that said, "This omission is called a lack of attention to detail. Before a proposal goes out, you will (underlined twice) check it for completeness," as though, after twelve years, this was a new concept for her.

Even after Gabby acknowledged that he received the cost estimate from Irena along with the other master copies of the proposal for reproduction, Damien held Irena solely responsible for the omission in true scapegoat fashion.

Theoretically responsible as marketing manager to motivate and oversee team members, with no management support and no power of authority, Irena could not compel hostile engineers to produce technical input according to set and agreed-upon deadlines.

Damien did not care that the engineering project manager failed to meet his commitment. He simply expected Irena and Gabby to perform miracles. They did perform the miracle of getting the proposal out the door to meet the client's deadline, but they failed to create time where there was none.

Prior to Damien's unrealistic demands, Gabby and Irena, as a production team for years, had never missed a deadline or omitted any element of a proposal. Had Damien supported Irena's request for technical input in the agreed upon timeframe, there would have been time for perfection without threat.

But Damien refused to support marketing or even discuss the engineer's irritating lack of cooperation. He refused to acknowledge that proposals are a team effort, and he refused to consider that proofing and cross-checking are only possible when team members live up to their commitments.

To demonstrate that she and Gabby were a team responding to his concerns and on top of the situation, Irena copied Damien with a note she sent Gabby reminding him to be diligent, to double check future proposal tables of content to be sure every element is accounted for, and to remind him that, as team members, they needed a failsafe cross-check of the greater team's efforts.

Gabby was as offended by Irena's written reminder to be diligent, regardless of her reason for the note, as she had been by Damien's reminder to cross-check.

Chapter Thirty-Two

By May, Irena was in crisis with worsening sleep problems, headaches, and chest pain.

She met with her primary psychotherapist weekly, but felt a greater need and began meeting with a second psychologist outside her health maintenance organization.

As circumstances at work continued to worsen, Irena began having frequent nightmares. Startled awake most nights for years, even on that pseudo-vacation in March, Irena did her best to regain control of her heartbeat and go back to sleep. Lately she felt like she was dragging herself over craggy boulders, creeping ever closer to the edge of an unstable cliff with warriors in hot pursuit.

*   *   *

Continuing to deteriorate in June and July, Irena remained plagued by Manny's influence, subject to Darrell's Manny-like bullying, with Arden's dirty looks thrown in for good measure.

Fiona had been out on state disability since April for her broken arm when Damien called her at home in June, six weeks to the day after she was injured. He told her she needed to come back to work. The day she returned and approached her desk, Arden never let her sit down, handing her termination papers, and poof, another woman was gone.

June and July plodded on. Darrell and his subordinate engineers continued to reject marketing support, producing worthless, unsuccessful proposals like the three discussed previously. When Irena reminded Damien that the engineers were rejecting her support, he told her that her workload was diminishing "because engineering contract work is diminishing."

You can't be serious. Irena thought.

If Damien believed what he said, or thought Irena would believe what he said, he was crazier than she would ever be. Declining revenue and diminishing backlog typically calls for an increase in multi-level marketing efforts by a cooperative team, to woo clients and stimulate requests for proposals, and to ultimately win new contracts.

But again, Damien was either clueless or deliberately trying to drive Irena crazy. Trying or not, he was driving the remaining nails into her psychological coffin as he continued to demonstrate a lack of understanding and respect for marketing.

While women were systematically being eliminated, no engineer was laid off or suffered a cutback in hours, because Damien expected engineers, as billable staff, to sooner or later generate revenue.

As engineers did little, if anything, to keep clients happy or even satisfied during project execution, the company continued to deteriorate. Irena kept trying unsuccessfully to make Damien, Darrell, and Jacques aware that clients were dropping the firm from their list of consultants not because there was no work, but because they were dissatisfied with the firm's services

*   *   *

Night after night, Irena slept fitfully. Seven years with Lupo's partnership of six had been professionally challenging and interpersonally agonizing, tested as she was by Lunice, Manny, and other factors. Lupo's sole proprietorship between regimes had been like holding her breath. And Damien ushered in the worst of circumstances.

Adding to the psychological impact of her workplace, while agonizing that July, Irena's eighteen-year-old son left home— amicably, but nonetheless difficult for a single mom. Her older son had already left home for university, and her school-age daughter was and had been suffering from a malady that mystified doctors. While waiting for a definitive diagnosis for her daughter, Irena's doctor speculated that she herself might have a melanoma that could kill her in three years.

When her daughter left for school one morning, Irena broke down. After a twenty-minute crying jag, she pulled herself together enough to call in sick to work. She dressed, drove to her health maintenance organization's mental health facility, and called from her car, explaining between sobs that she was in the parking lot and needed help.

The telephone attendant, like an unfeeling automaton, told her that her usual therapist was not available, the department did not take walk-ins, and she needed to make an appointment. Feeling as though her skin was losing its ability to contain her, Irena blubbered: "You don't understand. I'm in the parking lot. I need to see someone now. And I'm coming in."

By the time Irena reached the third floor, a therapist had been located who had time to talk. Irena poured out her story and this psycho-pharmacologist wrote a prescription to help Irena overcome her crisis. After stopping at the pharmacy, Irena went home and cried herself to sleep, sleeping until her daughter got home from school. An expert at faking it, especially to her children, Irena put on her happiest face and pretended that everything was just peachy.

*   *   *

August brought a world of change. The line between Irena's personal and professional lives had begun to blur more so than before.

The years of mistreatment—the manipulation and pressure— the impact on her health, family and social life—and the effort it took to simply survive every hour of every day, was destroying Irena's ability to think and eroding her ability to respond. She could no longer imagine a way to extricate herself from Yutz & Dunne. Unable to envision survival, Irena found it increasingly difficult to eat or sleep.

With hostile forces circling like a hurricane, Irena tried to suppress her terror while men causing her anguish remained at liberty to do so. She believed she had to ride out the storm to some unknown end while bleeding to death on a battlefield in the eye of a hurricane, in the inescapable grip of a giant fist squeezing the life out of her.

Fight, flight, or death, and death seemed most appealing. Embracing the imminence of demise, Irena watched herself collapse in excruciating slow motion, wanting nothing more than to drift into eternal slumber. She saw herself transformed from intrepid professional, to tolerant employee, to victim, to corpse.

Descending into an abyss of madness, Irena experienced a death surge and lobbed one last death-defying volley, cackling hysterically in her head like the lunatic she had become. Truly over the edge, Irena wrote one last memo to Damien, Jacques, Arden, and Darrell asking for a salary increase, justifying her actions by telling herself *it's been three years... again.*

Of course no one responded, but Irena had the glorious if insane pleasure of imagining their astonished disbelief that she would ask for a salary increase under the circumstances. Requesting an increase was the most hilarious thing Irena could imagine at the time. But when she stopped laughing, she began to grieve the futility of it all.

*   *   *

Irena's last year with Yutz & Dunne was the year from hell. September was Satan's pitchfork. Every day, every hour, every incident that month was a critical thrust to her soul in Damien's final assault against her, executed with military precision.

While sitting at her desk on the morning of Friday, September eighth, organizing her work for the day, Irena's phone rang. Damien summoned her to his office for an unprecedented meeting about marketing works in progress. Irena's heart thudded in her chest.

Immediately upon entering his office, with no prelude, Damien demanded to know what requests for proposals were in-house and what she was currently working on.

Despite Damien's belief that such was a waste of time, Irena had continued to produce her weekly go-no-go report and ongoing status report, and took copies with her. Therefore, she was able to respond with a minimum of conversation and the meeting took less than five minutes. Nothing else was said or required of her and she was dismissed. Leaving Damien's office, Irena was virtually paralyzed with shock and fear of what that conversation signaled.

Same day, seven hours later, having had no further interaction with Damien, he walked by her cubicle and, without saying a word as usual, tossed a document on her desk and kept walking.

Irena paid little attention and went on writing, designing and producing a proposal Damien had given a go the previous afternoon—Thursday, the seventh—for delivery to the client Monday afternoon, the eleventh. The proposal required Irena to work the weekend of the ninth and tenth to assure a reasonably worthy proposal delivered on time.

*   *   *

At the office on Sunday, Irena made time to read the document Damien had tossed on her desk. The document, addressed to him, was the previously mentioned consultant's appropriately critical but misdirected evaluation prepared in April of those three disastrous proposals Darrell prepared back then.

Obviously, Damien failed to tell the consultant that an engineer wrote and produced those proposals. Or perhaps he told her that marketing staff had done so. Either way, Irena agreed with the consultant's comments, but was infuriated by the implication that she, Irena, was the author.

The consultant criticized the "marketing author" rather than the "proposal writer" and stated that the proposals were "abominable"—which they were—and "lost opportunities"—which they were—by the "incompetent marketing staff"—"dismal failures" for which the "marketing author should be terminated."

Irena had no doubt that Damien planned to use the contrived content of that evaluation to justify terminating her, and she developed a written response before leaving the office. She fantasized about asking Damien, with every bit of spitting, biting sarcasm one might imagine:

Well, Damien, if Darrell wrote, formatted, and produced those appalling proposals rejecting my input, who then was incompetent, Damien? Who was the evaluator really criticizing, Damien? And if Darrell was hostile and uncooperative with me and you refused to support marketing, who then failed to exercise his responsibility to manage, develop clear lines of authority, and intervene with appropriate consequences when necessary, Damien?

*   *   *

On Monday, September eleventh, Irena completed the proposal she was working on and dispatched it to the client at three thirty. Having worked the weekend and through lunch, and considering her level of anxiety, Irena went home early to rest up and prepare for the inevitable confrontation with Damien the next day.

*   *   *

On Tuesday morning, September twelfth, Irena arrived at eight-thirty expecting to finalize her comments about the evaluation. Before she could deliver those comments to Damien, he summoned her to his office.

Feeling his cold iron grip around her throat, Irena knew instinctively that the end was at hand, and that Damien had merely tolerated her presence in the office the previous day to get that proposal delivered.

Sitting across from Damien that morning, he silently handed her another memorandum to read in front of him—this one from him addressed to her.

The memorandum stated that, effective the next day, her hours would be reduced to a maximum of twenty per week at her current hourly wage (she had been salaried), with no benefits and no guarantees. She would work only on proposals at Damien's discretion upon Darrell's request.

What a joke, Irena thought.

Perhaps Damien thought Irena would enjoy the privilege of serving as an hourly consultant at less-than-inspiring half the market rate with no benefits and no guarantees. Perhaps he thought she might relish the idea of being strung up like a puppet on a hook to save him in a crisis at some future time in the obscure chance no one else was available.

Since Damien had forbidden Irena to talk to Lupo, Irena risked immediate and indefensible termination if she approached him about what was going on. And since Lupo gave Damien carte blanche with his company, she and he were bound by Damien's decision.

Under no circumstance could Damien's proposition have ever been genuine, because Darrell refused to work with Irena and Damien made it clear he disliked her and wanted her gone. Damien had to know that his proposition was unsustainable for her as breadwinner for a family of four.

And disastrous for the company, Damien should have known that maintaining no-one on staff with capable marketing or clerical skills would seriously impact the quality of future proposals—unless, of course, he planned to immediately replace Irena with someone else.

*   *   *

Damien's memorandum, cleverly written with obvious help from an attorney in quasi-legalese to protect the firm, did not link Irena's performance with the consultant's evaluation of Darrell's proposals. Damien, no doubt, was keeping that evaluation as his ace in the hole in the event Irena refused to cooperate, sued for severance pay or anything else, and he had to charge her with something.

As that evaluation was written, Damien could claim that Irena was never terminated and therefore was not entitled to severance pay, unused sick or vacation pay, unemployment benefits, or any other compensation. In other words, there was no requirement for any corporate outlay of cash to get rid of her.

To conclude proceedings, Irena's work hours were to be calculated from the previous Saturday morning, and as of this meeting with Damien, she had already worked twenty-two. He was effectively terminating her in summary dismissal.

Damien's coup.

To deflect the look of pure hatred on Irena's face, Damien reiterated his previous comment, this time telling her that Lupo suggested reducing her work hours as a consequence of "dwindling revenue and insufficient engineering workload."

He added the ridiculous postscript "not to worry" because "you're not the only employee whose hours are being reduced." This last comment was probably his best knee-jerk attempt to make his proposition sound less absurd and to assuage any guilt he may unlikely have had.

Irena was well acquainted with Lupo and Damien's modus operandi. Over the years, she had counseled numerous troubled employees being constructively discharged (i.e., when an employer makes working conditions intolerable, forcing an employee to quit).

At Yutz & Dunne, when partners or principals wanted a salaried employee gone, they would convert that employee to hourly wages and then reduce work hours to where the employee could no longer economically survive, forcing the employee to find work elsewhere and resign—presumably of their own volition. Most employees took this illegal practice for granted, but it made Irena's blood boil.

Damien very obviously considered Irena a useless (because engineers could do anything she could do, couldn't they?), noisy (because she complained about mistreatment), and costly (because she was not billable) female thorn to be removed. When he isolated her from Lupo, Irena knew in her heart that Damien would eventually succeed at getting rid of her, saving the company the cost of her salary and the cost of severance, simply because he had more power than she ever would.

Eliminating women and their respective salaries was Damien's most expedient way to improve the firm's profit margin and impress Lupo. But Damien seemed unaware that eliminating Irena would wipe out the strides made in marketing during her tenure. He also failed to consider the long-term impact of his decisions. He obviously had so little experience that he could not foresee how much the company stood to lose from dismissing established marketing policies and procedures developed along industry guidelines, and turning marketing over to a phobic engineer like Darrell with no clerical support.

Damien seemed unable to comprehend that saving Irena's salary would never make up for the contracts never to be won as a result of poor proposals, poor presentations, and engineers who did not give a damn because they knew they would remain employed no matter what.

*   *   *

Irena sat across from Damien in shock, hypnotized by the pencil he tapped along the edge of his desk as he waited for her to grasp his message and leave.

Contemplating his words and the impact on the company and her life, Irena was consumed by a wave of grief as she tried to accept that Damien wanted her gone—that she would never see another day's work for Yutz & Dunne—a company she viewed almost like her child.

Tears threatened to spill down her cheeks as she realized that her systems and efforts will have been for naught but transitory success. And then, the beast of Irena's rage bridled in her gut. Damien may have gloated over winning this battle, but he had no idea the war was far from over.

Chapter Thirty-Three

Damien felt safe terminating Irena on Tuesday, September 12—or reducing her hours, as he would say—only after that proposal was completed, dispatched and delivered the day before.

He may have been afraid that had he spoken with Irena beforehand, she might have stormed out, leaving the firm with an incomplete proposal and another lost opportunity. He may have wanted her to storm out afterward so he could point to her behavior as one more reason the firm was better off without her.

Rather than give in to the vengeful alter ego that wanted to rip off Damien's limbs, Irena's more benevolent alter ego, Princess Charming, emerged to help her detach from her rage. Remaining in her seat across from Damien, Irena ever so politely asked him, "What is the criterion for returning to work full time?"

Furious that Irena was still sitting before him and still talking, Damien's body noticeably contracted, his color deepened to the crimson Irena knew so well, and he tapped that pencil faster along the edge of his desk, alternately fidgeting with the eraser.

In response to Irena's question, Damien barked that he planned to outsource marketing in four to six months. Irena heard that she was not wanted back, there was no longer a place for her in the company, and she should quit now or be formally terminated in four to six months.

As politely as she could, Irena asked Damien why any marketing manager would be targeted for reduction when backlog is down and the firm is winning fewer contracts. She added that logic would have marketing working longer, more intense hours to help cultivate more work for engineers with little to do.

Gritting his teeth and breaking the pencil he now held with both hands, Damien appeared positively apoplectic that she dared to question him or challenge anything he had to say.

After a lengthy pause, during which Irena did her best to suppress her disgust and the subliminal urge to do him harm, even knowing her comment would enrage him, she reiterated her previous observation that, as a firm, they might have been more successful if the principals and marketing ever talked to each other.

Irena's statement drove Damien to infuriated silence so deafening she had to leave the room. Meanwhile, Damien was unaware that Princess Charming had leapt across his desk, had her hands around his throat, and was achieving great pleasure from squeezing the bastard to death.

*   *   *

Irena took that pseudo-vacation in March, afraid to call it sick time because she believed, realistically enough, that she would have been terminated upon return (as was Fiona) or that Damien would reduce her hours so she could not economically survive (as he was doing now).

Irena imagined herself in slow motion, hitting a wall and flattening out into a huge dark splat, oozing down the wall into a black puddle of despair. She allowed the awareness that there was no possibility of professional survival to seep into the remaining shreds of her consciousness.

Irena's hopes were shattered, including her childish delusion that if she worked hard enough, did a good job, and was a good girl, everything would turn out fine. Trying to accept the fact that she was no longer in a position to make a difference for Yutz & Dunne, she experienced a fleeting pout of *after all I've done...*

Irena left the building that Tuesday burning with shame, feeling like a failure, and terrified by the implications of her situation. She was a woman over fifty and unemployed; a single parent with three children to support, with a mortgage, car payments, and all the other expenses of maintaining a household.

Later that day, between bouts of terror, Irena phoned her psychotherapist who had been encouraging her for years to take time off. In consensus with her other care providers, Irena was placed on state disability.

*　　　*　　　*

Irena's first night on disability, she dreamt of mass murderers like Dylan Klebold and Eric Harris who killed thirteen and injured twenty-four at a high school, Gian Luigi Ferri who killed eight and wounded six in an office building, and James Eagan Holmes who killed twenty-four and injured seventy in a movie theater. As her dream unfolded, she thought, *if they could do it, so can I.*

The years had taken a toll and Irena dreamt that she had to act. She knew her opportunity was the annual Christmas luncheon held in place of the weekly staff meeting on the second Thursday of December in the conference room. Friends still on the job confirmed the date, having no idea what Irena had in mind.

Consumed by the thought that another year of holiday cheer was lost to this sick and evil group of people, Irena considered it her responsibility to put an end to the misery these people dished out, particularly to female staff. Years of abuse convinced her there was no other solution. This was her opportunity and she was ready.

With everyone gathered in the conference room, it was easy for her to slip into the office unnoticed through a back door that remained unlocked during business hours. Eerily quiet, Irena heard only the murmur of voices up ahead emanating from the conference room.

Making her way through the monotonous space, moving quietly along the dirty beige carpet, Irena took each step slowly and carefully so as not to be heard. The sounds ahead were nearly drowned out by the beating of her heart and the rush of air as she inhaled and exhaled, afraid to take each succeeding breath. Her face was hot and she could feel beads of perspiration forming along her hairline, on the back of her neck, and trickling down between her breasts.

Prepared to carry out her plan that cold December day, Irena had taken time to find just the right weapon, even buying some Agrip so the gun would not slip in her hand. Glancing down at the clip of thirty rounds, her heart was pounding and her head hurt. Her hands were cold and clammy, and her fingers ached as they clenched the gun. And she trembled, just a little, as she inched closer.

Quietly approaching the big brown doors of the conference room, the right door ajar so the receptionist could hear the phone at her desk, Irena peered into the room to locate her targets, careful to remain out of sight. In a few brief seconds, it was over.

Irena entered the room, aimed in the direction of those she considered the worst offenders, and fired, killing six before she was subdued. Irena was livid that she had not exterminated more of the bastards.

Sad that innocent people had to suffer along with the guilty, Irena was ecstatic that at least some of those who had to pay for their sins did so. In her dream, Irena was confident they would never again treat another employee like they had treated her.

*   *   *

In the habit for years of getting up and going to work, Irena woke the next morning at the usual time, exhausted by her dream and distraught by the fear that she might never overcome the torture of disdain, hostility and indifference, and what had felt like slavery—juxtaposed by anguish that her children had been denied her time, love, and attention while she sacrificed for Yutz & Dunne.

Had Damien legitimately terminated her, the end might have been easier for Irena to accept. But his allusions to future work made it difficult for Irena to fully comprehend the situation. She failed to realize that keeping her confused was part of Damien's devious plan.

Given her history with the firm, Irena found it inconceivable that Damien truly considered her expendable. Unrealistically hoping for a different outcome, she went to the office on Wednesday morning to meet with Damien for more information. After waiting several hours, Irena was forced to accept that Damien would not meet with her or respond to her requests for information, and in fact would never speak with her again. He was done with her, as anyone in their right mind would have known.

*   *   *

Irena spent the next day—Thursday, September fourteenth—at home in bed feeling like a shattered mirror, shards reflecting details of past employment crises and future financial calamities. Irena could barely function enough to care for her children, terrified that this disruption would cost them their home.

Her mind erupted again and again. She felt beaten. She felt squeezed to emotional death. She felt like she was falling off a cliff and needed to protect herself from splattering on the rocks below. Irena wanted to escape. She wanted to run. She wanted to hide. She wanted to sleep. She had a difficult time stringing two thoughts together. She had difficulty finishing a sentence. She had difficulty containing her overwhelming fear and distress.

Irena suffered a massive depressive episode, also known as a nervous breakdown.

On Friday, September fifteenth, Irena met with her care providers to complete the remaining paperwork necessary to facilitate state disability. A workers compensation evaluator, provided by her health maintenance organization as part of the team evaluating her case, believed Irena sustained a psychological injury as well as two physical injuries, each of which he said likely constituted an actionable workers compensation claim.

The evaluator provided Irena with a list of attorneys with whom to consult. Stuffing the list into her purse, and unable to take constructive action on her own behalf, Irena eventually lost sight of the evaluator, his comments, and that list.

On Sunday evening, confident of an empty office, Irena went back to hand-deliver the state disability paperwork to the center of Damien's desk where he would presumably see it first thing Monday morning. Walking through the quiet, dimly lit space, Irena looked over her shoulder often, like a thief, to be sure she was not observed.

Familiar with hanky-panky by the principals over the years, Irena had chosen not to risk or waste time with the United States Postal Service, concerned that Damien might misrepresent the real timing of her paperwork's arrival, or that the paperwork might make a trip around the office for the gossips to see before landing on Damien's desk.

*   *   *

While in the office, Irena gathered her personal belongings, believing she might not have another chance. At home, she discovered that some personal documents were missing. Emboldened by her visit Sunday evening, she went back again Monday evening to find or print out those documents.

Entering her familiar cubicle, now stripped bare of anything reminiscent of her, she discovered that her computer was gone. Attempting to use the rogue, she discovered that her network password had been voided. Unable to print out her missing documents, Irena resisted the real or paranoid conclusion that her documents had been appropriated with sinister intent.

If Irena harbored any doubt that the reduction in her hours was in fact termination, her missing computer and voided password confirmed it—cemented the next day when the accounting clerk called her at home to say that Damien wanted her office keys.

The accounting clerk told Irena that Damien was outraged to discover the disability paperwork on his desk, no doubt because Irena still had access to the office after he terminated her, and because disability meant that he and the firm would not be free of her for the foreseeable future.

Irena grinned as she mailed in her keys.

Chapter Thirty-Four

I rena had a nervous breakdown. Doing her best to recover at home, she had a difficult time psychologically letting go of her former co-workers and her experiences.

Struggling with the chaotic chatter that echoed in her head like pebbles in a tin can, Irena did her best to establish some calm and quiet in her life. But that calm and quiet was shattered when staff made it clear that they had difficulty letting go of her, too.

Thirteen days after going out on disability, seven days after her final covert visit to the office, and five days after the accounting clerk called for her keys, Irena sat cocooned in her comfy reclining chair at home, having fallen asleep while reading, only to be startled from her reverie by the loud ringing of her telephone.

Wiley James, a part-time railroad engineer, was calling her for help with a major proposal to compete for a noteworthy and potentially lucrative rail project for a regional transit district, the kind of project Lupo yearned to include among the firm's accomplishments. The request for proposal was received three months before Damien terminated Irena.

She had been urging Damien and Jacques weekly to make a decision to go or not go after this worthwhile project before she left, but the request languished on their desks and no decision was made.

Listening to Wiley pleading her for help, Irena felt trapped between trying to act like a sane individual and the urge to slam the phone down hard enough to rupture his eardrum. His call confirmed one of Irena's greatest irrational fears—that she could never protect herself from her former co-workers.

She felt like she had been beaten to a pulp, kicked a few times, and left for dead. Vultures were stripping away her flesh, yanking out her fingernails, and plucking out her eyeballs. Not even her carcass could rest in peace.

Since Damien precluded Irena from contact with Lupo, one might assume Lupo remained unaware that this opportunity was in house, perhaps until now. Considering his enthusiasm for rail projects, one might also assume that when he learned about this opportunity, he demanded that Damien go after it.

Part-time Wiley had a respectable reputation in the rail industry, and Lupo may have tried to convince Damien that Wiley was a golden calf whose name and reputation alone could win the project. Lupo likely pressured Damien, and Damien likely pressured Wiley to pursue the project on his own.

But Wiley was smart enough to know that any proposal he could produce under the circumstances would make him and the firm look foolish at best. So, Wiley called Irena for a Hail Mary.

However, the proposal was now due in seven days, the firm employed no rail staff other than part-time Wiley, no marketing staff, no clerical staff, and the competition had had three months' head start building their sub-consultant teams.

Producing and delivering an attractive and winning proposal within a week adhering to the transit district's requirements was virtually impossible for even the most capable marketing staff, project manager, relevant staff engineers, and willing sub-consultants dedicated to working as a team. With no team in place, Irena knew that developing a proposal would be futile and she wanted no part of it. Even if it were a slam dunk, she still wanted no part of it.

Trying to wrap her weak and wounded psyche around her conversation with Wiley was also futile. A voice inside her head was crying *too bad, so sad,* and a much louder voice was screaming *leave me the hell alone! I'm gone! I was driven out! I had a nervous breakdown and went on disability two weeks ago! And you ask me to work on a major proposal under impossible time constraints? AARGHHH!*

Calmed by Princess Charming, Irena listened to what Wiley had to say, then reminded him she was out of the office on disability and was not available to help him.

Responding in pseudo-threat or desperation, Wiley told Irena that if she would not help him, he would have to tell Damien he did not want to be involved because, without appropriate marketing assistance, the submittal would be an embarrassment.

Irena wondered how much longer Wiley was with the firm.

Yutz & Dunne did not submit a proposal for the project, and Irena learned later that Damien was enraged because she refused to help. In subsequent legal proceedings Damien claimed that Irena "left the firm high and dry by going out on disability and losing them the opportunity to pursue the project."

*   *   *

Two days after Wiley's call, again enjoying some calm with a book, Irena received a call from Kitty, the receptionist. Kitty asked her, "What did you do with the electronic files for Broadson Property Developers (the firm's primary source of revenue at the time)?" and "Do you have electronic backup files at home?"

What? Irena thought.

Totally confused, the hair on the back of Irena's neck bristled with apprehension, and she asked Kitty what she was talking about. Kitty said that Jim Masterson (the information systems technology technician or IT guy) asked her to call with those questions.

When Irena called Jim, he said that Damien had asked Gabby (the reprographics manager who advocated gossip) to find certain electronic files. When Gabby could not find them, he told Damien, "Irena must have deleted them or taken them home."

@#&!%!!!

Being subjected to false accusations even in absentia compounded Irena's feelings of persecution and rage, but rather than act on her primal instinct to track down Gabby and beat him to a pulp, she solved the problem. She told herself she did so to clear her name, as if that could happen.

Irena called Gabby who said he was trying to locate project descriptions in a land development statement of qualifications she prepared for Broadson Property Developers, and that electronic marketing files from A through L were missing.

Gritting her teeth, Irena walked Gabby through the process, proving that he had failed to scroll back to the beginning of the alphabet, and that the marketing files were exactly where they were supposed to be and undisturbed.

Gabby never thanked Irena for her help, nor did he apologize for disparaging her. And Irena wondered if Damien ever learned the truth.

Like a ship at the mercy of a stormy sea continuing to break apart, Irena felt like she was being pulled down into a black void. She could not quiet her mind just as she could not quiet the sea. She had already drowned in defamatory gossip, was out of work, was in physical and psychological pain and declared disabled, and still she was being discredited and devalued. People wanted her gone and she was gone, but she felt like she would never be free.

Leave me the hell alone! reverberated in the cavern of her skull. Why was she unable to let the words escape? Why was she unable to let go? Irena sought therapy to learn the answers to these and other questions.

*   *   *

Twenty-seven days after Irena went out on disability, fourteen days after Wiley's call for help with a proposal, and twelve days after Kitty's call about the Gabby/Broadson file fiasco, Irena received a third phone call, this time from Jenny Rodriguez, the engineering field technician mentioned earlier, the last woman employed by Yutz & Dunne in any capacity outside administrative support.

Jenny told Irena, "They're finally squeezing me out too. But before I leave, as a friend, there are some things I thought you might want to know.

"I overheard the surveyors talking about Damien and his efforts to figure out a way to fire you. And even though Damien told you that other staff hours were being reduced, nobody's hours have been cut but mine. The receptionist and accounting clerk got raises, probably divvying up your salary, and so did Hank Jeffers, a surveyor, because he threatened to quit."

Jenny told Irena that Darrell, her supervisor, interviewed Roy Kentfield, a former surveyor, who wanted to come back to the firm. "I told Arden that Roy grabbed me inappropriately the other day and Arden thanked me for the information. He said another woman also complained about Roy. I told Darrell because Roy and I would be working together if he were rehired. And that was when my hours were cut."

And then there were none.

Chapter Thirty-Five

W hen Irena first went out on state disability, she applied for workers compensation benefits. The claims adjuster told her, "You need to be patient because your claim can take up to two years to resolve because your health maintenance organization is so slow at providing medical records." Irena learned much later that medical providers are mandated to respond quickly, usually within fourteen days. The longer Irena waited for feedback, the more her annoyance became obsession with holding Yutz & Dunne accountable for the wrongs perpetrated against her.

Motivated to file a civil lawsuit, Irena sought legal representation. Wanting to present her grievances concisely, she prepared a legal brief of sorts, consulting years of personal journals where she recorded events as they occurred along with her responses. Her first draft was sixty-three pages. Hilarious, even to herself, Irena consolidated to what she considered a manageable seventeen pages, and proceeded with her search for legal representation.

Each attorney she consulted said, in one way or another, "Yes, you have an actionable item (a legitimate complaint), but not for me because your case is too complicated with insufficient assets available." In other words, Yutz & Dunne was too small a company with not enough money available for settlement to be worth their effort. The injustice of being denied representation for a legitimate complaint compounded Irena's frustration.

One attorney suggested that Irena contact the United States Equal Employment Opportunity Commission, which she did. Phoning a local office, Irena made contact with Tina Franklin, a compassionate Commission representative. After Irena explained her situation as succinctly as she could, Franklin told her that, given her allegations, if Yutz & Dunne were a larger firm with sufficient assets, a lawsuit could result in a "huge" financial settlement.

Franklin also told Irena that, despite comprehensive employee protections provided by the Civil Rights Act, small businesses like Yutz & Dunne are more loosely regulated by the United States Department of Labor than big businesses and can breed greater and more frequent abuse.

She said that employees of small businesses often find it difficult to know their rights and/or resolve disputes short of parting ways. However, the Equal Employment Opportunity Commission and affiliated state Fair Employment Practices agencies are available to work with employees and employers to provide unbiased mediation for claims of discrimination, harassment, and other grievances.

Franklin directed Irena to her local Illinois Fair Employment Practices agency where she met with Jill Wittington. Wittington had Irena complete a pre-complaint questionnaire, then offered her two options.

The first option provided for civil litigation, where an individual files a grievance, obtains a right-to-sue letter from Fair Employment, retains a private attorney to litigate in civil court, and forever relinquishes rights to assistance from the Equal Employment Opportunity Commission or any Fair Employment Practices agency.

The second option provided for assisted mediation, where an individual files a grievance with the Equal Employment Opportunity Commission or a local Fair Employment Practices agency. Fair Employment then considers the grievance and, if deemed appropriate, provides a mediator to assist the employee and the employer reach a mutually satisfactory resolution at no cost, with oversight by the Equal Employment Opportunity Commission. And while legal representation is an advantage, it is not required.

Unable to secure legal representation, Irena opted for assisted mediation. Once that decision was made, her pursuit of justice took a few extraordinary twists and turns.

Chapter Thirty-Six

When Irena told Wittington of Fair Employment that she decided to seek assisted mediation, Wittington told Irena she could not go forward until she resigned from Yutz & Dunne. Irena understood that resignation would terminate her state disability and leave her with no other source of income. Trusting Wittington as the authority, Irena did not consider a need to verify her comments.

When Irena asked Wittington about filing a workers compensation appeal in addition to Fair Employment mediation, Wittington advised her to "wait until mediation is done." Irena spent more sleepless nights contemplating her options.

While agonizing over what to do, Irena received a phone call from Cal Chauvin, former president of Yutz & Dunne and her former supervisor. Cal told her he recently joined Emerson Construction Management as president, they needed a new marketing manager, and he hoped she would consider working for him again.

Cal knew Irena's qualifications, knew her affinity for marketing, and knew she could get along with difficult people. He knew she was on state disability and knew about her financial insecurity. He lured her with an appealing starting salary that was twenty-five percent more than her final salary at Yutz & Dunne, further illustrating her economic abuse at that firm.

Cal was offering what seemed like an opportune position paying a top salary, one of few available close to home, but Irena told him she needed a few days to think about his offer. She tossed and turned that night and the next as her mind roiled with the pros and cons of his offer.

Resigning would allow me to proceed with my complaint (a positive), would sacrifice state disability (a negative), probably preclude me from unemployment benefits (a negative), and replace my income (a positive). Accepting Cal's offer would have me working closely with him again (a negative), would allow me to perform work I love at a good salary (two positives), would satisfy my need for financial security (a positive), reasonably close to home (a positive), but would leave me psychologically vulnerable (a negative).

Should I accept? Will the position be in my best interest? Will I have regrets? Will I have time to go forward with my complaint? Will I be successful at either or both? How long will my complaint take to resolve? Do I have the stamina? Am I smart enough? What if I hate the job? What if the people there hate me? What if I can't get along with Cal?

Irena chose not to discuss this dubious opportunity with her care providers, afraid they would advise her not to quit which, according to Wittington, would mean she could not pursue her grievance.

Enticed by Cal's offer and determined to pursue justice, Irena ignored her apprehensions about reintroducing Cal into her professional life and formally resigned from Yutz & Dunne, terminating her state disability.

Only after resigning and accepting Cal's offer did Irena learn that Jill Wittington was dead wrong and she was screwed. Accepting Cal's offer was an error in judgment that gravely impacted Irena's long-term ability to recover from her ordeal at Yutz & Dunne—physically, psychologically, legally, and financially.

*   *   *

Emerson Construction Management leased space on the sixth floor of a modern glass-and-steel office building in a well-maintained suburban industrial park with lots of trees, groomed lawns, and planter beds.

Irena arrived on her first day of work excited by this new opportunity and the associated salary. Sitting across from Cal in his warm and sunny office, he welcomed her and provided her with some generic background about the company.

And that was when the first ghost of Yutz & Dunne paid Irena a visit.

Cal told Irena, "By the way, I am reducing the salary I offered you by five percent, but I promise to raise your salary that five percent after six months." Familiar fireworks went off in Irena's brain.

Six years had blurred the boundaries of her working relationship with Cal, and even as she was delighted by this new position, she shuddered to realize that Cal was still playing compensation games. She wondered if he played to determine whether she still liked him enough to work for him again, or if he just enjoyed the power to do so.

Irena felt manipulated and deceived, but rationalized by telling herself that six months was not long to wait for a mere five percent, that she would still be earning a great salary, that she was nonetheless happy to accept the position, and that Emerson had to be an improvement over Yutz & Dunne.

Confident she could manage inside marketing for this firm and confident she could work well with most people, Irena was optimistic that she and Cal could cooperate and manage new challenges together despite her resentment.

And so, Irena embarked on this new piece of history with this dichotomous individual who, while lifting her up, needed her to lift him higher; a man who failed to protect her from defamation and harassment; a man who continued to suppress her salary.

*   *   *

Emerson staff offices were positioned along a swath of windows with a view. Assigned one of those offices, Irena looked forward to restoring a career she loved at a market rate salary in a gorgeous environment.

Cal's first assignment for Irena involved reorganizing electronic files to make them more user-friendly. An urgent assignment, he said. Eager to make a good impression, Irena began immediately. At her first monthly staff meeting, with everyone gathered around the conference room table, when attendees were invited to contribute, Irena proudly announced that she had completed reorganizing the electronic files.

The room went deathly quiet. Time seemed to stand still. Irena felt queasy as everyone looked back and forth between her and Ralph Emerson, the firm's owner, very obviously expecting a reaction from him. After a long and nerve-wracking pause, during which Cal failed to mention he had assigned Irena that task, the meeting continued.

When the meeting ended, Irena was blindsided by the second ghost of Yutz & Dunne. Ralph called her into his office and, glaring at her, stood with both palms placed firmly on the desk in front of him, leaning forward to emphasize his point, and declared slowly and emphatically through nearly clenched teeth, "You – will – never – again – take – any – action - without – my – prior - approval. Do – you - understand?"

Sensitized to threat, appreciating the virtue of silence, and painfully reminded of the personalities and relationships she left behind at Yutz & Dunne, Irena nodded in agreement, bowed her head a tad in submission, and backed out of Ralph's office with a lump in her throat that would have rendered her speechless anyway.

A month or two later, Ralph reneged on a commitment he made to Irena when she was hired: that so long as she worked more than eight hours a day, she could start work at nine-thirty, allowing her to minimize her work-direction commute time.

In a total about-face, in response to a resentful receptionist, Ralph demanded that Irena "start at eight like everyone else," thereby increasing her morning commute from thirty minutes to over sixty while she continued to work beyond six-thirty or seven most evenings.

* * *

Irena was ostensibly responsible for developing proposal content. However, without warning, daily and often hourly, Ralph would review and radically amend Irena's emerging content, which had to be perfect at all times, including spacing, punctuation, and initial capitalizations.

Proposal development slowed to a frustrating crawl as her content became his, reducing her to little more than a typist with graphics capabilities. Ralph considered any discussion of his changes to be a direct criticism of him, which of course was unacceptable. If you did not agree with Ralph you were simply wrong. No questions. No room for discussion.

Emerson paid Irena a good salary for what she originally believed was her intellect and talent toward winning competitive contracts. But it became increasingly clear that she was being paid to type and tolerate Ralph, which was disappointing at best.

With a deadline looming, Ralph and Irena were going back and forth several times a day for several days in a row, requiring Irena to often run the forty feet or so between her office and his, revision after revision, section after section. Irena's patience wore thinner every day.

During one of their more intense go-rounds, Ralph pushed Irena beyond her post-Yutz & Dunne breaking point with a harsh criticism about a missing punctuation mark. He barked, "I pay you a lot of money to be a professional, and this is absolutely unacceptable!"

Irena contemplated laughing in his face, but instead, unable to control her newly liberated tongue, she said, "OK, Ralph, so get out the wet noodle and beat me to death!"

Ralph did not find Irena's comment amusing and insisted that Cal terminate her immediately. And Irena's psyche took another blow. But even as the words were coming out of Cal's mouth ending her employment with Emerson, she began to laugh uncontrollably, suddenly relieved of pressure she had not fully realized she had been keeping in check.

When filling out internal termination paperwork, the human resources officer confided to Irena that Ralph's obsessive need to control everything had resulted in voluntary and involuntary terminations company-wide every six to eight months for years. Only two office staff of nine and one field staff of fourteen had been in Ralph's employ for more than a year. Irena survived six months.

Walking out the door that day, Irena painfully realized that she had foolishly sacrificed state disability benefits to accept Cal's offer of this terrible brief employment experience. Panic set in as she contemplated a bleak economic future.

Had Irena turned down Cal's offer, had she not resigned from Yutz & Dunne, and had she remained on state disability, returning to work at Yutz & Dunne to be terminated as she was confident would have happened, Irena could likely have pursued legal action for retaliation. And she might have been spared from events at Emerson and elsewhere that unfolded over the next eighteen months, affecting her for years to come.

Chapter Thirty-Seven

L eaving Emerson gave Irena time to concentrate on pursuing mediation with Yutz & Dunne with the help of the Equal Employment Opportunity Commission and her local Fair Employment Practices agency.

Having heard nothing from Wittington or the Fair Employment agency for the six months she had been employed at Emerson, Irena called Wittington for a status report about her grievance.

The phone attendant told Irena that Wittington was no longer available, and Irena's heart skipped a beat. The attendant referred her to another Fair Employment representative who was unable to locate Irena's case file, and Irena's heart skipped another beat. When that representative in turn referred her to yet another individual also unable to locate her file, Irena nearly had a heart attack.

Trying to suppress her rising blood pressure, Irena refused to give up. She insisted on speaking with someone who might be in a better position to help, and was referred to Senior Director Gabriel Zander who promised to look into her case.

Zander called her a week later to say that Wittington had abandoned her case file on a vacant desktop without notifying anyone. Without saying how long ago that was, Zander assumed management of Irena's case, which only then began to move forward.

Meanwhile, six months was lost.

*   *   *

The dynamic process of assisted mediation began when Fair Employment notified the principal parties—Irena Nowak, Damien Hartless, and the contract mediator—that a meeting was scheduled two weeks later at Fair Employment offices on Randolph Street.

That day, Irena sat alone at one end of an oval oak table in a dimly lit conference room on the fifth floor. Damien, with Arden

Champion as his support person, sat at the other end. The mediator sat in the middle.

After written arguments supporting each side's position were submitted, reviewed, and debated, offers and counter-offers flew between participants for hours. At the end of the inconclusive day, participants left the meeting agreeing to continue negotiations by United States Postal Service.

The entire process took fifteen months, from submittal of Irena's pre-complaint questionnaire to resolution and signing of a settlement agreement. However, resolution implies that both sides are satisfied, and Irena knew better. Retaliation would play out in the wording of the settlement agreement Lupo's attorney was privileged to craft.

The agreement threatened Irena with a lawsuit if she disclosed details of the mediation process or the agreement which was written to deny her right to workers compensation.

Since Irena had a nervous breakdown, was under duress, and had no attorney representing her interests—having been told an attorney was unnecessary—those stipulations might still be arguable in a court of law as coercion or an abuse or usurpation of power.

Chapter Thirty-Eight

During Fair Employment mediation negotiations by United States Postal Service, with time to spare between offers and counter-offers, Irena contacted the Workers Compensation Commission, eager to discuss her injuries, the lack of response from her employer and the insurance company to her claim for benefits, the potential for denial, the relevant statute of limitations, and any overlap with Fair Employment.

Workers Compensation Commission Director Carl Jordan agreed to meet with her on the unforeseeably heinous date of September 11, 2001.

At seven fifty-six that morning in Chicago, eight fifty-six in New York, Irena was awakened by a phone call from her cousin Laura in Brooklyn Heights. Calling from her twenty-second-floor apartment with her unobstructed view of the twin towers, Laura said, "A plane just flew into the World Trade Center. Turn on your TV." The first plane had flown into the first tower at eight forty-five.

Believing they were witnessing a terrible accident, Laura and Irena remained connected by phone, with Laura watching events live and Irena watching on television, when the second plane flew into the second tower.

Beyond horrified, Irena and Laura watched as events unfolded until both towers of the World Trade Center collapsed. Weeping together, they agonized for those killed and injured.

Now believing they were witnessing an act of war, Irena and Laura feared for the rest of New York and for the country, a fear that changed them and the world forever. Images of the end of life as she knew it flashed across Irena's mind, as particulate matter carried by the wind found its way into Laura's apartment through the seams of closed windows.

It was in Irena's associated state of disbelief and grief that she met with Carl Jordan later that day to discuss workers compensation, wondering if anything familiar mattered anymore.

*   *   *

After commiserating over events of the morning, Jordan told Irena, in one of the greater dichotomies, that even though she never received a documented denial of her claim for workers compensation benefits, in order to protect her rights, she had to file an application for appeal of the denial she did not receive within one year of the date of injury or the date medical treatment was first sought.

Jordan determined September 12, 2000—Irena's documented date of disability—to be her date of injury and said, "You must file your application for appeal today, September 11, 2001, one day before the statute of limitations will expire for you."

Jordan added, "If you leave this office or wait to be done with mediation or wait for Newman National to officially deny your claim, you will forfeit your right to appeal."

Jill Wittington of Fair Employment had advised Irena to wait until mediation was done before proceeding with a workers compensation appeal. Had Irena followed Wittington's advice, she would surely have missed her opportunity to file an appeal.

Given the monstrosity of September 11, and given her stress about Fair Employment mediation, and given her apprehension about what would be expected of her once she filed her appeal, Irena had a hard time concentrating on Jordan's comments. Princess Charming, her saving alter ego, helped her gather her wits, and Jordan completed the application with her input, which she signed, shaking like a leaf.

Irena was comforted to learn that filing her application for appeal did not begin the arduous process but rather protected her right to proceed, like a bookmark.

Chapter Thirty-Nine

C al Chauvin continued calling Irena periodically "to keep in touch." She never knew whether he thought of her as a personal friend or a professional associate; whether, having allowed her to suffer slander at Yutz & Dunne, he was motivated by guilt to find her work when she was unemployed; whether he had some peculiar fantasy resulting from the speculation about her sex life; or whether he was keeping tabs on an employment ace in the hole. She entertained his calls because, in turnabout fashion, she just never knew when *he* might come in handy.

After resolving her Fair Employment grievance and subsequent mediation, and before proceeding with her workers compensation appeal, Irena received another call from Cal with another opportunity. Unemployed and suffering her perpetual fear of economic disaster, she again considered what he had to say.

Cal told her he was negotiating with the engineering department at the City of Chenowith to become a contract project manager, and in the process met Wally Perez, another contractor providing those same services. Cal told Irena that when Wally expressed a need for help, "I told him you were unemployed and would give him a call."

Dismissing Cal's presumptions, but excited by the possibility of new work she again did not have to search for, Irena called Wally. They met the following Thursday at his quirky little office on Glen Boulevard: a two-bedroom, one-bath house conveniently located three blocks from city hall, among other small and aging residential and business properties.

With oddly undulating floors, the house had a tiny lawn out front sporting two trees big enough to consume the house, and a flagpole poking out of a deep blanket of dead brown leaves. The old kitchen had been divided, preserving a wall of cabinets, a sink, refrigerator, and hot water heater in a long, narrow, functional space. The rest of the kitchen and a porch had been combined to form a room, with windows along two walls, that may once have served as a dining room. Wally occupied one bedroom as his office. The other served as a storeroom.

Wally told Irena that Cal recommended her to provide clerical help and Irena's excitement gave way to irritation. Cal may have believed he was doing her a favor, but Irena's mind reverberated with the demeaning comments he had made over the years denigrating the capabilities of women.

Irritation gave way to delight when Wally said, "Even though Cal recommended you for clerical work, after looking over your resume and talking with you, I believe you can do a lot more." Wally then offered Irena work as an engineering project assistant and they agreed upon a satisfactory hourly rate.

Irena filed a fictitious business name to set up a small business as a vendor providing hourly services. She bought furniture and equipment and set up her office in that quirky little house, content to work in the homey, non-threatening living room with its fireplace, front door access, and picture window overlooking Glen Boulevard.

*   *   *

Wally later invited Cal to join their little consortium several weeks after Irena started working there. Her heart sank, but she took the path of least resistance and accepted Cal as a business associate yet again. He set up his office in the kitchen-porch-dining room.

Cal would occasionally throw Irena scraps of clerical work—like a gesture of kindness or charity—like the bones of engineering design he threw Manny Handler before hiring him at Yutz & Dunne—paying her an hourly rate considerably lower than Wally paid her. Otherwise Cal did his own clerical work and billed the city his regular hourly rate.

The City of Chenowith also hired Irena hourly at an acceptable rate, to review and edit reports and write grant applications. Irena billed Wally, Cal, and the City monthly.

Wally and Cal worked more than forty hours every week while Irena worked about twenty. Their three-way split of rent, utilities, and security was considerably disproportionate to their incomes, but Irena rationalized that the arrangement allowed her time to pursue her workers compensation appeal. She had no way to know how many years of legal wrangling lay ahead.

*   *   *

Alone in her office one afternoon, Irena received a phone call from Dixie, the City of Chenowith's engineering department secretary. Dixie said that Manny Handler, Irena's old touchy-feely nemesis, was there and wanted to meet with Wally to review some project plans.

Irena began to tremble, yanked back to Yutz & Dunne where she suffered eight miserable years of exposure to this belligerent sexual predator. Two years had elapsed since their last encounter, but to Irena it was like yesterday.

This cretin should be penniless, incarcerated in some federal penitentiary, and some inmate's bitch; miserable, and unfortunately safe from his wife who could justify being out to kill him, Irena thought.

Once again. she wanted to bash his brains in, this bully who got away with so much hostility and sexual abuse at her expense. Once again, she regretted not having known her rights at a time when she might have acted.

Irena felt like a red rubber ball, the kind attached by a rubber band to a kid's wooden paddle—to be smacked out, snapped back, smacked out and snapped back—again and again and again—between Yutz & Dunne and freedom—between crazy and sane.

Irena calmly told Dixie that Wally was out of the office and asked her to have Manny leave the plans with her. Hanging up, Irena broke out in hives, dreading that Manny might show up at her office looking for Wally, not knowing she was there, where she was alone and would have to interact with him. She held her breath and waited to see if Manny would show up, wondering, if he did, would she go for his throat, freeze, or throw up on his shoes.

To regain control of her mind and body, Irena called Dixie to confirm that Manny had left the plans and departed. He had, but it was not enough to alleviate her anxiety. Had Wally or Cal been in the office with her, she might not have reacted the way she did next.

Irena called Dixie back and asked her to notify everyone in the department that no-one should ever refer Manny to the office she shared with Cal and Wally. She told Dixie that she had filed a sexual harassment complaint against Manny—true enough—and that he was not to contact her or come near her.

Dixie told Irena she should e-mail staff herself, which Irena did, expecting feedback. One city staff member told her that Manny "had a history" at the city, and Irena told herself, *someone will eventually hold Manny accountable and punish him appropriately. I only hope it's in this lifetime and I get to watch.*

*   *   *

On a glorious Tuesday, a few months later, Cal walked into Irena's office bursting with excitement, wearing an ear-to-ear grin like she had never seen on his face before, looking every bit like a child who wanted to jump up and down with glee. Cal told Irena that Yutz & Dunne would cease to exist at the end of the month. After a moment of astonished disbelief, Irena wanted to jump up and down, too.

While sad for the good guys who lost their jobs, Irena considered the demise of Yutz & Dunne to be joyful news of universal justice. And while she thought of herself as a spark in the meltdown, she preferred to imagine herself as a blowtorch.

Perhaps one day Lupo will consider the path his company might have taken had he respected the talents and efforts of others. Instead of struggling with minimal staff and suffering crisis after crisis, his company might have reached his heart's desire of three hundred or more employees. Yet even in defeat, Lupo no doubt continues to decry his superiority, Irena thought.

According to Jim Rohn (d.2009), "Failure is not a single cataclysmic event. We do not fail overnight. Failure is the inevitable result of an accumulation of poor thinking and poor choices. To put it more simply, failure is nothing more than a few errors in judgment repeated every day."

Wally, Cal, and Irena worked together sharing that quirky little house on Glen Boulevard in Chenowith, Illinois, for eighteen months, parting ways when the city cancelled all contracts for outside services.

Chapter Forty

I rena's pursuit of workers compensation benefits began when she submitted her claim to Newman National Insurance Company, her employer's insurance provider. Destiny, their claims adjuster, called Irena to confirm receipt of that claim, to arrange for her to sign request forms to have her medical records sent to them, and to arrange for her to be examined by their contracted doctors.

Destiny told Irena, "You need to be patient. Your claim will take about two years to resolve because your health maintenance organization is so slow to produce medical records."

Irena did not know for years that health maintenance organizations and care providers are federally mandated to provide copies of medical records upon written request of the client, usually within fourteen days.

Irena did not know for years that insurance companies are similarly mandated to advise an injured worker/claimant in writing within fourteen days whether a claim for workers compensation benefits is accepted or denied. And if the injured worker is not notified within ninety days, the claim is presumed accepted.

And Irena did not know for years, impacting her claims process, that along with written acceptance or denial, insurance providers are obliged to notify the injured worker/claimant in writing about the one-year statute of limitations for filing an appeal. They are obliged to provide preliminary information in writing about the procedure for filing that appeal. And they are obliged to advise the injured worker in writing to contact the Workers Compensation Commission's information and assistance officers for guidance through the appeal process.

Irena learned too late that the Commission will usually provide injured workers with a flow chart outlining the claims process and stipulating insurance company obligations, upon request if one knows to ask for one.

Irena learned, also too late for her to take advantage, that the American Bar Association provides information about "limited scope representation" as opposed to full representation, whereby an individual unable to afford an attorney or who wants to represent himself or herself can retain limited legal assistance at reduced cost.

Newman Insurance failed to notify Irena about acceptance or denial of her claim, and failed to provide her with any of the other informative documentation. They also failed to provide her with copies of their contracted doctors' reports. And so, Irena patiently waited in ignorance to be contacted by the insurance company, not knowing what she did not know.

*   *   *

With no legal representation protecting her interests, Irena waited nearly a year to hear from Newman or her employer about her claim. She made several unsuccessful attempts to reach Destiny, the claims adjuster, keeping detailed records of those attempts, her patience wearing thin. Had she followed Destiny's advice to wait two years, or had she waited even one day longer than three hundred and sixty-five to attempt contact, she would have exceeded the statute of limitations and would have lost her right to appeal. The attempt played a vital role.

Irena spent three more years trying to contact Destiny or any Newman claims adjuster who would discuss her case, eventually reaching Gomer Gett, an adjuster unfamiliar with her case but willing to talk.

After a quick electronic search, Gett told Irena that her now-four-year-old claim had been formally denied two years earlier and her records moved off-premises. Familiar rage flashed through her brain. She had not been notified or contacted by Newman or her employer in any way.

Gett agreed to provide copies of relevant documents and called Irena once after their conversation to clarify certain details, but she received nothing. And Gett was never again available when she called—leaving Irena breathless with irritation and frustration. She speculated that Lupo Yutz, her former employer, and his attorney had influenced the insurance company and sabotaged her right to workers compensation by virtue of the cleverly worded Fair Employment settlement agreement.

*   *   *

As mentioned, the statute of limitations for filing a workers compensation appeal is one year. Irena would appear to be three years beyond her opportunity to file an appeal of a denial she never received.

Aggravated and confused by Gett's comments and behavior, Irena plunged ahead in her quest for justice. Her notes about her original conversation with Destiny, her unsuccessful attempts to reach Destiny or anyone else at Newman willing to talk to her, and her conversations with Gett would serve as evidence at trial.

Determined to attain justice, Irena tried calling Carl Jordan, the Workers Compensation Commission director she met four years earlier.

The telephone attendant could not track him down by name. The title of "director" had been discontinued. The Commission office in Chenowith where Irena met with him had closed. And when the attendant finally discovered who he was, he had retired.

Irena felt like she was wearing a blindfold at midnight with no moon, stumbling her way barefoot across a minefield covered with broken glass. But she refused to give up.

*   *   *

Researching how to proceed with a workers compensation appeal, Irena discovered a report prepared in the late 1990s for a project that (1) analyzed the process injured workers faced when navigating the workers compensation system, and (2) evaluated injured workers' experiences and the services available to inform and assist them.

Project team members specifically examined problems injured workers faced when trying to gain information; examined public and private services established to inform and assist them with their claims; evaluated effectiveness and weaknesses of those services; and recommended improvements.

The executive summary for the project pointed out that injured workers entitled to benefits were theoretically provided with those benefits quickly and easily. However, evidence suggested that many injured workers were unable to obtain those benefits because they did not fully understand their rights and the process.

The project appears to have resulted in documented reformation of the workers compensation system beginning in the early 2000s, implemented during the years in which Irena filed her claim for benefits, filed her application for appeal, and proceeded with adjudication (also known as arbitration, negotiation, or mediation).

If the consequences of the project made it easier for injured workers to navigate the system, the previous process must have been virtually impossible without legal representation, especially for injured workers like Irena.

Irena was made aware of no public or private services available to help her, other than the Workers Compensation Commission itself and their information and assistance officers, who were of limited help.

One improvement to the appeals process may have been the establishment or re-identification of those information and assistance officers, replacing the previous title of director, which would explain Irena's difficulty locating Carl Jordan. The reformation might also explain the passivity of the information and assistance officers during her appeal.

*   *   *

With Jordan no longer available, Irena phoned Workers Compensation Commission headquarters, explained her situation, and was directed to Gladys Jeffreys, an information and assistance officer, although Irena did not know that at the time because Jeffreys did not identify herself as such when they spoke.

Irena explained that she signed an application for appeal four years earlier and was prepared to take the next step, whatever that might be. Jeffreys asked no questions nor engaged in any further discussion, and simply replied non-specifically telling Irena to "gather your papers and submit them to the Commission."

Believing that "her papers" had to summarize and constitute her entire case, Irena began to assemble her evidence, carried along ignorant and exhausted by the momentum of her passion for justice. Much, much later, Irena realized that Jeffreys meant legal documents about which she was and remained somewhat confused, but certainly not evidence.

*   *   *

Irena began gathering her papers by obtaining medical and psychological records from her care providers for the duration of her employment with Yutz & Dunne.

The Commission usually considers only those records going back one year from the date of injury, usually the first date treatment is sought for a particular injury. But Irena believed more was better because cumulative trauma and psychological injuries are not as clearly defined as a broken bone.

Destiny, Newman's claims adjuster, had told Irena that her health maintenance organization was slow at producing medical records, but Irena received all of her records within two weeks of her request, as mandated.

Those records arrived in somewhat haphazard chronological order, and included a few records for five unknown individuals. Setting the unknowns aside, Irena organized and analyzed her records and created a line graph illustrating patterns of treatment.

While engaged in that process, Irena received a copy of a legal petition to the Commission to dismiss her appeal, filed by Leah Jameson, a defense attorney for Newman National Insurance Company.

Jameson stated, "This worker has obviously lost interest in pursuing this case." Jameson's petition to dismiss Irena's appeal was dated four years and eleven months from the date of Irena's original application for appeal, leading her to conclude that an applicant or injured worker has five years from the date of an application for appeal to proceed or to quit.

Agitated by the sudden imperative, Irena immediately faxed Jameson a letter stating that she had not lost interest in pursuing her case, had been trying to make contact with Newman for years, and was ready to proceed.

She visited Commission offices the next morning and met with an information and assistance officer who told her that her fax to Newman meant nothing, and that she had ten days from the date of Newman's petition to dismiss, to respond by filing her own petition not to dismiss.

Irena completed her petition not to dismiss on the spot, had a copy stamped as received by the Commission, and deposited a copy in the appropriate receptacle in their office. She mailed a copy to Jameson as she left the building, as advised, and kept a copy for her records, triggering a sense of urgency and anxiety that would remain with her for years.

Shortly after filing her petition not to dismiss, and still operating in a relative vacuum, Irena filed "her papers" by delivering to the Commission a behemoth of documentation incorporating everything she believed necessary to substantiate her case, including a written summary of her injuries, her allegations, and her supporting documentation or evidence.

Having obtained, analyzed, and filed everything with the Commission, and feeling tentatively ready for whatever was next, Irena filed a formal declaration of readiness to proceed.

Irena had no idea she was a long way from having to produce evidence, and that by filing everything she had, she was giving Newman National what they needed to try and undermine her appeal.

Chapter Forty-One

Irena was unaware that once she filed her declaration of readiness to proceed, she was the party to request a preliminary hearing at which to advise all parties of case particulars. By waiting for the Commission to act, Irena surrendered power of authority to Leah Jameson, Newman's attorney, who requested the preliminary hearing at a time that could have been inconvenient.

The preliminary hearing took place in a small colorless courtroom about twenty-five feet square, filled with a dozen or so attorneys and applicants all vying for the judge's attention. The judge sat at his elevated mahogany bench fronted by two small mahogany tables, one for an applicant and attorney, the other for a defense attorney. Gray steel side chairs competed for the remaining space.

On her own and overwhelmed, Irena became lightheaded by the din in this room with little ventilation as she waited anxiously for the judge or someone else to call on her. As the crowd thinned and nobody approached her, she began to panic, having assumed she would be told what to do and questioned at this hearing. Unprepared to describe her case to the judge and the defense attorney, she muttered through some unmemorable discussion.

The information and assistance officer she talked to about submitting her papers, who might have guided her through this hearing, had offered no information about procedure. As a result, Irena arrived unaware that it was her obligation to know procedure before entering the courtroom. From this day forward, each time she became aware of something she might have known had Newman lived up to their obligations, she became more angry and despondent.

Irena believed that the information and assistance officers were available to help applicants file an appeal, which she considered done when she filed her behemoth of documentation. She remained confused about their function and availability once that paperwork was filed, and lost sight of those individuals. By the time she understood they were available to help during these and future proceedings, if she knew what to ask for, she believed it was too late.

Remembering little from her conversation with the judge at the preliminary hearing, Irena does not recall how the hearing ended, except that it did, and that she survived to engage another day. With little guidance from the workers compensation commission or the information and assistance officers, it never got any easier.

Chapter Forty-Two

Immediately after the preliminary hearing, the period known as discovery commenced. Discovery allows parties time to gather evidence to support their position. Irena had already acquired the majority of her evidence, but Newman possessed and controlled certain medical records vital to substantiate her claim: records they repeatedly failed to produce, even under pressure by the Commission.

Periodic status conferences were convened to track the evolution of Irena's appeal, held in small courtrooms attended by Irena, the two defense attorneys, and a Commission judge who was, disconcertingly to Irena, seldom the same, although each judge seemed in possession of relevant information.

The process of appeal and acting in ignorance without an attorney exacerbated the damage done to Irena's psyche by her employment at Yutz & Dunne. The greater the pressure, the more she suffered. When a judge or attorney asked her a question, Irena's breathing slowed down so far that she became disoriented, *like I just walked in on the final moments of my own scary movie*, Irena thought. She remained virtually mute, unable to formulate her thoughts or speak up.

To compensate for her inability to verbally represent herself, Irena did her best to submit everything to the Commission in writing. She held copies in her hand during proceedings, and when faced with the need to articulate she could have read from her copy. But Irena was frequently overcome by fear and a desire to flee.

*　　　*　　　*

When Irena filed her original application for appeal, she claimed physical and psychological injuries. When she filed her declaration of readiness to proceed five years later, the Commission directed her to amend her application to provide greater detail about those injuries. A year after that, the Commission again directed Irena to amend her application, this time to re-file as two applications, citing physical injury on one and psychological injury on the other.

The next step for Irena was verifying insurance company liability. Workers compensation insurance is state-regulated, and different agencies in different states maintain and provide information differently, sorted at some point by employer and year.

Irena learned that Newman National, to whom she submitted her original claim for workers compensation benefits, was Yutz & Dunne's provider when she incurred her psychological injury. Newman was therefore liable for that injury. She learned that Hazard Relief was Yutz & Dunne's provider at the time of her physical injuries. Hazard was therefore liable for them.

After Hazard joined the case, Irena found herself navigating two applications for three injuries with different dates of occurrence, two insurance companies, and two defense attorneys—with no legal representation of her own, and without the guidance that would have come had the insurance company lived up to their obligation to provide that guidance in writing from the beginning.

*   *   *

During adjudication, each party has the right to request documentation or information from another by United States Postal Service via formal requests for information filed with the Commission. Each party can also request a status conference to follow up on unfulfilled commitments or when events are not proceeding at an acceptable pace.

The Commission was compelled to schedule periodic conferences to motivate Newman to provide information Irena requested. Even so, proceedings dragged on. As Irena's energy and ability to persevere waned, she found herself having trouble maintaining focus and enthusiasm. Shame and exhaustion kept Irena from seeking help from her care providers, and she chose not to consult anyone at the Commission about her state of mind.

Forging ahead in a never-say-die haze, Irena's ignorance and state of mind became fertile ground for manipulation by defense attorneys who took full advantage. Irena remained oblivious that her only presumably constant and available resource was the information and assistance officers.

*   *   *

Defense attorneys—Leah Jameson for Newman National, liable for Irena's psychological injury, and Bertie Krap for Hazard Relief, liable for Irena's physical injuries—went to great lengths to protect their insurance company clients from having to pay benefits. Both assessed Irena's claims and each developed a strategy to undermine her appeal.

Jameson, a responsive-when-mandated, passively pleasant enough woman, allowed Irena's appeal to evolve from Newman's original mistruths and apparent misconduct, expecting Irena to fail from ignorance, insufficient evidence, or personal inability to see the process through. Jameson's strategy: lie, deny, and manipulate.

Krap, determined to protect Hazard from paying benefits by virtually any means necessary, dominated discussions at hearings and conferences and spoke as though for both attorneys.

Knowing Irena suffered psychological injury and was intimidated by face-to-face confrontation, he demoralized her during hearings with antagonistic and demeaning derision, out of earshot of any judge, of course. He criticized her ignorance about procedures she could hardly be expected to fully or even marginally understand. He even harassed her at home leaving condescending and intimidating voice messages.

Like an animal that smells blood and goes for the kill, Krap appeared to sadistically enjoy his work. He seemed dedicated to destroying Irena's appeal, and perhaps her as a person in the process, in an obvious attempt to coerce her into giving up in despair.

Krap's strategy: undermine and intimidate.

And Jameson appeared content to let Krap play bad cop.

Chapter Forty-Three

Workers compensation benefits hinge on medical corroboration. An injured worker who files a claim for benefits must be evaluated by a medical examiner retained and compensated by the employer's insurance provider.

That medical examiner, retained like a defense attorney to protect the insurance company from having to pay benefits, reports back to the insurance company validating the worker's injury, substantiating the claim, and recommending payment of benefits; or invalidating the injury and recommending denial of benefits.

An injured worker denied benefits who files an appeal of that denial with the Workers Compensation Commission, must similarly be evaluated by a Commission-qualified medical examiner.

The Commission provides an injured worker with a list identifying medical fields of expertise. The injured worker selects the appropriate field of expertise and is then provided with a panel of three practitioners from which to select one to perform an examination.

If the Commission-qualified medical examiner agrees with the insurance company examiner that the injury is invalid and benefits should be denied, the appeal ends and the case is closed. However, if the injury is validated by the Commission-qualified examiner, regardless of the insurance company examiner's conclusions, the appeal moves forward.

*   *   *

Irena selected psychology and orthopedics for her Commission examiners. Psychology was appropriate because she consulted with a psychologist within her health maintenance organization on-and-off for years in response to the interpersonal drama at Yutz & Dunne.

As the interpersonal drama escalated during her twelfth year with the firm, Irena also consulted a second psychologist outside her health maintenance organization on a weekly basis during the six months immediately prior to her care providers' determination that she suffered a major depressive episode called a nervous breakdown.

During the legal period of discovery during her appeal, Irena obtained her medical and mental health records from her health maintenance organization with no problem.

However, when Irena contacted Jennifer Darwin, the psychologist she consulted outside her health maintenance organization, she learned that a recent fire had destroyed Darwin's office and all of her patient records.

Darwin's records strongly supported Irena's claim of employer-induced psychological injury and were therefore vital to her appeal. Without them, Irena was subject to significant disadvantage.

Darwin reminded Irena that Newman had already obtained copies of her records, which became the only copies in existence. And because those records strongly substantiated Irena's claim of psychological injury, Newman passively refused to produce them, even when pressured by the Commission.

Attorney Jameson simply repeated through every relevant status conference that they were "still trying to locate the psychologist's records, which are missing." Irena could not prove that Jameson was lying, and found it curious that Jameson seemed to have every other relevant document about the case.

*   *   *

Irena selected the discipline of orthopedics for her cumulative and acute physical injuries, which would prove to be a mistake.

Her cumulative injuries can be traced back to her task chair and work station. An ergonomist from Irena's health maintenance organization, sanctioned by Yutz & Dunne, concluded that years sitting in an inadequate task chair and working at an inadequate work station had likely caused cumulative injury to Irena's lower back, neck, shoulders, and arms including her wrists. Along with her documented history of relevant treatment, the ergonomist's report was included among Irena's evidence.

Rather than co-operate with the ergonomist's recommendations for an appropriate chair and work station, Lupo had narcissistically elected to purchase a costly but inadequate chair *he* thought she should have. Then, rather than spend more money on the recommended work station, he had a handyman construct one that failed to meet ergonomic criteria.

Irena's acute injury can be traced back to a directive from Cal when he was president. In response to the hostility between Irena and Manny Handler, her sexual archenemy, Cal naively directed them, along with other staff, to go on a "team building" hike, expecting this simplistic exercise to restore a positive working relationship between the two of them. Cal, to be expected, opted not to participate.

Loathing the thought of being in Manny's company, Irena nevertheless agreed to participate because, in ways comparable to battered person syndrome, she could not set herself up for additional mistreatment by refusing to cooperate.

While on the hike, Manny repeatedly came around behind her like a non-commissioned staff sergeant enforcing discipline on bivouac, or more like a cattle driver, repeatedly commanding her to "Hurry up. Hurry up. You're not keeping up."

His provocation resulted in Irena overexerting already tense muscles resulting in sudden excruciating pain in her calf. Convinced she ruptured a tendon or a ligament, Irena sought prompt medical attention. The injury was reiterated in her medical records spanning years of treatment to alleviate chronic pain.

As a sedentary middle-aged mother of three with a pre-existing limp, averaging more than sixty intense hours every week at an inadequate work station, subject to repeated disdain and abuse on the job, Irena was hardly fit for the exertion of that hike, either physically or psychologically, much less with a militant harasser and other mostly male co-workers averaging a dozen years her junior.

*   *   *

Irena's choice of orthopedics for her cumulative and acute physical injuries was a mistake. Physical medicine and rehabilitation would have been the more appropriate choice. She made a bigger mistake when she selected the orthopedic practitioner to examine her. Naively assuming Commission examiners performed comparably, Irena based her choice on proximity to home.

Because Irena was acting "in proper" or legally representing herself, the orthopedist was obliged to review and consider her evidence and written arguments in the same way he was obliged to consider submittals from the insurance company defense attorneys. But he refused to do so, telling Irena, "I have seen all I need to see."

His haphazard report prepared for the Commission illustrates that he merely thumbed through more than five hundred pages of non-sequential and disorganized medical records for Irena (provided by the insurance company as obtained from her health maintenance organization) stopping on occasion to cite from a particular page.

He failed to comment on, apparently never noticing, the lack of chronological order and the erroneous inclusion of medical records for five unknown individuals. He even referred to one of those records, making a snide remark about "a woman Irena's age riding a skateboard."

When Irena eventually got to read the orthopedist's report, she was infuriated because he ignored her claim of cumulative trauma and the years of relevant treatment shown in her medical records. He implied that the doctors who treated her were incompetent in their diagnoses. And he declared her claim of tendon/ligament injury to be "invalid." He even accused Irena of lying, claiming her injury "could not have happened the way she said it did."

Irena still wonders how such a doctor remained a valid Commission-qualified medical examiner

Chapter Forty-Four

D efense attorneys take advantage of certain freedom to stall, manipulate, and passively deny an injured worker's requests for information in an attempt to drive the applicant (particularly an applicant without legal representation) to abandon his or her appeal in frustration.

Irena's appeal proceeded slowly, largely because Newman, despite repeated formal requests, passively refused to provide her with copies of their original medical reports upon which they based their as-yet-theoretical and undocumented denial of her claim.

As Irena contemplated whether or not to request another status conference to apply more pressure, the Commission, eager to speed up the process, ordered Newman to provide her with those reports.

Not knowing if or when she might receive them, and feeling pressured to respond to judicial impatience, Irena scheduled her Commission-required medical examinations in advance of receiving those reports.

Under the erroneous assumption that she was required to inform participating parties of her activities, Irena naively notified Jameson, Krap, and the Commission in advance of the date and times of her examinations. She believed that Jameson, Newman's attorney, would feel compelled to deliver those reports to her in advance.

Hardly.

Having been stalled for so long, Irena had lost sight of the fact that a defense attorney is an enemy who will use every opportunity to undermine an injured worker's case. And this was a matchless opportunity.

Had Irena known she had the right to receive, review, and comment on Newman's medical reports seven or more days in advance of her examinations—and had she known that her only opportunity to address relevant corrections, refutations, and other issues was at those examinations—she might have waited until after she had Newman's reports in her hot little hands.

But she did not know and she did not wait, and she blithely proceeded to her Commission-required physical and psychological examinations scheduled for the same morning, without Newman's medical reports, unaware that she was about to miss her only opportunity to address them directly with her examiners.

*   *   *

Arriving home after her examinations, Irena was surprised to discover that a thick package of documents had been delivered to her home while she was gone—conveniently, and no doubt pre-meditatively, and oh so propitiously for Newman and Hazard.

The package included the original medical reports Irena had been trying to obtain for years, a copy of Newman's "denial" dated two years after she submitted her original claim, the flow chart illustrating how workers compensation claims for appeal should proceed, information about the one-year statute of limitations, preliminary information about procedure, and the directive to contact information and assistance officers for help—none of which Irena had ever seen before.

When Irena reviewed Newman's medical reports, it became clear to her that their doctors (by virtue of their brief examinations and their dramatically flawed, radically skewed, and clearly incorrect medical reports) had been charged with contriving a basis for denial.

Considering Irena received those medical reports too late to address during her examinations, considering Newman refused to produce the only copy of her secondary psychologist's records, and considering the orthopedist did what he did, Irena realized too late that informing Jameson and Krap of the date and times of her examinations was a mistake of monumental proportions.

Irena knew she'd been had and it was bad.

*   *   *

The Workers Compensation Commission allowed Irena to request supplemental reports from her Commission-qualified examiners to consider her comments about the original medical reports. The psychologist complied and produced a brief report but did not change his position, claiming no new evidence was presented. The orthopedist simply refused.

When Irena complained about the orthopedist during a status conference, the presiding judge said, "Oh my goodness, you used *him*? We here at the Commission know all about him. You have to be dead to get him to agree to any injury."

Irena investigated having him replaced on her case, but by the time she learned the correct and only acceptable terminology for replacing him was "a request for set-aside of the qualified medical examiner," the Commission had scheduled a date for trial, setting in motion a few other matters to resolve first.

Chapter Forty-Five

C ase rating is a complex process that assigns a financial value to a substantiated claim to provide the judge, applicant, and attorney with a suggested range of reparation. Rating occurs just before settlement negotiations which, if successful, renders a trial unnecessary.

Even in the absence of Darwin's records, Irena's Commission-qualified psychologist found that she sustained a psychological industrial injury, and her claim was rated for $47,000. Had Newman produced Irena's records from Jennifer Darwin, the psychologist who had the fire, a higher case rating might have resulted.

Irena's claim for physical injuries remained unsubstantiated or deemed "invalid" by the orthopedist, and was therefore not rated.

Following case rating, the Commission scheduled a settlement conference, sending Irena's anxiety into overdrive at the thought of negotiating a settlement with Jameson and Krap.

After years in occupational hell, followed by years of frustration pursuing justice, Irena had little energy or ability to advocate for herself. Awake most nights, by the morning of the settlement conference Irena could barely speak coherently.

Throughout her appeal, Irena had yearned to avoid stressful face-to-face confrontations and to address issues in writing, but she did not seek formal authorization to do so. The Commission might have agreed, but more likely would have invited assistance from an information and assistance officer. But that is not the way it happened.

A week before trial, Irena and the attorneys convened for the settlement conference in a small anteroom adjacent to the main courtroom at Commission headquarters. Handicapped by anxiety and limited negotiating skills, Irena felt threatened by Krap's antagonism as Jameson continued to allow him to speak for both of them. Irena minimized interaction, withdrew into herself like a turtle, and said little, feeling as though she would be guillotined as if she stuck her neck out.

Leaning in to emphasize his points, like one more bully, Krap pressured Irena to settle for half the rated amount of her case, "...which is all you're entitled to...," he smugly declared, "...and virtually all of that..." he uttered with an air of self-satisfaction, "...will be reimbursed to the State Employment Development Department for compensation you received while on disability."

Krap cackled like a witch knowing his offer would leave Irena with virtually nothing after years tolerating her employer, having a breakdown, pursuing Fair Employment mediation and workers compensation benefits.

Raging internally at Krap's condescension and successful intimidation, unable to negotiate, and anxious to escape his tyranny, Irena refused to settle and opted for trial, much to Krap's very obvious dismay. She chose to put her faith in a judge she trusted to consider the facts objectively.

Leaving the building after that unsuccessful attempt to negotiate a settlement, Irena experienced painful heart palpitations, chest pain, shortness of breath, and dizziness. Thinking she was having a heart attack, she drove to the nearest hospital where doctors in the emergency room concluded she was having an acute anxiety attack brought on by the stress of her confrontations with Krap and the prospect of trial.

*　　　*　　　*

One can correlate Irena's experiences with the work of Elisabeth Kubler-Ross, MD, a Swiss American psychiatrist. Dr. Kubler-Ross, working with terminally ill patients, introduced the hypothesis commonly referred to as the five stages of grief in her 1969 book, "On Death and Dying."

Dr. Kubler-Ross asserts that individuals who face the reality of impending death or other extreme awful fate experience a series of emotional stages including denial, anger, bargaining, depression, and acceptance. While Dr. Kubler-Ross's hypothesis is not absolute, and stages do not necessarily occur in specific sequence, one can form an analogy.

- Irena's long-standing *denial* that her workplace at Yutz & Dunne was intolerable.
- Irena's protracted *anger* at her tormentors that carried through Fair Employment mediation and her workers compensation appeal.
- Irena's *bargaining* that everything would improve if she just ignored what was happening around her and worked harder at her job and during appeal.
- Irena's *depression* when she realized there would be no survival at Yutz & Dunne, where the bastards would win; at Emerson Construction Management and the City of Chenowith, where her dysfunctional relationship with Cal Chauvin would continue; and with regard to her workers compensation appeal, where the insurance company defense attorneys maintained the upper hand.
- Irena's ultimate *acceptance* that she could lose her fight and still survive.

Chapter Forty-Six

I rena's trial took place on a Tuesday morning, eight years after filing her original claim for workers compensation benefits, seven years after filing her appeal, and more than two years after filing her declaration of readiness to proceed. She and the defense attorneys were required to submit arguments and supporting evidence to the presiding judge in advance. Irena trusted the judge to be fair, compassionate, and familiar with defense attorney tactics.

At the appointed hour, she, Jameson, Krap, the judge and others convened in the main courtroom with Irena's heart pounding like a war drum she was sure everyone could hear.

On one hand, Irena's spirit was soaring. She was confident she had assembled, analyzed, and charted her evidence: confident she had clearly summarized her arguments to prove she suffered on-going physical, psychological, familial, and economic repercussions from her injuries: and confident she had substantiated that her employer and the insurance companies failed to live up to their respective obligations and were perhaps criminally complicit.

On the other hand, Irena had trust issues. She worried whether the judge had read everything she submitted, or even enough for her to prevail. And most frightful of all, Irena feared the judge would dismiss her case because she signed that Fair Employment settlement agreement presumably sacrificing her right to workers compensation.

Irena was well prepared on paper with strong arguments and evidence in hand and before the judge. Still, she was an emotional wreck. Tension mounted as she and the others waited for the judge to begin, like that moment reaching the peak of a roller coaster and preparing for the drop.

Soothing herself, Irena fantasized that the judge, having reviewed and evaluated each side's written arguments and evidence, would see and get a feel for the participants, render his judgment, and dismiss them in short order.

Then she began to beat herself up, feeling defeated even before proceedings began. Her throat constricted, her heart raced, and she perspired like a leaky sponge. She could not feel the floor beneath her feet and she could no longer hear well from the pounding of blood in her ears. Irena watched herself, the applicant, carried along by the momentum: and watched herself, the observer, frozen in time and place.

As the morning progressed, Irena became increasingly overwhelmed and should have asked for a break, at least to use a restroom, but she could not and did not. Conditioned by family, by Cal, and by society-at-large to get along, and anxious not to make waves, Irena forged ahead in a foggy haze, oxygen deprived and exhausted because she tends to hold her breath under pressure. She kept telling herself, *just get it over with, and when it's over I'll be done, because I just can't take it anymore.*

When the judge called everyone to order, Krap literally leapt out of his seat to argue, "Your Honor, Ms. Nowak's appeal should be dismissed because she signed an agreement forfeiting her right to workers compensation benefits."

The judge replied, "I don't care what she signed."

Irena's heart leapt with joy as Krap skulked back to his seat defeated, having to face the rest of the day like everyone else.

*   *   *

First on the docket was identification of witnesses. Irena mistakenly believed that depositions were preferred over witnesses. But even if that were true, she had been unable to locate anyone who could or cared to remember events that occurred eight years earlier relevant only to her. With neither witnesses nor depositions, Irena arrived at trial with only character references for herself, accepting whatever risk that presented.

Taking her breath away like an unexpected punch to her mid-section, Krap presented Lupo Yutz and Cal Chauvin as witnesses. Having no idea how she would interact with them, Irena felt instantly pulled back through a wormhole to re-experience her historic vilification.

Irena was sure Lupo was angry when she filed for workers compensation benefits way back when; was furious when she filed her Fair Employment grievance; was incensed when she filed her workers compensation appeal; and was livid to be summoned to trial. She had no doubt he looked forward to making her regret her choices.

Every moment in the courtroom seemed to stretch out interminably. Irena had no idea what to do and could probably have sought assistance from an information and assistance officer. But feeling as though all opportunity for survival had already been lost, she sat there virtually paralyzed, thinking of nothing but gritting her teeth, getting through the nightmare, and rushing forward to the conclusion of her association with Yutz & Dunne and with her workers compensation appeal. She only hoped to see justice prevail, preferably without her participation.

Irena would have benefited by having a therapist or an attorney with her that day at trial: someone who might have taken her by the hand as she began to panic: who might have stepped in to request a break when she did not or could not: who might have facilitated time for her to breathe and regain her composure.

She did not know she could have hired a therapist or attorney on an hourly basis to do those things, and she never learned how much support might have come from an information and assistance officer.

*   *   *

The judge spent the morning going over what he called "housekeeping issues," including the rejection of Krap's argument for dismissal and the identification of witnesses. Irena was blindsided when he asked that she and the attorneys leave the courtroom for one last effort in private to negotiate a settlement. She remembered their last attempt to negotiate and her subsequent anxiety attack.

Seeing the panic on Irena's face, the judge looked her in the eye and said, "You *do* (seemingly with emphasis and compassion) want to come back in here and testify." Irena understood him to say, "Do not settle, come back here and testify, and you will not regret it."

Excited by what she believed the judge was telling her, Irena was also terrified to leave the security of the courtroom and once again be subject to Krap's antagonism. The judge had no way to know the degree of Irena's anxiety, and she had no way to explain it to him.

Weak and ashamed over her inability to negotiate, Irena did, however, have enough composure to explain to the judge that she and the attorneys had been unable to arrive at a fair settlement earlier, and that she did not believe they could do so now.

Had Irena stopped talking and refused to leave the courtroom, the judge might not have insisted, and they might have moved on with the trial. Had she talked to an information and assistance officer, she might have learned that she was within her rights to refuse to leave. But neither of those things happened.

Instead, Irena's anxiety and her compulsion to cooperate caused her brain and her mouth to collide, and she continued to talk, somewhat disjointedly, hoping to discover a way to escape what was about to happen.

A burst of adrenalin gave Irena the courage to ask the judge if he could provide a neutral third party to help keep Krap's crap to a minimum. The judge explained that the Commission did not usually provide such assistance, but he made an exception and located another judge to sit in.

*   *   *

Stepping out of the courtroom with the attorneys, Irena was incapable of rational thinking, rational action, and rational conversation in the same context. At first, she felt like a child losing touch with her mother's hand in a crowd. A few steps later, she felt like she was walking the green mile to her execution. Irena told herself to agree to nothing and to return to the courtroom to take her chances.

It should have been that easy. The judge had her written testimony in front of him and she had copies in her own hand to read if and when her mind went blank. She had rebuttals to everything she thought the defense attorneys might possibly argue. And she very much wanted to testify, to state under oath that what she presented in writing was the truth, so help her God.

But Irena was no longer in control of herself or anything else.

The judicial babysitter waiting for Irena and the attorneys in the small anteroom nearby knew nothing about Irena's case and had no basis for comment. Nevertheless, he voiced his variously distracting comments and opinions, dominating rather than mediating the discussion.

His thinly disguised hostility, perhaps for being asked to babysit, perhaps wishing to be done with us as soon as possible, became evident when he told Irena, "You should accept the offer of a compromise and release because you probably won't do any better." When Irena questioned how he could make that statement without knowing more about the case, the babysitter abruptly stated, "You'll just have to accept my opinion."

That was the moment it was over for Irena.

Facing Krap's antagonistic behavior along with a hostile, assertive, egotistically authoritarian judicial babysitter who overstepped the boundaries of his role as peacekeeper, Irena felt like she was suffocating. Her heart was racing, and again she felt like she was having a heart attack. Irena needed to escape. She needed to end the day or she was sure she would die.

Having lost sight of everything, most especially the seemingly supportive judge who encouraged her to return to the courtroom to testify, Irena was overcome and collapsing under the weight of the situation. Primed and ready to agree to almost anything, she choked and made the positively catastrophic mistake of agreeing to Krap's offer of a compromise and release.

The split second she agreed, Irena knew it was a mistake, especially when Krap nearly broke his neck snapping his head toward her in surprise. Agreeing to the compromise and release felt like a fatal, self-inflicted dagger wound to her heart.

By agreeing, Irena forfeited any opportunity for the judge to make an award, and she wound up settling for a small portion of what the judge might have awarded had she been able to return to the courtroom to testify.

Irena settled for $36,000, immediately reduced by $24,000 to reimburse the Employment Development Department for payments she received while on state disability. Irena was left with $12,000 after eight years of turmoil engaged in her appeal for workers compensation benefits—far less than half what her psychological injury alone had been rated for.

Had Irena been able to testify, the judge might have taken into consideration not only her rated psychological injury, but also the consequences of the Commission orthopedist's questionable evaluation of her physical injuries.

He might have considered Newman's manipulation of their obligations, withholding of evidence, and likely criminal misconduct; misconduct and abuse by her employer; lost income; lost ability to earn an income; future impact on social security benefits as a result of lost income; anticipated loss of home and lifestyle as a result of lost income; plus, impact on family relationships.

*   *   *

With details of the compromise and release worked out, the necessary paperwork completed, the judge advised, and court proceedings at an end, Leah Jameson approached Irena in the corridor to ask if she wanted to say hello to Lupo.

Hell no, Irena thought, but said instead, "I don't think so," and headed for the elevator. If Lupo wanted to say hello to her, she was sure it was only to gloat.

Irena later learned that the compromise and release might have been eligible for reconsideration by the Workers Compensation Commission, considering Krap's abuse of her state of mind and other factors. But Irena was done, and promptly planned a party to celebrate the end of proceedings with family and friends.

Epilogue

Years after trial, Irena was surprised to encounter Lupo in the reception area of a medical facility. Viewing him as the manifestation of the grief she endured at Yutz & Dunne, she had hoped never to see him or interact with him again. Realistically, living in the same county, she knew she would come in contact with him sooner or later and wondered what might happen.

On this particular day, having registered for her appointment, Irena turned and came face-to-face with Lupo sitting in a chair directly in front of her. She started to smile, then giggle, then succumbed to a hysterical fit of uncontrollable laughter, harder every second until tears were streaming down her cheeks, and she fell to the floor rolling in laughter with stitches in her sides.

Internally.

Externally, she just grinned.

Having no choice but to walk toward Lupo, and feeling safe in the company of others, she looked directly at him and said, "Hello, Lupo," her greeting possibly tinged with a hint of sarcasm she had a hard time suppressing.

He sat there like a stone, with a smirk on his face, looking beyond Irena, which made her want to laugh even harder.

Having worked with this man for so many years, Irena knew that Lupo's win had to be someone else's loss, someone else's win was an affront, and nobody got the better of Lupo without retaliation. She was convinced he ignored her because it pleased him to do so, and smirked because he got off easy. She hoped this was his best shot.

The intervening years left Lupo noticeably heavier, nearly bald, his head and lined face spattered with age spots. Universal justice, Irena thought, or maybe she just wanted to see him as pathetic.

She continued to smile because she did what she set out to do. Irena had her day in court. In fact, she had two.

She documented her grievances about mistreatment at Yutz & Dunne and thoroughly enjoyed Lupo's real or implied admittance of guilt by signing the Fair Employment settlement agreement supposedly "resolving" their differences.

And Irena took comfort knowing that, had she been able to testify before the judge at trial during her workers compensation appeal, she would likely have been awarded much more than she was.

Irena's lengthy ordeal was excruciating and reparations comparatively meager, but Irena is satisfied that the outcome will always be good for a laugh—knowing that macho Lupo lost to a woman who fought him and his attorneys without an attorney of her own, and legally prevailed not once but twice.

And when Irena occasionally berates herself for her limitations, she can always recall her victories, along with the image of an adolescent codger in that waiting room.

www.ingramcontent.com/pod-product-compliance
Lightning Source LLC
Chambersburg PA
CBHW070327260626
47160CB00003B/969